Unfaithful

Unfaithful

DEVON SCOTT

KENSINGTON PUBLISHING CORP.
http://www.kensingtonbooks.com

DAFINA BOOKS are published by

Kensington Publishing Corp.
850 Third Avenue
New York, NY 10022

All Kensington Titles, Imprints, and Distributed Lines
are available at special quantity discounts for bulk
purchases for sales promotions, premiums, fund-rais-
ing, and educational or institutional use. Special book
excerpts or customized printings can also be created
to fit specific needs. For details, write or phone the office of the Kensington special sales manager: Kensington Publishing Corp., 850 Third Avenue, New York,
NY 10022, attn: Special Sales Department, Phone: 1-
800-221-2647.

Dafina Books and the Dafina logo Reg. U.S. Pat. &
TM Off.

ISBN-13: 978-0-7582-3897-9
ISBN-10: 0-7582-3897-5

First trade paperback printing: May 2008
First mass market printing: March 2009

10 9 8 7 6 5 4 3 2 1

Printed in the United States of America

PART ONE

Chapter 1

Olivia—

I've tried for days to tell you what, for me, is an absolute new feeling. I've been asking myself if what I dare to express is real and worth fighting for, given our circumstances and the fact that we've been friends for so long. But I've come to the point where I can no longer NOT let you know how I'm feeling.

I know a letter is not the best way to communicate affairs of the heart, but in the interest of so many things, I feel this is the only way to start.

So, here goes . . .

Something changed within me that night at the party. Two weeks ago, almost to this day, my life was indelibly altered. I can't tell you exactly why it began, but all I know is I don't look at things the way I did before. I find myself dreaming about new things—whole new realms of possibilities, and each one includes you.

Olivia, what happened between you and me that night cannot be ignored. It was profound. It was deep. And I pray that it happens again and again

*and again. Yes, Olivia, for me it was so much more
than just physical . . . it affected me that much. . . .*

Ryan doesn't hear the door open until the footfalls are inside his cage. He glances up to find his
boss, the president of the company, standing before
him. He swivels away from his laptop and quickly
closes the clamshell, ensuring no one will witness
this spilling of emotions.

"Ryan."

"Rodney. Have a seat."

"No, thanks. This won't take but a second." He
glances back toward the door as if expecting company.

Ryan witnesses Olivia's dark locs rise into view. Before he can breathe, she is moving through the door.
Russet-colored skin and toned calf muscles, sculpted
flesh that curves upward to the hemline of her short,
yet fashionable, skirt. The crisp white buttondown top
is fitting, following her curves the way a sports car
does a winding road. Eyes drift upward to her full
breasts pressed against cotton—no, that is not right.
They are straining against the fabric—yes, straining.

"Ahhh, perfect timing, Olivia," Rodney says.

She grins at Rodney before flashing her alluring
smile in Ryan's direction.

Rodney begins without preamble. "I need the two
of you in New York, tonight. Sorry for the late notice,
but, Olivia, your guy is having second thoughts—
something he's hearing on the street about a manufacturing defect with the optics. Pure bullshit, of
course, but we need to squelch this thing before it
gets out of hand."

Olivia is nodding, as if she expected this. Ryan is
turning a sour face, as if he has no idea what they are

talking about. He opens his mouth to speak, but Olivia beats him to the punch.

"Rod, Ryan and I met earlier today regarding this issue, and I've already had my staff prepare a briefing just in case. So Ryan and I can finalize it on the shuttle going up. We'll be ready, no problem. Just tell us when and where."

Ryan remains silent. He is observing her, cool under fire. Her stare is unwavering, her smile captivating. He feels himself stirring, readying the switch that turns the windows opaque so fast it would make her head spin. He longs to push Rodney out of his office, then rush to her the way a cheetah attacks its prey.

"Outstanding. Jackie has all the details." He turns to leave, swatting Ryan on the shoulder. He winks at Olivia as he says, "As usual, the two of you make quite a pair." Then he is gone, leaving Olivia alone with Ryan, a smirk painted on her sensuously full lips.

Six hours later, he sits across from her, forty-seven floors up from Broadway, enjoying the tastiest broiled salmon of his life. She is dressed casually: tight jeans, dark boots, and off-white sweater showing off her curves. As she excuses herself to go to the restroom, he stares silently at her perfectly shaped ass, thanking God for answering his prayers.

When she returns, looking more refreshed than before, he focuses on the gap between her thighs, that sweet spot, attempting to make out the cleft that forms her core. He knows what it feels like. He has committed its form to memory . . . has touched it . . . even slipped a finger inside.

God, what a night that was.

He hopes tonight he will finish what they began.

The biz trip to New York was a godsend.

He is drinking rum and Coke. The buzz he is feeling helps his thinking along. He stares at her, pondering just how alluring she can be. They talk casually about stuff, already exhausting the technical problems that sent them there. Once again, he is barely listening. Instead, he remembers a scene very similar to this one.

Months ago, the two of them were out on a client call . . . another late night, one of many. For some reason, he was feeling depressed that night. Can't recall why—but it was one of those times when self-esteem was at an all-time low. Perhaps he was just going through a midlife crisis—or reexamining his life from a different angle. We all need to do that from time to time. Right?

Regardless, he was feeling down, and needed to believe in something else for a change.

Warmth.

"Do you find me attractive?"

He recalls blurting out the question over dinner. She had glanced up, incomprehension etched in her usually smooth brow.

She was thinking.

"What do you mean?" she asked cautiously while setting down her wineglass stem and giving him her full attention.

"Just what I said. Do you find me attractive?"

He was thinking about her husband, Miles. How could he not? They had been talking about him earlier. And Ryan found that he was comparing himself to the man. Ryan was thin and lanky, like a ball player, whereas Miles was muscled, stocky. Ryan was light-skinned; Miles, on the other hand, richly brown. Ryan wore his hair short, tapered, professional, almost boring to a fault, whereas Miles wore his to fit his personality—wild, free, unencumbered. His locks were thick, dark, and long. Women loved his hair. He re-

ceived stares and comments from women everywhere he went. Sometimes it made Ryan sick.

Olivia stared at him for a moment, pondering the question, and in the ensuing silence, he wondered, Could I have gotten her? Could I have been her man?

Her brow furrowed. She smiled and then said something simple that blew him away.

"I think you're beautiful."

Ryan considered her words for a moment. Head tilted down, he pondered their meaning.

He didn't see her get up, didn't notice her move to his side of the table until she was bending down. He glanced up, meeting her stare as her mouth opened. Before he had time to consider further action, her mouth was upon his, kissing him, loving him with her mouth, those luscious lips pressing against his with a passion that ignited something so deep and primal he hadn't felt in decades.

When she was done—he wasn't sure if it took mere seconds or minutes—Olivia finally pulled back, wiped the locs from her eyes, and sat down. She then picked up her wine and took a sip. No words were needed. He knew now how she felt. . . .

"Penny for your thoughts?" she asks, bringing him back to reality.

He smiles in remembrance. "Just thinking."

"About?"

"You. Me. The party a few weeks ago."

Olivia grins. "Fucked me up."

His breath catches in his throat. Then, he smiles. "Yeah. Almost."

Olivia stares at him unknowingly. "What do you mean?" she asks.

He ignores the question. Instead, he drains his drink and places the glass down, staring into the kaleidoscope of ice patterns for a split second before sucking in a breath, then exhaling loudly.

"Let me ask you a question."

"Shoot . . ."

"That night, did you want things to go all the way?"

Again, that look. Furrowing brow.

"Pardon?"

"You . . . me . . . the party. Hel-lo?"

She laughs. For a moment, the tension had risen to the point where one could cut it with an axe. Seconds later, thanks to her mirth, it had dissipated. So, he laughs with her before turning serious.

"Something funny?"

Olivia responds. "Yeah. As I recall, we were all pretty fired up. You, me, Carly—oh, my god—"

"This isn't about Carly," Ryan states, interrupting her, willing her to stay on track. To not talk about his wife.

She pauses. Stares at him hard.

"Okay."

"I've known you a long time, Olivia. We go way back, right?"

"Right."

"So, no sense in pussy-footing around." He chuckles at his own joke. "I mean, it's something we need to discuss."

She opens her mouth to speak, then thinks better of it and nods instead.

"That night at the party, something happened between us. Something that can't be denied. Two weeks later, we've yet to fully acknowledge it. I don't know about you, but I can't just waltz around here like nothing happened, 'cause that's not the case."

"Ryan—look, I know—"

The annoying clamor from her cell phone cuts the conversation short. Olivia reaches for her hip, mouthing her regret as she answers it. Her face changes—a glow emerging in place of a frown.

Miles . . .

He stands, slaps some bills on the table, and is walking away before she stops him with a brush to his elbow.

"Miles wants me to remind you about Friday. He's made reservations at Bluespace for noon," she says, gesturing to her phone. "Don't be late, he says."

Olivia smiles in an attempt to cut through the apprehension that has risen again between them. He smiles in return, but their conversation is done. Dejected, he heads for his room.

Chapter 2

He was standing by the refrigerator, the door open and shielding his lower body from view. To someone standing across the room, one might assume he was naked. Fact is, he was wearing boxers—the Scooby-Doo ones Carly gave him for his birthday as a goof.

He was just standing there, head pounding from a night of crabs, Coronas, apple martinis, and cigar smoking. Just the last two were more than enough to make his head spin.

One-thirty in the morning, standing in the kitchen of his best friends' home, Olivia and Miles asleep upstairs, Carly crashed on the futon in the basement below—and Ryan, his cotton mouth and tongue begging for moisture as he rummaged through the fridge searching for something to drink. He found a liter of Sprite and, not having the strength to search for a cup, tipped the bottle to his lips and thirstily drank.

As he dropped it back into the slot in the refrigerator, he stepped back to close the door.

That's when he saw her.

She was standing motionless, observing him silently.

He was caught off guard. What he saw took his breath away.

Olivia was clad in a button-down shirt—little else. The shirt hung open and he could see the dark patch of pubic hair that spread over her mound—and a large purplish nipple peeked out from the side of the shirt. Her hair hung free, locs surrounding her beautiful darkened face. Between her lips hung a burnt-out cigar. She moved forward on her toes, like a dancer; she seemed to glide toward him effortlessly. He glanced quickly toward the closed doorway that led to the basement stairs. Behind her, the back of the family room couch was sprinkled in shadows; the rest of the room was indigo.

He couldn't wrestle his gaze from her body, which seemed to writhe as she moved near—the illusion of a serpent— and the fullness of her spoke to him. Not like Carly's slender form, certainly not overweight. Just curvy hips, meat on the bones like his mama. Legs and thighs that spoke of substance and full breasts that hung invitingly. When she was within touching distance, her eyes never leaving his, the cigar now inches from his face, his cock swelling in his boxers with the certainty of a raging flood, he reached for her. Her legs parted; her eyes were unblinking. His fingers traced a line down the cotton fabric of the man's shirt, past buttons, parting the halves, and resting a hand lightly on her breast. Gently, he circled the hard nipple before dipping down farther past her navel, which he traced gently with his fingernail before meandering through her dark patch of hair. Finally, after a splendid minute, he felt the rise of moistened flesh that met his touch.

She reached out and expertly slipped her hand inside his shorts. His cock came alive as she palmed the bulbous head, stroking the shaft, raking her fingers lightly over his balls. He found her opening effortlessly, slipping a finger inside.

His cock stretched out in front of him, gently bobbing beside her waist. She stroked it with her palm, then, just as she found her groove stroking him, she ceased and moved to the back of the couch that was dappled in darkness. Her hands spread lengthwise along the edge of the furniture as she bent forward and down, lifting up the shirt in the process— Miles' shirt, the same one he had been wearing earlier that evening—and spread her legs wide, exhibiting in all of its splendor her heart-shaped, chocolate-colored ass.

He groaned contentedly, marveling at the exquisiteness on display before him. He could clearly see the lips to her sex, which glistened even in the half-darkness. He thought of the kiss they had shared months before, her intoxicating scent that night in the elevator, the way her skin felt when he massaged her shoulders in his office, the electricity that coursed between them. He gripped himself decisively, readying to impale his hardness into the wetness of her sweet cavern. Suddenly, unable to contain his hunger, he lunged forward with a purpose that surprised even him.

In that same moment, they clearly heard the rustling coming from upstairs, the weighty, uncoordinated footfalls, and Miles' unmistakable deep voice calling out, "Olivia, baby, is that you I hear?"

Chapter 3

The hallway is silent. He stands in front of the door to her room, glancing down at his feet, listening for sounds, willing his breathing to slow. It is after one A.M.; the hotel and most of its occupants are fast asleep.

He has been standing there for the better part of five minutes, not moving, fingering the letter he holds in his hand. He's ready to slip it under her door, but each time he musters up the strength to bend down and release it, an ache appears out of nowhere, righting him.

He knocks on the door. Hears rustling. Knocks again. More noise, then footsteps. Locks and bolts undone. The door opens, and he finds himself facing her.

"Know what time it is?" she inquires, wiping at the corner of one eye. She is clad in a wrinkly, man's button-down white shirt, way too big for her frame. He looks her over, musing about what, if anything, she wears underneath. Immediately, his thoughts return to the party two weeks ago, and the night that made him a man obsessed. Even at the lateness of this hour, her sensuality reaches out and tickles his skin, caressing him in the lonely hallway. He smells her, takes in the smoothness of her skin, the roundness of her cheekbones, the surety of her stare. Her graceful curves cannot be concealed by another man's shirt.

All of this conspires to confuse him, tear him down, and make him weak, a slave to the physical. Yet, it is his stare that is unyielding now. He can hear the pulse in his ears. He is growing hard, can feel it tighten his jeans, and is certain she can sense his awakening, too.

"Anything wrong?" she asks, her gaze washing over him hastily, hand on her hip, making no move to let him pass.

"Need to talk—didn't get to finish what we started earlier."

"This can't wait?" she inquires, somewhat exasperated. The hour is late.

"Obviously not."

They stare each other down for a moment before he hears her sigh. She retreats, and he enters the room.

The bed is unmade, oversize pillows and thick comforter haphazardly situated. She climbs onto the bed, exposing thighs. A hint of white emerges—and he conjures up images of silk panties, erotic g-strings, and other sexual things. She witnesses his stare. Asks him what it is exactly that he wants.

Silently, he hands her the letter, which has occupied his time for several evenings.

"What is this?"

"How I feel." With nothing more to say, he sits on the edge of the bed, facing away from her.

She repositions the comforter over her legs, ensures she is buttoned up top, unfolds the letter, and glances over at him. Then she begins to read.

It takes her a minute to complete. He is silent watching her. Her expression doesn't change, as if she has been expecting this. When she is done, she refolds the letter slowly and glances up.

"Ryan."

"Yes." He is waiting, breathless.

She is cautious with her words.

"This is my fault," she says. "I've led you on. Things happened after that party which cannot be undone. I would be lying if I said I regretted them all, but the truth is"—and here she pauses for a moment to search the ceiling, as if she can find comfort there—"they shouldn't have happened."

He is silent. She takes his silence as an approval to continue.

"For several reasons, Ryan. One, I am married. We both are. We love our spouses, and are not about to jeopardize what we have."

A statement, not a question.

"Two, you and I are friends—been that way for as long as I can recall. Don't want to mess that up—right? I mean, what good can come of this? Lose a friendship for twenty minutes of pleasure?" She stares at him, yet he looks away. "Ryan, is it really worth it?"

She barrels forward, finding the strength—the energy to go on, regardless of the effect it has on him.

"Three, we work together. We're on the same team. You and I built this company together. I love what I do, and I know you do, too. Don't want to do anything else; don't want to work anywhere else. I know you feel the same."

She spreads her hands wide, palms upturned. "So you see, Ryan, what happened that night was a mistake. All of it a serious error—I realize that now. I was being selfish—enjoying the attention, the stares, and the energy you threw my way."

Olivia smiles weakly.

He has been sitting patiently, rubbing his palms together. He stands now, goes to the window, and parts the curtain to glance down at the street life below. He turns toward her to speak, his voice a whisper.

"You said I was beautiful." Mustering up the strength to continue, he barrels forward. "I know things aren't simple. I wish to God they were. I wish there weren't these obstacles in our way. I wish we could just finish what we started. I'm not disagreeing with what you've said, nor am I implying that your reaction doesn't make any sense—'cause it does. But affairs of the heart never make sense. They defy logic, Olivia.

"I know what I feel—what I felt that night, when you took me in your sweet mouth. I know what you felt, too—know it as sure as I'm standing here."

Her expression has changed. It has suddenly soured and forces him to pause. She is staring at him as if he is not of this world. Instinctively, he waits.

"What are you talking about?"

"Kind of late in the game for coyness. You know what we shared."

He moves forward, a wave of elation surging through him as he remembers the sweet details of their last encounter.

Reaching the foot of the bed, he climbs on. Olivia retreats to the headboard, back pressed into the veneer wood, hearing it groan.

"I think you should leave," she says with sudden finality.

He strokes the lump where her thigh is positioned under the cover. She recoils like a caged animal.

"Stop it. This isn't going to happen. Not tonight. Not again."

He pauses, hand in mid-stretch. His gaze is galvanized with hers; her locs seem to tremble along with the rest of her body. In that moment, he feels extreme pity . . . and intense pain.

"Do you deny how you felt? How good it felt when we were together?"

Silence.

He reaches for her again. She lets his hand rest on the comforter. His lips are upturned.

"You said I was beautiful. . . ."

Her head thrashes, but in slow motion. She opens her mouth to speak, and is interrupted by the high-pitched scream of the smoke alarm.

Hands immediately rise to their ears; both are shaken by the intensity.

It is close to 1:30 A.M., and the fucking fire alarm is wailing.

Unbelievable!

The next thirty minutes pass in rapid-fire succession—into the hallway, down countless flights of stairs, out into the pouring rain, away from the hotel complex that has been maddeningly roped off by the NYFD. Sirens, fire engines, police vehicles, hoses, hotel staff, and guests are everywhere. The guests scatter; already clogged streets become choked to near bursting with equipment and panicky, half-dressed out-of-towners. By the time he leads Olivia hesitantly to an all-night diner four blocks away, Miles' shirt is soaked to the bone. Her nipples shine like beacons. Either she hasn't noticed or no longer cares. She is freezing, dead tired, and drained of all emotion. At 2:18 A.M., they have only each other for comfort.

That thought alone is sobering.

They sit across from each other now, Olivia and Ryan, in a cramped, dingy booth, sipping lukewarm coffee. The silence and wobbly table are the only things separating them, as she tries unsuccessfully to forget this night, this man, this situation.

She is thinking, *How on earth did things get to this point?*

Chapter 4

He enters her slowly, feeling her expand as he fills her up. He groans in response to her grabbing his ass and pulling him inside of her. He glances down; Carly's caramel skin is aglow with the sheen that accompanies lovemaking. Her body writhes underneath his frenzied thrusts. Her small breasts, with dark erect nipples, beckon him near. Her pubic hair is trimmed neat, and he loves to watch himself thrust in and out of the sweet spot between her legs.

At this moment, he is thinking of her.

He is savoring the moment of being inside his wife. Yet, he ponders *her*... Olivia's legs, thighs, navel, breasts, neck, ass, and beautiful face.

He longs to drink her in, consume her in one bite, so he can carry her around inside of him wherever he goes. Since this is not possible, he dreams of her instead. Constantly. At work, during the commute home, while having supper, afterwards as he and his wife sit on the couch watching television, and even while they are having sex.

Now as he thrusts deep inside of his wife, he imagines he is making love to *her*. He thrusts harder, giving it to her the way he supposes Olivia would want it . . . deep, hard, and long. Carly's eyes are glazed as he pummels her, mouth open, tongue poised at her lips, but no words emerge. She is not one to talk during sex—not even a whimper or a moan. She only makes faces, ushering him onward with a gesture here and there. She's not shy—not afraid to take his dick in her hand and put it where she desires.

But she doesn't moan.

And this is okay with him. It never even crossed his mind. Until the one evening when Miles and Olivia stayed over . . .

The rain pounded the roof with a vigor that frightened even him. He was huddled on the couch with Carly, while Miles and Olivia sat cozily across from them on the love seat. With the electricity out and half the city in the dark from the storm, their faces were bathed only by candlelight. It had been pouring for hours—started just as they arrived. They were supposed to be going out for dinner and a movie—and now had no choice but to change plans, deciding instead to dine in. Then, the power went out. They listened to the reports on a portable radio about the roads becoming flooded.

Ryan told them to stay over in the guest bedroom. No way were they going to attempt to drive anywhere in that deluge.

Later on that night, after exhausting the supply of chardonnay, merlot, and margarita mix, they retired to their separate rooms. Carly, as usual, drank a bit too much and had to be put to bed. So, Ryan lay beside her, stroking her smooth belly with one hand, tugging on himself with the other. In the next room, Miles made love to his wife. It was clear they tried to keep the noise down, but Ryan had no trouble discerning Olivia's moans through the thin wall.

Ooooooooh.

Ahhhhhhh.

He imagined Miles taking her from behind, her round, heart-shaped ass flattening against his harried thrusts as she moaned and groaned.

He heard it all—Olivia begging for more, commanding her husband to give it to her deeper. Her whispers became increasingly frantic until she cried out, a single muffled scream that caused Ryan to spurt onto his own belly, her orgasm mixing with his as Carly snored peacefully beside him.

He never forgot that night. Never forgot those sounds of love that haunt him even to this day. He longs to hear those words, soft melodies that alighted from her lips.

Ooooooooh.
Ahhhhhh.
Mmmmmmmm.
Yeahhhhhhhhhhhh.
Sounds of love . . .
From this woman . . .
The object of his obsession . . .
Another man's wife.

The huge, warehouse-like space is littered with cubicles and conference tables made of steel, mesh, and chrome. Four elevated offices located in the four corners of the building; the domain of management—hers—Olivia's diagonally across from his. The staff, he recalls with a smirk, calls them birdcages, and that is exactly the way he sees his office, as a cage—because everyone, all the staff, can watch the intimate actions of their superiors just by glancing up at the elevated space and four sheets of glass.

While sitting in his cage, re-reading an e-mail thread from a throng of engineers, his cell rings. He absently glances down and notices he has three missed calls. Answering on the fourth ring, he notes the time. Well past 3:00 P.M.

Miles. No preamble.

"I waited for close to ninety minutes . . ."

Ryan clenches his teeth and swears.

"Oh, shit, man, I totally forgot. Got tied up with this defect shit."

"Whatever. We need to talk. It's about Olivia."

This stops him dead in his tracks. He is silent.

"Hear me?" Miles demands.

"Yeah." A million scenarios run through his head at warp speed. Of course, she told him. Ryan would have been naïve to think otherwise.

What to do?

Deny it?

No, she has the letter . . . his words on a page.

He wonders if Carly knows yet.

If not, it would only be a matter of time.

Oh, Christ.

"I have to take care of a few things," he hears Miles utter, "but will be free later on. We need to talk. Tonight—can't put this off any longer."

"Okay."

Miles provides the when and where, then hits End. Ryan stares at the cell in his palm. Glancing up, apprehension covering his face like stubble, he peers toward her office. It sits vacant.

He punches the switch angrily, bathing his cage in privacy.

Men always focus on the physical to a fault.

He does that now.

Reliving, in excruciating detail, how she took him— inch by delicious inch—into her awaiting mouth.

He recalls with razor-sharp clarity the feeling of absolute pleasure he took in slipping inside her mouth. The feeling was so exquisite and overpowering, as he knew with a surety he would not last, couldn't hold back the passion surging forward like a wailing, out-of-control sandstorm. No longer caring, his mind ceased to perform the analysis, to evaluate what he was doing there and then, or the dire consequences of his actions.

When exactly did he compromise his marriage? He should have paused to consider this simple question.

But he could not.

Was it months back when he began, seemingly unconsciously, to notice her in a different light—looking forward to the times when she sashayed into his cage, flashing her signature smile, her touch alighting on his shoulder in passing, but the feeling remaining for several hours?

When was it?

She had kissed him that night—and that single act had changed him. His internal fire turned up high—no longer smoldering, but an all-out four-alarm blaze; he was no longer able to contain his emotions.

Was it minutes or hours earlier when Miles' gruff voice interrupted their pleasure?

He did not know. Nor did he care.

The two of them, Olivia and Ryan, had scattered like rats, retreating to their separate lairs to wait—he knew—counting the seconds until her husband's snoring returned to normal. Then creeping back up the carpeted steps slowly, hands extended in front of him as he moved stealthily, his mind a daze, no longer thinking of her—his wife, Carly, who lay sleeping and unaware below.

When he reached the first floor, he found it bathed in darkness. No matter how long it took, he would feel his way, inch by inch, foot by foot. He did so, fingers outstretched, remembering where the couch and other furniture lay. Found the couch quickly and sat down slowly, aware of every movement and every sound his body and the fabric made. He

*willed his breathing to return to normal, but it would not
comply. He was that fired up.*

Then he heard her.

Every sense was tuned to an ultra-high frequency.

Progressing down the stairs—he was sure.

Returning to him.

*He squeezed himself and stifled a moan. His heart
raced. Soon now—nothing else mattered. It was messed
up—this situation—if one could call it that—if he allowed
himself one split second of reasoned thought to consider—
but he did not.*

He was too far gone for that.

*She approached. He silently inhaled, smelling her scent.
It was overpowering—the musk that accompanies passion—
raw, primal sex smells. His fist rushed to his mouth. She was
ready for him, meandering around furniture silently, footfalls light on the thick carpeting.*

*A woman's touch. He felt it on his face and chest, mov-
ing downward, experiencing the fingernail as it grazed skin
and navel before ending at the top edge of his boxers. He
held his breath, and held his cock in his palm, as in offering. Take it, he willed her, before I go insane.*

*Then he alighted from the couch as she silently complied,
taking him gently inside.*

*The feeling was indescribable. Her mouth was an oven
and he thrust toward the back of her throat as he reached for
her locs, the ferocity within causing him to tremble. Toes curling on the cool carpet, legs outstretched, holding her head in
his hands while bucking his hips slowly. Darkness had settled around them like a blanket. Occasional house creaks
and groans interrupted the otherwise silent hush of the night.*

*He bucked harder, increased his thrusts. She met him
with an expert touch, wrapping her fingers along his shaft,
squeezing him back inside.*

To a place that was warm, wet, and cozy.

She was increasing the tempo now, upping the pace, let-

ting him know in that unspoken language lovers use, it was okay to unleash. I know what you want. I know what you need. Use me, baby. Don't be afraid to let go. I'm willing to take anything you send my way.

How long, he could not say. Wasn't very long, though. The time they had spent all came down to this—a single physical act—an instant in time that forever changed things.

A tidal wave rolling.

An avalanche barreling down an ice-covered mountainside.

It all came down to this—a delicious blow job, an end of the line, fantasy turned reality.

He couldn't have stopped it if he tried.

He rose up, toes digging into the carpet, grasping the sides of her head, locs trapped between fingers as he came, unleashing an outpouring of emotion and everything else he had to offer. Until there was nothing left to give.

It took everything he had and every ounce of strength he possessed not to scream.

Then it was done, as quickly as it had begun.

Her sweet mouth contained his manhood for an instant more before allowing it to slip out. While rising off her haunches, she tucked his member safely inside his underwear before leaving him alone, giving him back to his spouse quietly before returning faithfully and silently to her own.

Chapter 5

The interior of the sedan is warm. He scans the dash, noting the time. Over an hour late to this preordained meeting, his eyes pan across Miles' smooth, shadowy face. Even dappled in darkness, he is ruggedly handsome—strong angular lines, piercing eyes, inviting smile. He knows why she chose him.

Miles is chewing on an unlit cigar, the image propelling him back to the party—and to her, clad only in a man's button-down shirt—her wares spilling out enticingly.

Stop it.

That precious moment, captured eternally in midflight, emblazoned in his mind like a high-resolution photograph, is gone forever.

Never to return.

He understands that now, yet ponders how everything went wrong so quickly.

Back to the present. He's late.

Miles' clenched jaw line tells him so, and that the man in the driver's seat is not amused.

Patience running thin.

Gas tank on reserve.

He's been driving around the city, attempting without success to find a solution to this problem.

His situation.

But situations like this don't have easily defined solutions or answers.

He's been avoiding Miles as if he were the plague, knowing he has to face his demons, his nemesis, sooner rather than later.

However, he never counted on it all crashing down this soon.

"Hey," he mutters, breaking the silence.

Miles turns the radio down, glancing his way.

"Expected to see you about an hour ago."

He grins nervously. Raises his shoulders as if to imply that shit happens.

Miles clears his throat, then lowers the window and chucks out his now-cold cigar. Turns to Ryan and says, "Time we talked, you and I, don't you think?"

He merely grunts.

Miles launches. "I'm aware of this . . . this thing with Olivia. Have known for some time, actually." He pauses, glances over at the passenger side, at the figure whose stare is riveted to his clenched hands, heart racing, afraid to breathe. Afraid not to—unsure of which is worse.

They are in a quiet park at The Point, a hundred yards from a lazy river, airport lights twinkling in the background. A huge sculpture is buried in the sand and dirt to their left, an outstretched hand reaching for the sky, veined and grotesque. At least it appears that way from his vantage point.

"Can't blame you, actually. I mean, look at her— what an incredible woman she is."

He listens. Wonders for a brief instant how this will end.

Knife in the heart?

Fingers gripping his neck until life ebbs away?

His candle blown out—way too soon?

"Even though you've got someone beautiful at home, a man's gotta roam, right? In the genes—innate to all males, handed down, species to species, since long before dinosaurs roamed the earth."

He continues.

"You're obsessing. Can't help yourself. Over your head. In too deep." Miles turns his body to stare at him, giving him his full profile. "Understand what I'm saying?"

He nods silently.

"Problem is, you're obsessing over the wrong one."

Sharp glance his way.

"I don't understand," Ryan says, finding his breath, fighting the demons that live within.

"Obsession—it's a terrible thing. Makes one lose sight of what they're searching for."

Slow, sharp exhale. Resolve—resolve to settle this thing, this situation, no matter what, no matter how fucked up it is, regardless of the outcome, like men— man to man.

"Listen, Miles, I didn't come here—"

"You need to know she wasn't the one who tasted you," Miles says.

He is rising out of his seat now, anger bubbling to the surface, unfettered. Facing Miles, he swallows hard.

"Just what are you talking about?!" he yells incredulously. "What the fuck are you saying?"

"I think you know. Search deep within your soul, and I trust you'll uncover the truth. I have—and I'm in a better place because of it. The truth, as someone once said, will set you free." Miles grins, emits a sharp laugh.

"You're crazy, you know that, Miles? What shit have you smoked?"

"Am I? I think you know it wasn't Olivia who took you deep into her mouth that night after the party . . ."

Split-second pause.

A smile—not wicked, but filled with something else Ryan's yet to comprehend.

"It was me that night, Ryan. Yours truly. Me."

Then Ryan is scrambling out of the car and running full force, arms flailing; branches and vines are stinging his face and cheeks as he sprints blindly into the darkness, eyes wide and mouth open in a silent scream. And Miles sits patiently, fingers tapping to some unnamed, noiseless beat, waiting for him to return, as he knows he will, sooner rather than later, to face his passions and his demons—two opposite ends of the same, god-damned spectrum—the same way he has—like a man. . . .

PART TWO

Chapter 6

She can still taste the salt air on her tongue—that is if she concentrates real hard, closes her eyes, shuts out the cacophony of noise coming from the machines in her office—three-quarter-inch tape; digital video; DVD player; audio; high-definition plasma screen hanging on one wall opposite her desk; another flat-screen on a stand to her left; laptop docked behind her, all vying for her attention. Her senses are on overload—what she's come to expect as a television producer. For a moment, she forces everything to grind to a halt and pushes it down defiantly, leaning back in her executive chair as she swivels, glancing out the picturesque window without really seeing the steel and concrete beyond.

Instead, she recalls the way warm, coarse sand felt on her toes as she maneuvered between lapping waves. Ryan's fingers interlaced with hers as they walked the shore every morning, his brown skin a stark contrast to the white sand beneath their feet. Ryan cracking jokes, stopping every several feet to bend down, examine a shell, a smooth piece of colored glass, or discarded beer bottle fragments caressed by

Caribbean seas. Leaning in, he runs a hand along the small of her back, kissing her neck at the spot that makes her instantly weak, under her chin just off the mid-line, knees faltering from his feather-like touch, and Miles rushing up behind them, patting her ass playfully as he directs them to "get a room" before taking off at a dead run. Olivia's not far behind, clad in a neon bikini, her muscular calves flexing and locs flying as she digs into the sand, attempting to gain on her husband. Ryan and Carly follow close behind, refusing to give up this daily ritual to Miles.

Later, they all sprawl onto hard-packed sand, panting and sweating, laughing and boasting of previous nights, drinking binges featuring liberal amounts of Mount Gay rum and "wukkin' up," that high-energy gyrating dance that Olivia and Carly have come to fancy—their husbands and Bajan (locals), too! Racing mini mokes across the island along meandering roads that turn back on themselves as acres of sugarcane pass them by; hour-long naps in oversize hammocks strung between silk cotton trees; and gin rummy played on the veranda of their ocean-front villa.

These thoughts alone make her smile.

The cottage she shared with her husband for nine days was breathtaking: open air, vaulted ceilings, an explosion of colors, whitewashed hallways; orange rust living room and pale yellow dining room both beachside; cinnamon red study/library and vibrant blue bedroom. Carly could lose herself in any of these rooms and the eclectic artwork of Barbados natives for hours, while sitting cross-legged on the hardwood floor leafing through a Zane novel, Ryan's face in her lap, eyes closed, a pair of headphones adorning his head as he bops to melodic jazz. In the evening, they dined on couscous and fried flying fish, made love on an overstuffed mattress, windows and drapes thrown open to the elements, slow spins from a ceiling fan, sea sounds invading their domain, washing over their damp bodies as Carly used a goose-down pillow to suppress her orgasmic-filled cries. Later, they'd meet Miles and Olivia at the bar, and the ladies would exchange knowing glances, as if their respective passion moans had carried between villas.

The phone on her desk buzzes. Carly checks the caller ID—an associate producer—and ignores it. It is not her husband. Not Ryan. Her eyes flicker over the darkness outside her window that is spreading like a cloud. Fourteen hours in the office, and still no end in sight.

A moment later, the cell on her hip vibrates. She hits mute to squelch it; again it's not him.

A few moments more . . .

That's all she needs today.

Sun-ripe days spent with her husband and best friends, Miles and Olivia, sightseeing, snorkeling, dancing, shopping, tanning, eating, laughing, playing—dazzling starry nights filled with rum drinking, catamaran cruises, and partying till dawn.

She recalls their last night on the island at an outdoor restaurant in Bridgetown, the four of them dining under the stars as live music played on in the background. Miles stood, a thin wineglass filled with merlot.

"To best of friends," he said, his low voice carrying across the expanse of sand as if on wings of doves.

"Hear, hear." They toasted each other and drank silently, each of them lost in memories of the previous week. When Miles sat, flattening his napkin against his linen pants, Carly cleared her throat.

"I want to say something."

All eyes were upon her. It was as if all conversation among the dining patrons ceased for that split second.

"This week has been so incredible. I can't begin to put into words how I feel. I mean, it's been so long since I've taken a real vacation, with work and everything. But my baby here," she said, reaching out to stroke Ryan's forearm, "knew just what the doctor ordered." Her husband beamed. "And, invit-

ing our best friends in the whole wide world was nothing short of genius."

Ryan nodded. *"Listen to the woman!"* he yelled, having had a bit too much to drink.

"I'm serious," she said, voice cut down a notch, eyes capturing each one's gaze in turn. *"Y'all my family—and I love you like you're my own. So thank you for this; thank you for everything."*

Hugs.

Tears shed.

Memories of their vacation together spilled on that final evening like lukewarm tea.

Memories that would be etched into their psyches . . . forever.

They would walk along the beach with its waning breeze one final time, the four of them gazing to the heavens above, silent with their thoughts of the previous week, and contemplation of their place among the stars.

And afterwards still, they found themselves wukkin' up, one last time . . . 'til dawn. . . .

Chapter 7

"Hey, girl!"

Olivia's heart skips a beat as she presses the phone to her ear. For a brief moment, her breath is caught in her throat—and she imagines her body lying on a gurney in a whitewashed emergency room stall; a green, pulsating line on the monitor dipping dangerously low; the pained, anguished look on the attending physician's face before Olivia blinks the thought away. She gulps a quick breath.

"Carly."

It's after ten on a Friday night and Carly's still in the office finishing up the edits for a segment she's producing—something akin to MTV's *The Assistant,* but with a darker shade of skin tone.

She's used to the long hours, the frantic, hectic life of working in television—the network on 24/7 . . . executives always looking for fresh new ideas, competition for viewers' attention always something fierce. Still, it's Friday, and she was hoping to spend some quality time with Ryan at some point . . . at least before the night was through.

He had called her earlier saying he and Miles were meeting. Was vague as to the particulars. Nothing new there. Ryan tended not to provide all the details of his comings and goings unless forced to. Not that he was trying to hide anything. Just his way.

"What's new? Haven't talked to you in a minute," Carly says, trying to dance around the real reason for her call.

She had tried to reach Ryan, but to no avail. He hadn't answered his cell. She left a message earlier—about an hour ago, around nine—and called twice since then, but the calls went straight to voice mail, which was strange.

Perhaps he and Miles are just in a bar someplace with lousy reception.

Happens all the time, doesn't it?

"Not much," Olivia responds, willing herself to calm down. Since this *thing* with Ryan surfaced, she hasn't communicated with Carly much, other than a quick "hi" and "bye." She feels guilty—incredibly guilty for her role in all of this—for leading him on. She's replayed that evening after the party over and over in her mind, examining it from every angle until her head hurt. Then, exhausted from the analysis—and with little wiggle room left—she went to Miles and told him with as little detail as she could muster that Ryan was becoming infatuated with her—that the night of the party she had indeed led him on—the alcohol talking way too loud; she quickly assured her husband while leaving out the sordid details of Ryan's hands traveling the length of her torso, his touch finding his way inside her.

And her hand discovering all of him . . .

"Been busy, as I'm sure you are." Olivia is in the kitchen, refrigerator door open, reaching for a can of Diet Coke when the memories come flooding back.

This is my best friend I'm talking to.

And I violated her trust.

I was intimate with *her* man . . .

Stop it, she tells herself as she takes a quick gulp.

"I hear you," Carly replies. "I'm still at the office, if you can believe that. BET is kicking my black ass without no let up in sight!"

"Damn, girl, sorry to hear that. It's Friday. Can't they let a sistah breathe?" Olivia asks while moving into the living room and taking a seat on the couch. The room is dim, quiet, empty.

Just like that night several weeks ago.

Miles has yet to return.

"As soon as I finish this piece, I'm outta here! Until then, call me Aunt Jemima, 'cause to them I'm just a light-skinned slave girl!" Carly chuckles to herself. Olivia is grateful for the reprieve. "Anyway, listen. I know Ryan and Miles are hanging out tonight . . ." She lets the sentence hang, as if her words were a road that suddenly ends, cars in an instant finding themselves hurtling through dusty air as if suspended by threads.

"Yeah," Olivia says, putting the can on the coffee table, "boys' night out. You know how they do."

Carly did. But Ryan almost always answered his cell.

"Just wondering if you'd heard from your better half. Haven't heard from mine, and I'm trying to figure out when to expect him home."

"Naw, girl. You know how those two get when they're together. Wouldn't surprise me if they're out at Camelot's or someplace like that!" She's referring to the strip club located on M Street, not far from the White House.

"Those fools better not be," Carly replies teasingly.
"Alright, girl . . . well, if you hear from them anytime
soon, have my man holla at his woman. Okay?"

"I got you, girl."

"I know you do."

The line goes dead.

A minute or two after the end of their conversation, Olivia's breathing returns to normal.

Miles returns home a little after midnight. Olivia's
upstairs in their bedroom, TV on, watching Lifetime.
She hears the closing of the front door, keys thrown
onto the hallway table before he heads deeper into
the house. She mutes the volume, listening. Moments
later, she hears his footsteps on the stairs. When he
enters the bedroom, she smiles.

"Hey, baby."

"Hey, yourself!"

Miles is dressed casually, yet stylishly. A pair of
auburn pleated slacks, boots, and an off-white, oversize, button-down made of some foreign fabric that
feels like silk. His locs are thick and held in a pony-
tail by a wide band. His chocolate skin is rich and
luxurious, and Olivia finds herself sucking in a breath
involuntarily. Her husband is looking so delicious that,
for a second, she gets jealous, thinking of all the women
who probably hit on him during the evening. The
moment passes as he bends down, kissing her lightly
on the lips.

"How's your night?" he asks while beginning a
slow undress. The shirt comes off first, floating to the
carpeted floor. Olivia watches him silently before responding.

"Good. Waiting for you, that's all."

Miles gives her a doubting look.

"Meaning what?" he asks, turning to face her. His upper body is still well conditioned considering his age—not from frequent exercising, but because Miles is predisposed to good genes. "You knew I was meeting Ryan tonight. Hell, it was your idea that I have a word with him."

Olivia retreats backwards into the comfort of the pillows. Her husband is right, of course. It had been *her* idea. She knew that her trying to talk to Ryan was not going to cut it. Therefore, she changed tactics.

"So, baby, how did it go?" she asks cautiously.

Miles had slipped off his pants and retreated to their walk-in closet to hang them, his ass and thigh muscles tight in the black boxer briefs he wears. Olivia feels a pang at her insides. Her husband still looks good—damn good.

He returns without responding, the front of his boxer briefs filled with a bulge that makes Olivia beam. She eyes him silently as he moves away from the bed toward the master bath. When he reaches the doorframe, she speaks.

"Not gonna answer me?" she says cautiously.

Miles turns. His facial expression is neutral, but something about him seems preoccupied.

"What do you want me to say? I spoke to him like you asked of me. Told him that this *obsession* with my wife was something he needed to get a handle on." Miles steps out of view and into the master bath, a large room with black tile, dark gray wallpaper, vaulted ceiling, skylight, and a raised soaking tub equipped with a separate shower stall enclosed by clear glass on two sides.

Olivia feels the tension in her gut radiate outward. She raises her voice to be heard over the din of the shower he's begun.

"Baby? You didn't say *obsession*, did you? Tell me

you didn't use that word!" A few seconds pass. Then a
few more. Olivia resists blurting out her dissatisfac-
tion, but this minimalist communication style of his is
not working for her right now. She counts to three
silently and then says, "BABY?"

Louder this time.

Miles walks out of the bathroom and into the bedroom. His boxer briefs are gone. He is nude. Olivia
blinks, eyes traveling down his torso, quickly dispens-
ing with his belly and waist. She never ceases to marvel
at his manhood—which is, in her humble opinion, a
true work of art. She smiles as she eyes his penis,
knowing he will be aroused soon, if she has anything
to do with it.

"WHAT?" he says, deflating any thoughts of inti-
macy and passion. He is staring at her as if she uttered something completely ridiculous. "What the
hell is this, the third degree?"

"No, baby—"

"Look," he says, one hand on his hip as he interrupts her, "you asked me to handle it, and now
you're attempting to dissect every single word? No—
I'm not having that."

Miles glares at her for a second, and for that moment, Olivia's thoughts are transported back to her
childhood—when her daddy used to chastise her for
doing something wrong. It was the same stare—almost the same pose—hand on hip, index finger outstretched toward her. Olivia gulps and remains
silent. Satisfied there won't be further discussion,
Miles pivots on his heels and returns to the bathroom.

The door slams shut.

Or perhaps she just imagines it does.

Olivia remains in bed, alone, not moving, and

quiet. Her mind is racing, thoughts ping-ponging between Miles, Ryan, and Carly.

Husband, lover, best friend . . .

Jesus.

Chapter 8

Olivia enters the clammy room. Steam wafts from the shower and is hovering just below the skylight like a cirrus cloud. The mirrors above the twin vanities are fogged; the glass stall is covered in perspiration. Yet, she can see her husband, his back turned to her, face to the wall, soap decorating his ass and thick legs. She is wearing a Japanese robe, a repeating pattern of blue cranes on white silk. Olivia considers crossing the three feet to the shower stall as is, but instead, she drops the robe where she stands by the vanity and goes to him on her toes, nude.

Olivia is one of those women who, as Miles is fond of saying, is far more beautiful unclothed than clothed. That does not take away from how smart she can look when she is dressed—but get her naked, and her true beauty shines like a flame.

Her body is thick—substance to her powerful, yet sculpted thighs, a slight bow to her legs, giving her a sensuous edge. She is equipped with an ass that any black woman would be proud of, large ripe breasts, and thick dark nipples that stand erect with the slightest breeze. Her sex is not shaved clean the way most men prefer. She doesn't have time to keep it trimmed nor could she care less, so Olivia lets it grow—not run wild, but enough that Miles has to part her pubic hair with his fingers in order to find her sweet nectar center.

Olivia reaches the glass door, grasps the polished steel handle, and opens it silently. Miles senses her without turning around. Yet, before he can react, she is pressing against him—her cool body on his hot, soapy one; heavy breasts connecting with his back, her nipples making twin soap trails as she maneuvers into position. Hands wrap around his waist, face nuzzling against his neck as he leans back into her and sighs.

They are silent.

Words are not needed.

Olivia's original plan was to wait for Miles to come to bed before continuing their conversation. But something didn't seem right. The fact that he had seemingly snapped at her for no reason didn't add up. It was reasonable for her to be curious about the conversation he'd had with Ryan earlier that evening, wasn't it? She had thought for sure he would come home and want to replay the details for her—allowing her to consider every sentence and response.

But that hadn't happened.

Miles had been drinking . . . that much was obvious.

So, she'd left him alone, giving him his space, until she couldn't stand it any longer.

The not knowing.

The unknown.

Olivia knew, that like most nights when Miles went

out without her, he'd return home ready for some action. Perhaps she could speed things along—get him in that vulnerable position where men would say and do anything their partners asked of them.

Olivia smirks as she readies her plans.

Her hands roam over his soapy skin, taking the loofah and body wash from him. Lathering it up, she proceeds to wash his entire body, beginning with his neck and shoulders, descending down his back to his waist, grabbing his ass in one hand, squeezing the flesh as she cleanses him, feeling his power and strength as her fingers and palm drift from one cheek to the other. Miles loves the spinning classes he takes several times a week at the gym several blocks from his office. Because of it, his ass, thighs and calves are well defined. Olivia spends some time on these parts before descending further. Miles stands there and allows her to take control, hands overhead and pressed against the sweating tile with his head thrown back. The rush of the spray is therapeutic. He sighs when she takes hold of his penis, her hands snaking around his waist, fingers gliding over dark skin, inching near until she feels him.

Miles is already erect.

Olivia smiles, rubbing the bulbous head with her palm, dropping the loofah so she can give him her full attention.

She begins to tug at him . . . a slow, deliberate motion that elicits a heartfelt moan. She kisses his neck and flicks her tongue around the fleshy part of his ear. She grinds her pelvis into him, letting him know she is turned on, as well. A moan escapes from her lips and she is cognizant of her own wetness that meanders down her thigh.

Miles turns.

His member brushes against her stomach.

Then his hands are on her ass, pulling her into him. He kisses her hard on the mouth, tongue darting between her teeth, and the beer taste is not undesirable. He is being aggressive, nibbling on her lower lip, hand rushing up and palming her breasts, tugging at the nipples before both hands dip back down and again find her ample behind.

Olivia's response is pure rapture.

Miles pushes her against the back shower wall, cool tile on her skin as he palms both cheeks, spreading them apart. Instantly, she feels the rush of water on her skin, an avalanche of passion racing downward, a powerful spray on her neck to the small of her back, and downward still. Miles is sucking at her neck as he grinds against her. The rush of water is like a river; it finds her vulnerabilities and rides her like a wave.

Downward.

And when the water licks against her, Olivia finds heaven.

Fingers, his, find her core, spreading her wings, and as Olivia closes her eyes and soaks up the intensity of this wondrous feeling, a thought embraces her. *I'm a butterfly,* she thinks, *with wings of honey.*

Olivia smiles at the imagery.

Then, in an instant, that icon is gone—disappeared, replaced by something else entirely.

Something she must grasp and hold on to.

Just for a moment.

Ryan's fingers had found her core, too. His digits spread her the way her husband is doing now, this delicious instant. And she finds she can't separate the two—as she stands this very second in the shower—knees ready to falter, legs all rubbery and about to give out, the lovely rush of hot spray against her clit, the tremor of Miles' fingers filling her insides, distinct from Ryan's smooth, slow, and purposeful touch.

Olivia remembers that evening with precision-like clarity—the way her best friend felt at that exact moment when he entered her. It was as if all the air had been sucked out of the room. Olivia wanted so badly to scream, but found she could not do so.

In an instant, she feels the tremor and gives in to its power. Before she can scream, Olivia is brought back to reality by Miles inside her, two bodies leaning against each other as the hot spray rains down, one leg hiked around his hip as he fills her in one flourishing stroke.

And that is fine, because Olivia is still sensing the aftershocks.

She grips her husband as he beats against her, hot breath on her neck, locs swinging to a silent syncopation, a slow groove that loses its rhythm.

Miles moves against her with abandonment, eyes closed, head thrown back, palms pressed on either side of her, fingers splayed and flat against the tile.

Holding on . . .

Holding back . . .

Then, no longer giving a damn, he grunts, groans, and comes.

It takes a moment for them to collect themselves.

Such is the way after really good sex.

Later, they towel off in silence.

Olivia suddenly longs for the warmth of her bed, and her husband's arms that shield her and hold her safe from harm's way.

She is hoping tonight, in the afterglow of their lovemaking, he'll share the intricacies of the conversation between husband and best friend . . . a gift, just for her . . . the details of which she longs to hear.

But it is not meant to be. . . .

At least not on this night. For Miles is uncharacteristically silent tonight. And there is nothing Olivia can do to change that.

Not a damn thing . . .

Chapter 9

Ryan blinks.

He is sitting on a high stool, a thick, dark bar curving away from him in both directions. The shiny surface holds an untouched beer in a tall mug, which has been set directly in front of him. He is staring at the glass, attempting to focus on the details, seeing without truly seeing. He has no idea how it came to rest there. No idea at all how he came to be here.

The bile remains lodged in his throat. Ryan winces and reaches for the beer, hoping to erase the taste. Hoping to erase everything about the evening. But so far, that's proved impossible.

How long? How long has he been sitting here?

Ryan does not know.

He glances around. A bar, for sure; name, unknown.

Low-lit, windowless, typical bar atmosphere almost to the point of clichéd: pool table towards the back, a few dartboards hanging on walls to his left, several patrons at the bar with heads down, lost in their thoughts or their sorrow. A few more at two-person tables. Mostly white folks; a few black people—none of them paying him any mind.

The bartender catches his eye and asks if she can get him anything.

Ryan takes a moment to consider her.

Brown skin, nice smile, hair done in afro puffs, slightly large—thick is the politically correct term these days—round ass in tight, low rider jeans. Pink Von-Dutch baseball tee showing off her D cups. A bottle opener stuck into the back pocket of her blue jeans. A short vertical stud bisects her right eyelid. Tiny diamond embedded in her left nostril. When she speaks, he observes a blue barbell in her tongue. When she turns and bends down, a hint of a tribal band tattoo peeks out, just above her café au lait butt.

Twenty-two, twenty-four years old—max.

Ryan's been staring during the few moments it takes to consider her request. Now, he merely shakes his head, feeling nothing—not hunger, not thirst. Only the bile in his mouth is constant, and it won't go away.

I received oral sex from a man . . .

The bartender nods and moves off. A second later, Ryan clears his throat and she stops in mid-stride, head turned his way. He waves her back over.

"Anything sweet," he says barely above a whisper, then winces, swallowing hard. "Nasty taste in my mouth." He starts to say something else, but shuts it down. Pushes the mug away.

She nods understandingly, and goes to work fixing him something else. A chilled martini glass is placed before him. She's grabbing this liquor and that—a clear bottle followed by others he does not recognize. She is watching him, silent as she crafts his drink, giving him a smile when they make eye contact. He glances away.

She shakes the concoction in a cocktail shaker, does a show of twirling the gleaming metal in one hand in a quick flourish before pouring the frothy mix. She wipes her hand off on her jeans before she extends it to him.

"I'm Reese. Let me know if I can get you anything else."

Ryan takes her hand, offering a weak handshake in return. Her hand lingers a bit before dropping to her side. He doesn't provide his name—and she doesn't press him for it. Reese walks away a moment later to attend to other customers, and Ryan watches her go.

The interior of Miles' car; the unspeakable things he said, and all it entailed; passenger door flung open; Ryan stumbling, running; leaves and branches stinging his face and cheek; guttural screaming—emanating from his throat. Ryan touches his face and winces in horror as he feels the welts on his cheek. *Engine turning over, tires squealing, Ryan peeling away; cars, taxis, streetlamps, government building . . . all a rush of imagery as he passes them by, seeing without truly seeing.*

How he got here, he does not know.

He remembers pulling over beside some trash-strewn, vacant liquor store in D.C., thick black bars on the doors and windows. His driver's side door left open as he went to the curb and vomited, the grotesque foul-smelling chunks nearly missing his shoes as he retched. He remained doubled over for nearly a minute, the pain so deep and intense he thought he would pass out, then righting himself because he suddenly felt the chill associated with premonitions— hair on his forearms standing up straight as if his life

*would momentarily be snuffed out on some nameless, ghetto
street. So he bolted—reached the car in three quick strides
and careened away, almost hitting a parked car as he
fought to control his vehicle.*

Not feeling safe.

Pulse not recovering until he was miles away.

Ryan blinks.

Reese is standing in front of him, stealing a quick
sip from a glass of water.

"Drink okay?" she asks.

Ryan hasn't touched it. He does so now, takes a slow
sip . . . testing the waters, so to speak. He nods. Reese
nods in return, then hands him a bar napkin filled
with ice chips.

"For your face," she says, gesturing towards him.
He cautiously takes hold and applies it to his cheek,
eyes never leaving hers.

I received oral sex from a man . . .

Am I a faggot?

Ryan scrunches his face as he considers the cold
ice pack and the question that looms in front of him
as clear as day.

Reese watches him, but says nothing.

He has regarded this question and the associated
thoughts over and over for the past two and a half
hours. Has pondered Miles' words—dissected them
over and over, reviewed them from left to right and
then again from right to left—looking for an opening, a weakness he could exploit.

Nothing.

Miles was fucking with him. Telling lies.

Had to be, right?

Guys fuck with one another, right?

Poor choice of words, considering the circumstances. But the answer still is no.

There's no way what Miles said could be true. What Miles was implying couldn't be true—not in Ryan's case.

Could it?

A woman's touch. He felt it on his face and chest, moving downward, experiencing the fingernail as it grazed skin and navel before ending at the top edge of his boxers. He held his breath, and held his cock in his palm, as in offering. Take it, he willed her, before I go insane.

Could what Miles be implying be true?

Ryan didn't know.

So, he forces himself back to that evening.

Measures the details as if he were reliving the entire episode frame by frame.

The feeling was indescribable. Her mouth was an oven and he thrust toward the back of her throat as he reached for her locs, the ferocity within causing him to tremble. Toes curling on the cool carpet, legs outstretched, holding her head in his hands while bucking his hips slowly. Darkness settled around them like a blanket. Occasional house creaks and groans, spiking the otherwise silent hush of the night.

And finds nothing.

Nothing of substance to clear him from the truth.

Am I a faggot?

Because I let another man . . .

"STOP IT!"

Reese glances up sharply. He is yelling—not at her. Not at anyone in particular.

He drops his head and shakes it forlornly. This whole thing has been blown *way* out of proportion, and if he just closes his eyes, blinks back the tears that seem to be waiting in the wings, he'll be alright.

He'll wake up tomorrow, snug and warm in the confines of his bed, Carly on her side, spooning him as she's fond of doing, everything the way it was before. Everything okay.

He hasn't done what Miles alleges.

Ryan blinks.

He did not allow another man to fellate him.

He did *not*.

Could *not*.

Blinks again.

No heterosexual man in his right mind would.

Or could . . .

Right?

Ryan looks to Reese for an answer.

She smiles sheepishly when their stares meet and lock.

Sorrowfully, she lacks the answer to this fundamental question.

Chapter 10

Miles listens to her breathing. It's like the slow, steady hand of a Swiss watch—predictable. She has been asleep for over thirty minutes now. Olivia faces away from him, covers pulled up to her neck, clad in a silk nightgown that comes down to mid-thigh. It is after one in the morning, yet Miles is wide awake. He stares at the patterns of shadow and light dancing off the stucco wall and listens to the wind howl. He can't sleep, not with things left in this unresolved state.

Miles considers the things he has to do . . . the people he has to see.

Ryan.

His thoughts have not strayed far from his friend this past evening.

Their conversation went badly. Not at all the way he had planned.

Miles had rehearsed it a thousand times. Was hoping and praying Ryan would understand . . . would see things his way, open his eyes to this new way of thinking, this new way of *existing*.

But not yet . . .

Miles, for one, marvels at his newfound freedom . . . this newfound lifestyle. It's amazing how differently things look now. Colors more vibrant, air more pungent. Miles is loving life. He is, in a word, a*live*.

His thoughts race back to his shower. Miles had wanted to be alone—needed time to decompress, to sort things out. But Olivia had violated the sanctity of his temple by entering the stall.

His shower . . .

But it was okay.

Olivia is his wife. He loves her. He still desires her. And above all else, he still wants her in his life.

No contradiction as far as he's concerned.

Miles smiles in the near darkness, then reaches down and takes hold of himself, feeling the blood rush.

Oh yes, it was fine that Olivia came in when she did.

For that is the beauty of this, this new *thing*—Miles can have his cake and eat it, too!

He suppresses a giggle.

Yes, he's having his cake and eating it, too.

Making love to his wife was exactly what the doctor ordered. In some small recess of his mind, he had fantasized about delicious things happening between Ryan and himself tonight, but he knew it was too early to happen. Ryan's response was typical, and Miles was not the least surprised by his reaction. Poor guy didn't know what hit him. He kind of liked doing that—witnessing the deer in the headlights look, all confused, unable to make any sense of what was being said. But then all the pieces suddenly dropped into place. And in time, sooner rather than later, Ryan would come around . . . just like Miles had.

Ryan *will* come to understand the power of male sensuality—the bond two men can share.

After all, he had passed the first test by allowing another man to take him in his mouth.

Oh yes, he will come to crave it the way vampires crave blood.

That he will. Miles was sure of it.

Miles pulls on his penis, which is semi-hard. Thoughts drift like tendrils of smoke back to that wonderful evening, the night when he was able to consummate his lustful fantasies with action. Ryan had been so far gone, so consumed with obsession that he would have fucked a stump if he'd thought it belonged to Olivia.

Miles wasn't stupid. . . .

He'd seen all along what was going down . . .

Carly had to be a fool for not seeing what was transpiring before her very eyes.

So, Miles took the bull by the horns and took advantage—not the way he had planned it—but sometimes you have to take hold of the situation and seize the moment. And that's exactly what he did.

He doesn't regret a thing.

Olivia stirs. She turns on her back, and then sighs heavily before turning to face him, breathe in his face, inches from his own. Still out. Arm draped over his shoulder before dropping to her side. Miles places one hand on hers, caressing the flesh, feathering the curve to her digits as he masturbates with his other. Slowly, methodically, he draws her hand closer.

Inching nearer to his engorged state.

Miles finally places her hand on top of him. Wraps her fingers around his girth.

Tugging at his hardening member with her slender fingers.

Miles is grinning now as he lifts the silken fabric. Finding the space between his wife's legs, he rubs her with the palm of his hand.

Olivia emits a slight moan, then parts her legs wider.

Miles considers his two lovers: Olivia and Ryan . . . Ryan and Olivia.

His wife is stirring, eyes fluttering before coming awake, feeling her hand on her husband's sex.

Miles is thinking, *I took Ryan that night and made him mine . . . just like I'm going to do to you tonight, my love.*

Olivia is thinking, *My husband is insatiable, but I can feel his cravings tonight, and this is something I can handle.*

She smiles in the near darkness and spreads her thighs wider.

One more time . . .

Chapter 11

The harshness of sudden light makes his head throb. Like a siren in the dead of night, it is piercing, painful. Ryan, head down, glances up quickly. And just the act of doing so makes him dizzy. The bar is vacant. The bartender, Reese, is cleaning up behind him. She is scooping up half-empty beer bottles, placing them on a drab gray tray. A cup of coffee is positioned in front of him. Gingerly, he reaches out for the handle, puts the mug to his lips, and takes a sip. Lukewarm. He grimaces as Reese walks behind him, her hand on his shoulder as she leans in.

"You straight?"

Ryan nods imperceptibly, and then considers the absurdity of the question, considering *his* present circumstances.

Am I? Am I straight???

"Closing time, man, you gotta get going," she says softly. "Coffee for the road?"

Ryan turns his head to stare at her. She is standing there, hand on hip, lower lip being mashed by her teeth. He watches her silently, nods. Reese moves behind the bar, removes the coffee mug, and replaces it with a fresh one. "Don't have any Styrofoam cups here, so this'll have to do. You can return it next time you're in the neighborhood. Deal?"

She is only a few yards away, smiling, and Ryan, for the first time since his terrible ordeal, smiles back. He gazes upon her, notes a certain attraction. She is not at all like his wife, who is tall and thin, light skinned, auburn-colored hair that is normally worn flat-ironed and pressed. This woman is the opposite. Reese is shorter, more filled out, but with sensuous curves, a healthy ass, and large breasts. Her look, though, is what Ryan is drinking in now. The way she broods over him silently; the steel in her brow, nose, and tongue erotic, the afro puffs retro—and yet, it all works for her. And works well. The whole package says: sexy, neo soul. For the first time since he ran screaming from Miles' car, he feels momentary peace.

Eye of the hurricane . . .

"You okay?" she inquires.

"Yeah, I'm gonna live," Ryan responds.

"Good, 'cause I was worried about you. You've got this . . . this lost look to you. Like you just lost your best friend."

Ryan considers her words. In a way, that's exactly what happened.

"I'll be alright. Thanks for the hospitality and the drinks."

"It's what I do," Reese answers. She thinks to herself, *There is something about this guy that I like . . . something intriguing.*

Ryan rises from the bar, falters, and reaches out for support. Reese is there with a strong hand.

"Whoa—you need to take it slow. Listen, you're in no condition to drive, so let me call you a cab."

"Naw, I'm fine," Ryan says, sucking in a quick

breath before standing on his own. He reaches for his wallet and fumbles around inside before pulling out two twenties. "Keep the change," he mumbles, palming them to the bar.

"You are too kind." Reese grabs the bills and places them in the register. "I'm serious, man, you can't drive. I'd take your keys right now, but then you'd have to wait until tomorrow evening to get them back. So, I'm gonna let you go—but only if you promise not to get behind the wheel."

Ryan is waving her away as he takes several steps from the bar. It is obvious he has consumed too much liquor. His gait is that of an elderly man or someone with a knee injury. Reese comes from behind to join him, leading him to the door and up the stairs to the street. The going is slow. He needs to hold onto the railing for support. His other hand wraps itself around her waist. The air hits him in the face when they reach the street—a stark contrast to the warmth below. He pulls the halves of his jacket closer around him as he shivers involuntarily.

Reese leads him to the curb and says, "Here you go. You can catch a taxi. Shouldn't be but a few moments before one arrives."

Ryan glances around. He recognizes the street, but has no recollection of getting here. Automobiles line the road on both sides. Yet he doesn't see his.

"What's wrong?" she asks, arms still looped inside his.

"Can't find my car," he slurs.

"Told you, no driving. Want me to take your keys?"

She is leaning close to him. Even after a long night of tending bar and slinging beers, she still has a womanly scent. Ryan closes his eyes to lose himself in her scents.

"Not gonna drive," he responds, his eyes locking

with hers. "Just wanna know where I parked, that's all."

Reese grins. "Worry about it when you've sobered up. Listen, I gotta go—gotta get back inside to close up. It's been real."

Ryan attempts a smile. "Yeah, it has."

She takes a half step away from him; Ryan wobbles; Reese stops.

"You sure you gonna be okay?"

"Yeah, yeah," he says softly, waiting for her to disappear, "as soon as I locate my ride."

The dash reads 2:15 A.M. Reese has cranked the engine twice before it fires. She sits in the front seat rubbing her hands together as she attempts to get warm. The heat is set on high, but this is a ten-year-old car, so it's going to take a few minutes for the interior to warm.

She is bundled in a brown leather jacket with oversize buttons. The worn backpack slung over her frame now sits squeezed between her shoulder and the driver's side door. Reese takes off slowly down the brown-stained cobblestone alley, which is strewn with overflowing trash bins. She makes a right, cuts through a mostly empty parking lot to the street, then pauses before steering into traffic. She is heading away from the bar, but as she steals a quick glance in her rearview mirror, she spies him.

Curbside, thirty yards or so away.

Coffee mug in hand.

Him.

Unmistakable.

Reese does a quick U-turn, accelerates to where he stands, and leans to roll down the passenger window. It is then that Ryan notices her.

"Dude," she says playfully, "you can't stand here all night. Why haven't you caught a cab?"

Ryan leans his elbows on the open window, grins, and shrugs. Takes a sip of the still warm liquid.

"Been trying, but nobody wants to pick up a black man this late!"

Reese eyes him, sucks her teeth, and then reaches over to unlock the door. "Get in," she says quickly. Ryan does. "And roll up the window," she adds. "I'm freezing over here."

She's still idling near the curb. They turn to face each other.

"Now what?" she asks, realizing she has no clue as to why she's offering this stranger a ride.

"I dunno. Still don't know where I parked my car."

Reese whistles. "Damn. I told you, no driving. Where's home?" she asks.

Ryan begins to rapidly shake his head. "Naw, the wife wouldn't appreciate a pretty young thang dropping me off. Nope."

Reese notices that he pulls incessantly at the ring on his left hand. She considers his words as she stares. Warms a bit when she hears the compliment. "Okay . . ."

Reese pulls out. Ryan is silent, mug between his palms, staring out the window. She sighs heavily.

Reese is thinking, *It is late. I have a stranger in my car. He has nowhere to go. And I have nowhere to take him . . .*

Nowhere, but home.

Chapter 12

Sunlight blazes into the kitchen, warming the dark ceramic tile floor. Olivia is at the sink preparing coffee; Miles is at the counter, halving a muffin, spreading margarine before placing it in the microwave. His wife is glancing out the window, watching the rustling of tree branches, an occasional cardinal checking the birdfeeder for seeds before flying off into the morning sky; Miles is keenly observing the margarine melt.

Another beautiful day—cool, judging by the wind, but delightful nonetheless.

Olivia sighs contentedly. She received a good night's sleep.

Well rested . . . well sexed.

A smile paints her full lips. She turns from the window to pour herself a steaming cup of java.

"Want some?" she asks her husband.

"Please." She pours a second cup.

"So, Miles," she says, handing him the mug with a smile, "you never finished telling me about last night."

Miles takes a cautionary sip and swallows before setting the cup down on the counter.

"What about it?" he asks.

"Come on, honey, why do I feel as if I'm pulling teeth over here? Just tell me. How did it go between you and Ryan?"

Miles is silent.

"MILES!" she says, a bit more forceful. Hands on her hips.

"What? Jesus . . ."

"Miles, I'm tired of having to ask you the same question a thousand times. You said—"

"Look, baby," he interjects, going over and placing his hand on her waist, drawing her near, "everything's cool, okay?" he says with a smile, temporarily deflating her sails. "You asked me to take care of it, and I did—it's done—nothing for you to worry about. Okay?"

"No, Miles, not okay. I need to know what went down. After all, it's me who's gonna see him first thing Monday morning when I get to work, and I don't want any surprises. Okay?"

Miles stares at his wife for a moment, then bends over to kiss her.

"Baby," he says softly, his lips inches from hers, "I said everything's cool. We talked, that's all. Ryan realizes what happened was a mistake. He's a man—and he fucked up. It happens. But it won't happen again. You don't have anything to worry about. We're all still friends."

Miles stands back and sips at his coffee. His wife considers him, clad in a robe, 18-hour stubble on his smooth, dark face. She smiles, reaches out to squeeze his hand, shards of last night entering her mind. Glancing at her watch, Olivia winces, realizing she's got plenty to do. Even though it's Saturday morning, she's an executive. Therefore, work never stops.

Hope my husband is right, she muses. *Hope this thing is over. Done with for good.*

A confrontation with Ryan is the last thing she wants or needs.

And then there's Carly to worry about.

Let this be the last thing Olivia or anyone hears on the matter.

Please, God, heed my silent prayers. Push it down deep, out of sight, and I will be eternally grateful . . .

Carly awakes with a start—jolting up, hair disheveled, back and shoulder aching, senses disoriented. It takes her a few moments to adjust to her surroundings. She finds herself on the couch—television across the room tuned to an all-news channel, sound muted, cell phone on the coffee table beside her. She glances quickly to the watch on her wrist . . . 7:17 A.M.

Oh God!

She glances down.

Favorite pair of sweatpants and Cornell sweatshirt in desperate need of ironing.

Flips open the cell. No incoming calls; nothing missed.

She jumps up, almost yelping from the back pain, the byproduct of a terrible sleep on the sofa, and races to the stairs.

"RYAN?" she yells, head tilted upward to their bedroom.

No response.

Stairs taken two at a time.

In high school and college, she ran hurdles.

Carly's still got skills.

At the top of the stairs, quick left into master bedroom.

Bed unmade.

"Ryan?"

Bathroom—empty.

"Ryan?"

Down the stairs, taken two, three, and then four at a time. She hits the bottom landing with a deafening thud. Skids on the shiny hardwood. Scoops up the cell and is speed-dialing his number as she races for the kitchen. Footfalls on tile as she reaches for the door leading to the garage.

"RYAN, DAMN IT!" Carly screams.

Two-car garage—left stall containing a black Range Rover. Call goes immediately to voice mail. She snaps the cell shut.

"DAMN IT!"

Two-car garage—right stall empty.

"Husband," she screams to the quiet house, "where the fuck are you?"

Olivia is stuck in Beltway traffic.

Un*fucking*believable.

How you gonna have traffic jams on a Saturday morning?

Not even 8 A.M.

Only in the nation's capital.

Her cell chirps. Olivia reaches for it, stealing a quick glance at the screen.

Oh shit.

Carly.

"Hello?"

"Ryan didn't come home last night."

No preamble. No formalities this time.

"And he won't answer his phone!" Carly exclaims.

"Shit, Carly." Olivia's mind is racing along with her heart. She can feel the pounding in her chest. Swears Carly can hear it through the phone.

"Miles. Time—what time did he get home?" she asks, words disjointed.

"'Round midnight, Carly," she says, trying to sound calming.

"Well, mine never showed. You have any idea where they went?"

Olivia swallows hard. This situation between them— Ryan and Olivia—this thing that occurred several weeks ago—something seemingly so innocuous, something she wishes to God she could undo and forget— suddenly looms in front of her.

It haunts her; it can't be undone; it *won't* go away.

This situation threatens to consume everyone she's close to—her husband, Miles, her best friend, Carly. This thing between them—Ryan and Olivia— spreading like a tumor, growing out of control with each passing minute.

Something about Miles' way-too-calm demeanor and his reluctance to talk doesn't add up.

Like he is hiding something.

Like he doesn't want her to know the truth.

"No, girl. Miles said they . . . talked . . . hung out . . . guy stuff, you know? I don't like to pry," Olivia adds.

"Well," Carly says, beyond frustration, "I want to know. Where the fuck can he be?"

"Calm down, Carly," Olivia advises. "Please, just calm down. We'll find him."

She switches lanes, brakes, heads for the shoulder. An exit several hundred yards away beckons her. Olivia takes it.

"Listen, I'm sure he's fine. I'm sure there's an explanation for all of this."

God, Olivia thinks, *what if something's happened to him?*

Could Ryan's *disappearance* be related to the conversation her husband had with him? Could it possibly all lead back to this thing with him and her?

Jesus.

Olivia needs to come clean now.

A feeling of sudden doom consumes her. She steers right, into a gas station, stopping by a bank of pay phones. Cuts the engine. Pain seizes her at once. She glances out the window, upwards, as if relief will come from the heavens above. It doesn't. The sky is a mixture of blues and white clouds. Olivia breathes deep, attempting to collect her thoughts.

Carly needs to know.

Now.

No. Carly can't know.

Not now.

Olivia exhales sharply.

"Carly, everything's gonna be alright. Let me call Miles," she says, "find out what he knows." Olivia speaks rapidly. "I'll check the office, too—see if anyone's seen him."

"You do that," Carly snaps.

And the line goes dead.

Chapter 13

At the exact moment Olivia's line goes silent, Ryan awakens.

He senses floors creaking, hears a door closing and a toilet flush.

Ryan rises up slowly to examine his surroundings. Feeling the throbbing in his head, he curses silently.

He finds himself in a darkened room—a small, cramped one—on the couch, covered by a light blanket, his feet pressed against the end of the hard sofa. Clothes still on and rumpled. The smell of cigarette smoke hangs on the fabric like cheap cologne. Looking around the living room, he sees a small TV housed in one of those entertainment centers made from wood veneer—the kind you find in Wal-Mart or Target. Several dozen DVDs are in the cabinet underneath the TV.

Hardwood floors, no carpet. A rattan chair in the corner by the window. A number of potted plants; a few prints hanging on walls—an apparent attempt to add color to the place. Small trinkets and miniature sculptures made of wood and stone adorn the coffee table and are positioned around the room.

Ryan places his feet on the cold floor. Hands to his face, holding his head. The pain is a dull roar—a throb that lessens a bit when he massages his temples with his fingers.

Checks his watch.

Seven-thirty A.M.

SHIT!

Door opens, floor creaking.

Ryan glances up and sees her.

Reese—clad in a white tank top and matching panties—caught in mid-stride. It is her thigh that Ryan attempts to focus on. Their stares lock before her head turns along with her body. Then her back is to him as she retreats to her room, and Ryan is left with the after-image of her round bottom, ass cheeks rising and falling in slow motion, the contrast of her white panties on dark skin—thrilling. For a moment, he forgets everything—the past and the present—as lust infuses his being, and he exists merely as a male. For a brief moment in time, he watches her silently, feeling himself swell and rise. However, as quickly as the euphoria comes, it is gone, and all the images, sounds, and feelings from the previous night come crashing down upon him—back to reality, shattering any sense of lustful thoughts that were beginning to take hold.

Ryan's head throbs as he rises. He wobbles un-steadily as he shuffles over to the coffee table where his jacket has been deposited. Reaching into the pocket, he fishes out his cell phone, powers it up, and experiences spikes of pain radiating throughout his chest as he sees sixteen missed calls.

Sixteen . . .

Five voice mail messages.

Ryan listens to them—all from his wife, Carly, her voice morphing from calm and collected to frenzied, harried, and then crazed.

He winces in pain, more so from Carly's words than his hangover.

He's got to call her. Let her know he's okay.

Got to get out of here first.

His mind races with detailed thoughts.

Got to get home fast.

This thing between him and Olivia is a snowball that's rolling down a hill, expanding in mass and volume as it goes. Soon, it will be an avalanche—nothing in its way stopping it.

The thought makes him pause.

Ryan realizes he no longer knows for sure who this thing is about anymore.

Is it Olivia—the object of his obsession?

Once upon a time, it was.

But now, with the icy words of Miles, her husband, creeping back into his psyche, Ryan no longer knows.

He can't even trust his instincts.

Oh God.

How did he get himself into this mess?

He snaps the cell shut, and then re-opens it. Contemplates calling his wife this very instant. Begins to speed-dial her number before snapping the phone shut again.

No, not here.

Not yet.

But she's got to be going crazy—wondering if I'm dead or alive.

He sits. Ping-pongs back and forth—should he or shouldn't he?

Get out of here—find the car. No, too much time.
Instead, get to a pay phone and call her from there—
appease her mind.

The cell phone is heavy in his hands.

He stares at it as if it is a meteorite—something
not of this world. Turns it over in his palms before
opening it and sighing heavily. Glancing at the empty
doorway, he speed-dials her number.

Carly snatches up her phone on the first ring. And
Ryan feels her fury.

"WHERE THE FUCK HAVE YOU BEEN???"

"Baby," he begins, the pain in his head threatening
to make him black out. He presses forward, through
the fire. "I'm sorry. I was too drunk to drive, so I slept
in my car. Phone's been off—battery dead—just have
a second or two of juice left . . ."

Carly is in the midst of a rapid-fire tirade that
Ryan can only half comprehend.

"Baby," he interrupts, "I'm on my way. Just have to
get something in my stomach before I get sick again.
Be home soon, okay?"

She is relentless, on fire. Ryan winces, turns the
volume down, lest the entire neighborhood hear their
back-and-forth exchanges.

"I know; I know, Carly. I'm sorry, but I was drunk.
Look, gotta go. Be home soon."

He closes the phone on her words. Shakes his
head as the cell is dropped into his lap. He exhales
slowly before glancing over to the doorway. Reese is
there again, shoulder pressed into the doorframe,
still clad in her sexy white tank and panties. Legs
crossed. Arms folded across her large chest.

She is staring at him. He is staring back. No words
are spoken.

He is observing her, the jewelry in her eyebrow and
sparkle at her nose. The steel, along with her full, moist

lips, is drawing him near. The outline of dark nipples pokes through translucent fabric, making him weak— a slave to the flesh. Ryan is unblinking. He is thinking about her—this stranger—wondering about her allure, if she has the power, the *authority* to take his hurt away.

If only for a moment.

Make him forget . . . make him right with the world. If only for a single solitary moment. He'd give his right arm for that . . . a moment of solitary peace.

But he's got to go—get home. Face Carly and her wrath.

Suddenly, everything is falling away again. This time, Ryan prays the instant will last.

Reese turns and walks away.

Her footfalls are heavy on wood.

Ryan's heart is pumping a mile a minute as he observes her retreat. Her fullness speaks to him again.

The sound is *loud* . . .

Seconds later, he rises unsurely.

Head pounding, blood flowing, he follows . . .

Like a slave.

Chapter 14

Pulling off the main road and into the sub-development, he feels what he always feels at this moment—peace, tranquility. It's as if he has been transported from one dimension to another—steel, concrete, brick; cars commandeered by hostile drivers; speeding taxis; everyone moving way too fast—giving way to fresh clear air, sunlight, the shrill of birds, the rustling of tree leaves, and best of all—urban silence.

Their house is on a cul-de-sac, a large reddish brick colonial; it sits on a slight hill, higher than the others—a mistake made by the builder—giving it an air of majesty. The grass front and sides are well manicured, the hedges well trimmed. He feels enormous pride every time he turns onto his street and spies his home.

Their home for five years.

Yet this feeling that satiates him is short-lived.

Ryan steers the car up the driveway, feeling his heart race as the garage door lifts. He enters his stall to the right. He takes a deep breath and sighs before hitting the remote to close the garage door. He exits his car, checking his rumpled clothes before sighing again. Ryan steps up and opens the door.

Their house features a large eat-in kitchen facing the deck and backyard. A bay window divides the room; beyond it is a sunken living room. The walls rise to the second floor where a balcony overlooks the room and the fireplace on the far wall. He pauses briefly to take in the expanse of the well-decorated first level.

She is there, like he knew she would be.

Her back is against the island, facing him, a steaming mug of herbal tea in one hand, supporting the cup in the palm with her other. Her favorite, wild berry. Ryan can smell it from where he stands.

Carly's showered, changed. The sweats are gone, and are now replaced by faded jeans and a flattering sweater that showcases her smallish breasts. Shoeless, white socks adorning her feet—the way she's most comfortable. Done her hair up the way he likes. Straight, smooth down her neck.

After all, she's had plenty of time.

It's now close to eleven.

Ryan lets the door close behind him.

Observes her.

She is eyeing him silently. She is in the act of taking a sip when he enters. She finishes, taking a soothing gulp, as if there is no rush.

Not a care in the world.

There is something on the counter behind his wife—thin molded plastic, reminiscent of a thermometer. His attention diverts back to her.

"Hi."

She stares, but says nothing.

Ryan advances, hands at his side. When he reaches

her, his arms raise up to embrace her, head tilting down to implant a kiss. Carly reacts by turning away as she puts up a hand, pushing him back.

"Don't come near me," Carly whispers, and for the first time, Ryan is scared. He has never heard his wife use this tone before and it chills him. For a moment, he looks away, past her into the living room, taking in the rest of their home, thinking, *I could lose all of this. I've already begun my downhill slide.*

"Baby," he begins, but Carly shuts him down.

"Ry, you can't be serious?" She puts the mug down on the counter behind her with a thud. Ryan takes two steps back. Her hands go to her hips. Glancing at her watch, she continues. "I mean, it's fucking eleven o'clock—almost three hours since you said you were on your way home!"

Carly glares at him. She purses her lips, then mashes them together as if she were squashing a bug.

Ryan doesn't like it when she curses. Doesn't like it one bit because it means she is beyond angry.

"I know, Carly, and I'm sorry. It's just, I had to get something in my stomach, had to get gas—"

"And all that took three fucking *hours?* Please!" She reaches for her mug. In the process, her wrist connects, sweeping it off the counter and onto the tile floor. It shatters on impact, ceramic shards and sweet hot tea expanding outward like a hydrogen bomb. In seconds, her foot is red and burning. Carly screams, hands to her toes as she sidesteps the impending wave. Ryan reacts, reaches out to her as she recoils as if in horror.

"Don't fucking touch me!" she hisses, hobbling backwards to the table and taking a seat. The sopping, now stained sock is flung away, narrowly missing him. Ryan backs away. He grabs a roll of paper towels to deal with the spill.

"Don't even come near me after some bullshit excuse like that."

Ryan is kneeling, silent.

Carly is rubbing her calf and toes, shaking her head.

For a moment, the two are still.

Then the tears begin to fall . . . down both cheeks . . . and Carly makes no move to wipe them away.

"Oh, baby," Ryan says, rising. "I'm so sorry for all of this. Please, believe me—"

Carly interrupts him. "You know what? I don't know what to believe. All I know is this: we've been together going on seven years and in all that time nothing like this has ever happened. You've never stayed out all night. You've never," she says, rising while wiping her cheek with the back of her hand, "never got so drunk that you couldn't drive. I have no idea what you are doing. No idea *whom* you are doing it with."

"Carly, it's not—"

"Let me finish!" she exclaims. "If you are doing something, only you know. I'll tell you this, though— I've been your devoted partner and wife for all these years. I've stood by your side, taken the good with the bad; never complained; never faltered in my love for you. But if you think for one second—"

He goes to her, wraps his arms around her frame, despite her protests, and holds her tight.

"I love you, Carly, I do. Wouldn't do anything to hurt you."

The sobs wrack her frame as Ryan holds her tighter, letting the moment pass. She pulls away, again wiping both cheeks and the tears that form in the corner of both eyes.

"I stayed up all night waiting for you," she says, slightly above a whisper.

Ryan leads her to a chair and sits facing her.

"Had some news I wanted to share with my husband," she says.

He swallows audibly. He knows he's fucked up.

"I'm here now," he offers, a half shrug.

She stares at him, taking in his features—his face, his hair, nose, jawline, eyes. Considers the right words to use—tongue against the roof of her mouth before exhaling and nodding imperceptibly.

"I'm pregnant."

Ryan is speechless. He is still, eyes scanning her face, searching for a sign, something that is all-telling. Carly is grating her teeth; he witnesses her jaw seesaw back and forth.

"You sure?" is all he can muster.

She nods.

Reaching over to the counter, she picks up the plastic thing and hands it to him. He stares down at it. Two small windows embedded in plastic at one end—one round, one square. Two parallel lines, one in each window. He glances up. She nods a second time, takes it from his hand, and lets it fall into her palm.

"We're going to have a baby," she confirms.

Ryan extends his arms, connecting with hers. For a full minute, they embrace.

Kissing her forehead, he repeats what she has just uttered. "A baby . . . a baby."

Carly leans back to look him right in the eyes.

Her eyes are wet, yet she is unblinking.

"Don't mess this up, Ryan," she says in a near whisper. "We're going to have a family, so please don't . . . mess this up."

Ryan nods slowly.

"I can forgive many things, but ruining this," she says, waving the plastic thing at him, "is not one of them."

Carly stands.

She reaches for Ryan, grasps his shoulder. "I don't know what is going on with you, but whatever it is, I hope to God it passes." Their eyes lock. "Because if you break this," she says, gesturing a second time with the plastic thing in her hand, "a lifetime will not be enough for my husband to be forgiven."

With that, Carly walks away, leaving Ryan there in the room alone.

His mind is a rushing stream; it races along. Visions enter his mind at light speed—his home, his wife, his burgeoning family.

All imagery coexisting in peaceful harmony.

Nagging at the edge, however, is a subtle thought. One that tugs at his insides, a new consideration—Reese. Her scantily clad body in silhouette, staring him down from across the room, taunting him, drawing him inside her web like a spider, infusing herself into his being.

A snowball rolling down a hill . . .

Ryan thinks himself incapable of slowing it down . . .

The thought both petrifies and ignites his soul.

Chapter 15

She is in her cage, watching him.

She arrived at 7:00 A.M. He arrived thirty minutes later, striding across the wide expanse of office space, meandering around cubes and conference tables with a purposeful step, briefcase in hand, a man on a mission. Didn't offer up a glance her way. Not even for a second.

She watched him climb the steps to his office, his cage diagonally situated from hers. Observed him drop his bag onto the low, leather sofa, the one she's so fond of. Monitored him as he went to his desk, settling into the chair, firing up the laptop before the walls went opaque. She'd swear their eyes locked for a split second before he punched the button.

Maybe. Maybe not.

It is now close to nine. Ryan's been behind closed doors since he arrived. She checked Outlook. Nothing on the shared calendar, but a few of his design engineers sauntered up the stairs close to an hour ago and have been sequestered in his cage ever since. She checks her cell phone. No text messages, no returned voice mails. Nothing.

She's called him—several times. The first was on Saturday morning after she'd hung up with Carly. Calling to see where he was. Wanting to know if everything was alright. Again, later in the day. Calls not returned.

Strange. Not like him at all.

She had spoken to Carly later on that afternoon, and learned her husband had indeed returned home that morning. Olivia had resisted the temptation to speak with him that very moment, the gnawing feeling regarding Friday and the conversation between Miles and he not sitting well in her midsection at all.

On Sunday, she ventured another call that went straight to voice mail. She left a short message, hoping all with him was well, and asking that he call her, needing to discuss a business matter, something that would be on the agenda at Monday's staff meeting.

That call was left unreturned, as well.

Finally, on Sunday night, beyond frustration, the knot in the pit of her stomach a constant dull pain, like a nagging headache that wouldn't go away, she text messaged him. Short and to the point.

R U OK???

Nothing.

Olivia checks her watch and sighs as she realizes it is time to get back to work. Forget Ryan, and whatever has crawled up his ass and made a home there. Too much to do. Work never stops; it doesn't even slow down.

Ryan will come around. He'll emerge from his funk; all will be forgotten; life will pick up its pace and they'll move on. He's just being a man—a Gemini, a regular Jekyll and Hyde.

Yeah, Ryan'll come around.

In time, all men do.

The video con call with the Malaysian plant couldn't wait. Problems with the line over the weekend dictated that Ryan handle the situation ASAP. So he got his team together and placed the call. No matter it was a 13-hour time difference. Business comes first.

He now sits in his chair, fumbling with the stylus of his Ipaq, half-listening to the back-and-forth banter between his guys and Chin, known to everyone as Chinny, the head of production in Malaysia. Ryan allowed his team to take the lead, as he is fond of doing, stepping away from the limelight, letting his guys run things, only inserting himself when leadership is needed.

As usual, the finger pointing is reaching an all-time high. Production blames Engineering for the defect, which has led to the slow-down on the line. Engineering, on the other hand, states unequivocally that their designs are sound. They have schematics and computer models to prove their case. So the drama continues.

R U OK???

Ryan stares at the screen. Taps the stylus against the glass quietly in time to a rhythm only he comprehends. Checks his watch. Sits forward, clearing his throat.

"Okay," he says, standing, pressing his tie against his starched blue and white striped shirt, "I think everyone's had ample time to make a solid case. Problem is, we still have an issue with the line. So . . . Jan, Chinny . . . I need answers and a game plan."

He stares at his Senior Design Engineer named Janice—a dumpy-looking white woman in her mid-twenties, who dresses terribly and has clingy brown hair. A permanent scowl adorns her face, yet she is brilliant, the best they have. His gaze pans to the plasma attached to the back wall. On screen, Chinny is sitting at his desk juggling golf balls. As usual, he is smiling, no matter how dire the circumstances. "Two hours—handle it offline, cool?"

Janice nods.

"You got it, boss," Chinny says a bit too happily.

"Great." He shuts the call down. Janice and the two others rise; they gather their things to leave. He turns back to his laptop when they are gone, scans his messages and the calendar for the day. Isn't feeling any of it. So, he picks up the phone.

"Sharon, I'm outta here. Let the department heads know, if you would."

"No problem, but did you forget about the staff meeting—"

He cuts her off in mid-sentence.

"Anything critical—I'm reachable on my cell." He kills the line before she can respond or complain.

R U OK???

Ryan picks up his briefcase, snaps his laptop shut. The sound is hollow, reverberating across the room. He reaches for the door, pauses momentarily, glancing back at his clean desk. He reaches it in two strides. Punching the button underneath, the walls go clear.

His gaze rises from floor to wall. Stare meets Olivia's for a brief moment.

But only an instant.

Then he is descending the stairs, meandering through the expanse of cube-space as if on a mission, briefcase swinging indolently. Moments later, he is out the door and gone, and Olivia is left with the same gnawing feeling that, like bile, rises in her throat, making it hard to breathe.

Once again . . .

Chapter 16

She is in her office, the sleek, black plastic phone cradled to one ear, her head cocked to the side, fingers splayed, rapidly moving as if playing an instrument. The clicks from the mini-keyboard are drowned out by the segment she's editing—displayed on the flat screen on the wall in front of her.

She is nodding her head, emitting short grunts in agreement to certain action items in the conversation—details lost as her assistant hands her pink slips of paper that she ruffles through absentmindedly. To the left, her BlackBerry is vibrating, the blue plastic case shuddering as if in orgasm. Behind her, Outlook is chiming, signaling incoming mail. Her mind is a jet fighter—traveling supersonic, pitching and yawing, evading enemy capture. This morning, she is multitasking to her fullest capabilities. It's what the job entails, and it is only after nine.

A shadow crosses her desk. Carly glances up, only to spy the grin of Tyler Nichols, dressed impeccably in a double-breasted, navy pinstripe suit. He is wearing a bright solid yellow tie, which is so incredibly vibrant that for a moment she ceases to hear the conversation from the associate producer in her ear. She discards the incessant vibrating like yesterday's newspaper; forgets the din coming from her laptop. Carly is suddenly transported back to the islands—the flavor and aura of Barbados invading her mind like a sea storm from out of nowhere. This sudden onslaught is quickly replaced by thoughts of her husband and her/their pregnancy.

All of this in the rapid blink of an eye.

She raises her finger to Tyler, telling him to hold on. He nods and takes a seat in front of the desk without being told.

Carly uses the time to consider him without being caught. She swivels to the left, checking something on her corkboard while still on the phone, observing him. Associate General Counsel, the youngest BET has ever had. Top of his class at Howard, number two at U. Penn Law. Tall, athletic build, smooth face and features that indicate a gentle soul; short cropped hair, never a strand out of place. Handsome in a boyish kind of way.

Always impeccably dressed.

Always.

The women in the company are forever talking behind his back, searching for a chink in his armor. He's been at BET for three years, and in that time, he has never dated an employee—never been seen with anyone outside of work. Still, he's a man. He's gotta have sexual needs—or he's gay! The rumors run rampant, yet Tyler just smiles as he goes on about his business—professional to the core.

Except when he's around her.

It's no secret that he wants her.

Knows he can't have her, but it doesn't stop him from trying.

Carly jots down some notes, makes another edit to her segment, and signs off.

"Morning," Tyler says cheerfully. "You're at it early today."

Carly nods, smiling momentarily before a scowl paints her face.

"I'm busy, Tyler. What is it?"

As soon as the words emerge, she regrets them, knowing she is being unkind. He hasn't done anything to offend her or make her mad, but this thing with Ryan has been gnawing at her insides all weekend.

No, that isn't right. This thing is now an open, festering wound.

Tyler continues to smile, showing off his white teeth. He is staring at her—never glancing away—always giving her or anyone he's communicating with his full, undivided attention. She likes that—shows he has nothing to hide.

"You alright, Carly? Weekend go okay?"

"Tyler—I'm fine. Just busy. Too much shit to do, that's all."

He considers her for a second, then breaks into laughter.

She stares at him as if repulsed.

"Naw, Carly, that's not it. Why are you always trying to front around me? You know that doesn't work, don't you?" He steeples his fingers on the smooth top of her desk and moves closer, eyes locking with hers. In that instant, she feels what she always feels around him—angst for this uncanny "gift" of his, for lack of a better word, this way he has of cutting straight through the morass of bullshit, seeing clearly, the way a laser cuts through smoke. She sighs, drops her shoulders a bit. Tyler watches her for a moment more before getting up to close the door to her office.

They are now alone.

Just the two of them.

Carly watches him silently as he walks behind her desk, his hands finding her shoulders. He begins a slow rhythmic massage of that spot where her neck meets her shoulder blade, tight unwieldy neck muscles. Strong, smooth hands glide along skin, taming the flesh, gently moving her hair out of the way.

She lets him.

Powerless to stop him.

After a few minutes of silence, he speaks.

"Husband of yours acting up?" Tyler asks, almost in a whisper. He questions her matter-of-factly, without the slightest hint of malice.

Carly's head leans back; their eyes lock; hand goes to his, putting an end to this . . . thing.

"Stop it, Tyler."

He backs away, hands in the air, a thin smile adorning his face.

"I'm just asking, Carly. No shame in letting me in. I'm one of the good guys, you know."

She exhales sharply.

"Don't have time for this shit," she says, swiveling rapidly to her laptop, pressing a few keys, making herself busy to hide her impending anguish. Turning around, she finds him back in the chair across from her: calm, composed, as if nothing had happened.

"Need to make time, Carly," he says.

Tyler moves in again. Steeples his fingers on the desk once more.

"You need to vent. It's as plain as the nose on your face that you're hurting. You might be able to fool some of these silly black people out there," he says, gesturing towards the shut door, "but you can't fool me. So stop fighting and fronting . . . and tell me what's on your mind. You'll feel better when you do."

She watches him. Ponders his words. Tyler continues.

"Let's do lunch. I know a place where we can talk. It will be good for you to get away, get you to relax a bit, unwind—and I really do want to hear what's troubling you, Carly."

Carly shakes her head.

"Can't. No time today." The words come out rushed, almost rehearsed.

Tyler's brow rises.

"Can't? Or won't? Even a gal with a gorgeous figure like yours needs to eat. It's all about proper nourishment, Carly. Surely someone with an Ivy League education knows that, right?"

Tyler is rising, smoothing his tie before opening the door.

"I'll make reservations for one o'clock and get your assistant to put it on your calendar in ink if I have to." He smiles, winks, and then is gone, leaving Carly to produce a smile that Tyler doesn't see—the first in close to seventy-two hours.

Chapter 17

Reese is fast asleep when the buzzer sounds. Never expecting anyone this early, the clamor catches her by surprise. She rolls over onto her side, pauses there as if out of breath, listening to the sounds emanating from the streets, the normal din of traffic—buses, cars, taxis, pedestrians, garbage trucks backing up, their incessant honking making it difficult to get any semblance of peaceful rest. Yet Reese has grown accustomed to anti-silence, allowing it to infuse into her being until she fears she cannot rest unless there is noise—as crazy as that may seem to some.

She waits a moment more, breathless. The buzzer returns. She rises slothfully, glancing at the cheap wind-up alarm clock on the nightstand.

Ten-eighteen A.M.

Shit, she's normally not up until way past noon.

She's clad in her normal bedroom attire, tank top and panties. She scratches at her stomach and pulls on the stud in her right eyelid while moving slowly into the living room. Place dark, window shades down, almost eerie in the half-light. Goes to the wall intercom and presses the button.

"Who is it?" she asks rather gruffly.

A second or two passes before an unwavering voice comes through the box, loud and clear.

"Me. Dude from the bar a few nights ago." A half-second before the voice adds, "Ryan."

Reese stares uncomprehendingly into the darkened space, her mind and heart whirling. Ryan's voice once again breaks the silence.

"Can you let a brutha up? It's kind of cold out here. . . ."

She sits across from him, staring into the space that separates them. He is looking good—well rested it seems, shaved, suit and tie. She hadn't expected that at all—figured him for a blue collar kind of guy, even though his fingernails were clean and clipped, hair well kept. Now, he sits across from her, looking a bit nervous, eyes darting left then right, a bit afraid, it seems, to settle his gaze on her. She has slipped into a thin, tattered robe, but with the thermostat broken, the heat cranked on high, she leaves the robe open. Her heavy bosom under the flimsy tee is in plain view, and she feels a surge, a sense of satisfaction, as she knows she is making him uncomfortable. But that's just the way Reese is . . . after all, this is her place—her world.

"Glad to see you made it home in one piece," she says. Ryan nods, holding a steaming mug in his hand from which he gingerly takes a sip.

Reese is watching him silently, leaning back, elbows on the rim of an adjacent chair. The act projects her breasts more than they already are, and she spies Ryan glancing over for a half-second. She smiles in self-assurance.

"So to what do I owe this honor?" she asks. Reese, of course, knew he would return—understood he couldn't stay away—but returning this soon was not anticipated.

"I don't know," Ryan begins, putting down the mug, looking uncomfortable in his suit jacket. "Hot in here," he adds.

"Yes. Get comfortable," Reese says. "You see I am." She smiles again, locking stares with him. And Ryan returns a smile, feeling himself being drawn into this thing he can't fully comprehend. He feels her power over him, and for a moment, he tries to wrestle with it, but then just sighs and gives in, feeling the rush, the attack, and infusion into his soul. With everything that's gone on these past few days, this is a welcomed diversion. Reese, out of everyone, *understands*. Saturday morning, there was nothing between them other than intense conversation—Ryan's insatiable need to gush what he was feeling—everything, every sordid detail to this total stranger because it just felt right—because Reese did not wrinkle up her nose in spite; she did not judge. And that is why he has returned. Because of how right it feels . . .

"Our conversation," he begins, jacket off, sleeves unbuttoned, tie loosened, leaning back, too, his position a mirror image of Reese's, "intrigued me. Does that make sense?"

"Of course. A lot was said."

Ryan nods his head. Considers, for the first time this morning, the totality of his situation—the snowball that is rolling down a hill.

"It's just . . ." and here he tries to find the right words, but falters. "I don't know—it's hard right now, trying to separate everything and make sense of it all."

"You're questioning your own sexuality," Reese says, sitting up, putting her mug down inches from his. She is cutting to the chase, not bothering to dance; no foreplay. "It's understandable, but only earth-shattering if you allow it to be."

"How so?" he asks, sitting up, fascinated.

"Isn't that the entire crux of your concern? Up until a few weeks ago, you were a normal guy who seemingly had it all—job, marriage, the works. Then this thing came at you from out of nowhere and knocked you on your ass. This thing that began with infatuation morphed into obsession. Now, that would have been fine—you and your best friend indulging in a bit of the pie that night after everyone had gone to sleep—except it didn't turn out that way. 'Cause brutha-man seemingly had been pining away for you—had you in his sights—yet, you didn't know it. That's when things turned ugly."

Ryan nods, eyes clear, knowing with full certainty that Reese has a better grasp of what is going on than anyone else in his sphere.

"And now you're hurting," Reese continues, "totally messed up inside because of what has transpired between you and this guy. It's understandable, but as I said, not earth-shattering."

"Easy for you to say," Ryan quips.

"Not really. You men need to stop being so damned homophobic. I mean, it was only a blow job, nothing else."

"Please! Just a blow job? You've got to be kidding!" Ryan exclaims. Suddenly, his arms are flailing wide.

Reese leans forward, placing her hand over his, which is now resting on the coffee table. "Listen, you need to chill. A blow job is a blow job, Ryan. You dug it. You sat back and enjoyed the hell out of it. Why? Because in your mind, this woman . . . what was her name, Nora?"

"Olivia."

"Olivia, right. In your mind, Olivia was making love to you, not anyone else. And that's what made it so special—so passionate. In your mind, it was her mouth, her hands, her throat. So, you didn't do anything wrong. You didn't make a conscious decision to stick your dick in another man's mouth—it just happened."

"Damn, Reese—do you have to be so graphic?" Ryan asks, and then laughs.

"I'm just saying . . . so chill, man. It's gonna be fine. Doesn't mean you're whole demeanor has changed. Doesn't mean you're suddenly gay!"

Reese is watching Ryan, observing his eyes.

"Yeah, you're right," Ryan says, sitting up, taking a long sip, nodding as he swallows. "I'm not gay. That shit ain't me. Nothing to worry about," he says surely.

"So, do you truly believe that, or is this just a bunch of lip service?" Reese has suddenly stood, stepped away from the table so she can remove her robe. Her nipples are the size of quarters. They are dark and push against the thin fabric. For a moment, Ryan does not answer. He stares, allowing himself to drink in her features. And she allows him, letting his gaze paint her body with its intensity. Finally, as she returns to her seat, he answers.

"No lip service, Reese." His eyes have not wavered from her bosom. "This is real."

She nods, tugging at the stud in her eyelid. Licks her lips absentmindedly. The act is not lost on Ryan. "Good," she says, "gotta get back in the saddle, then. Get some pussy and claim it as your own. Tame the

beast; forget all about this thing that's got you un-
nerved. You know?"

"Love it when you talk dirty." Ryan grins. Reese
just shakes her head.

"Got any more piercings?" he asks suddenly.

Reese considers his words. Her head is cocked to
one side, taking in this new persona—and Reese
likes what she sees.

"Perhaps," she replies, drawing the word out as if
it were a magician's scarf, its length seemingly without end.

"Where?"

He has placed the mug down and stands to remove his tie. He flings it to the chair beside him. Another button to his shirt undone, sleeves rolled to his
elbows.

"Aren't we the inquisitive one?" she whispers,
their stares locked in a tug-of-war.

The pulse in his forehead, neck, and chest is a syn-
copated fury that is exhilarating. Ryan remains standing, glaring at her silently.

"Well, let's see. There's this one," Reese says,
pointing to her eyelid, "and another," she adds, feeling for the stud in her nose, "and another," she grins,
a half second pause before uttering, "between my
sugar walls."

Reese recites these words in singsong.

Ryan closes his eyes for a brief moment before
pulling a chair over the bare hardwood floors with a
scrape until only inches separate them. His fingers
find the smoothness of her thigh, lightly running upward toward her panty line.

She does nothing to stop his advances.

"Show me," he whispers, his breath a hot flash on
her cheek.

Reese is unblinking as she counts the rhythmic

seconds to her own pounding heart, the muscle threatening to tear her apart.

But she remains whole, and breathes deep.

Slowly, silently, Reese leans back, fingers hooked under white cotton fabric, legs parting leisurely, sugar walls coming unhurriedly into view . . .

Chapter 18

"WHERE WERE YOU?!?"

The sound reverberates across the expanse of bathroom floor tile, Madagascar African stone, to be exact. Its rich, brown-indigo hues contrasting with the shiny, off-white porcelain wall tiles and glass shower stall. Ryan has his back to her—shampoo-adorned head thrown back when he hears the sound. He was in the midst of recalling his wonderful, stress-relieving morning and late decadent lunch, when she came in, messing up his revelry.

"Excuse me?" He turns slowly, soap on his face, hanging like a beard from his smooth chin. He lets a stream of water beat down over his forehead, cleansing his eyes. Carly stands on the other side of the shower glass, its water-laden streaks muting her visuals. She is beautiful; two piece olive suit, thin framed rectangular glasses, not a hair out of place yet, the image is flawed—hand on hip, head cocked to one side, lips pursed into a snarl. Ryan's member was rising past the nine o'clock hour, but hearing those words cutting through the steam and spray makes him instantly flaccid.

"Where were you?" Ryan's wife repeats.

He faces her, giving her full frontal nudity, no longer concerned about the state of his manhood. It looks at her as if she's lost her mind.

"When, Carly?"

"Don't fucking toy with me!" she snarls. Carly grabs hold of the stall door and flings it open, almost sideswiping herself in the process.

"What the hell is wrong with you?" Ryan asks, clearly agitated, slamming the stall door shut. He gives her his back and ass, finishes rinsing as his heart rate mounts.

"I called your office, Ryan—hours ago. Your assistant said you had left for the day. Interesting. You didn't pick up your cell—none of the times I called. You weren't home. I know—I checked. So, I ask you again, where were you?"

Ryan laughs, then instantly regrets it. "You're tripping. Serious tripping." He glances back at her over one shoulder. "Since when do I need to clear my itinerary with you?"

A loud thud rocks the shower stall. Ryan spins around, witnessing his wife pulling back her clenched fist from the glass shower. He stares at her incredulously, like she's out of her mind.

Perhaps she is.

He twists the water off with a vengeance, then storms out of the stall and grabs a towel from the rack, almost assaulting his wife in the process.

He towels off with verve, wiping a hand against his shortly cropped hair, showering Carly with water spray before spinning to face her.

"Just what has gotten into you?!" he shouts.

"What has gotten into me? What the fuck has gotten into *you*?!" She doesn't wait for a response. "Three nights ago, you decide not to come home—as if you're a single man—not living under the same roof as me—your wife—the woman who will have your child. I ask you where you've been and you give me excuses—treat me as if I'm still in high school! Please—do I look like I was born yesterday?"

Ryan opens his mouth to speak, but is shut down by the fervor of Carly's continuing tirade.

"Not even three whole days later, you leave work early this morning—disappearing for several hours—not picking up your phone—"

"Carly, stop! This is ridiculous! I was at an appointment—had lunch with a client. Since when do I need to clear that with you?"

Now it's her turn to stare at him incredulously.

"Negro, please! Do I look stupid? I checked with your assistant—had her triple-check your calendar—even had her talk to the staff under the guise of a family emergency."

He pushes past her into the bedroom. She is close behind.

"You didn't have anything with any client. This, Ryan, I *know*."

"You're crazy, you know that? You have taken this one situation on Friday and blown it way out of proportion—"

Carly doesn't hear him, for her thoughts are transported back to her lunch with Tyler Nichols a few hours ago. It was, as he had promised, just what the doctor ordered. Carly had never fully opened up to Tyler before—had no need to—nor did she want to encourage that kind of relationship with him—where he knew intimate details of her life and came to rely upon her as a friend. Today, however, she needed an objective voice—someone who could be her sounding board—someone neutral, not emotionally involved. In fact, the more they talked, the better she felt. Sometimes, one can get greater counsel from a stranger than a best friend whose judgment is clouded.

At first, she had been reluctant to talk. She just sat there at a quiet window table at Café Asia, picking at her food, watching Tyler eat: spicy Vietnamese spring rolls, Tom Yum lemongrass soup with shrimp, and sushi as their main entrée. As usual, though, Tyler had a way of coaxing from her exactly what he wanted, and in no time, she was talking about her marriage and the sudden change in Ryan. General stuff only at first, certain irritations and frustrations she had with her husband, but then, rather than diving into specifics, she would ask questions instead. Like: "Tyler, what would you make of a husband taking three hours to get gas and food in his stomach?"

In no time, Tyler got the picture and began offering advice.

"If it were me, Carly, I'd confront him. You have a lot to lose, and you don't want to set precedence by letting this slide—because that gives him license to do it again and again. You want to know the truth, and you *need* to know the truth. This is the person you've pledged to spend your entire life with—and dishonesty and mistrust have no place in any relationship, especially a marriage."

Words to live by.

Carly intends to do just that.

"You know what, Ry? I am not going to be one of those wives who turn the other cheek, especially when the shit is staring me in the face. So, you need to come clean. If you love me, you'll do that, right now, and cease this 'I don't know what's gotten into you' approach."

She folds her arms across her chest. Exhales and waits. Eyes locked onto his.

Ryan stands there, towel tucked and covering his midsection, water streaking his torso. He considers his wife for a moment. Considers telling her the truth . . . knowing the truth would open a chasm that could never be closed.

Never be mended . . .

"I took a client to lunch, Carly. Nothing more sinister going on. I think you need to calm down—"

"Who's the client?" she spits.

Ryan blinks for a second.

Thinks half as long.

"David Ramsey—in town from Arizona on business and tracked me down."

"Company?" she asks.

Ryan glares at her.

"I will not play twenty-fucking questions with you over how I spent my day! You can forget that shit! By the way, what did *you* do for lunch today, Carly?"

Her eyes flare.

"I was at Café Asia with Tyler Nichols, associate general council for BET. We discussed many things— most of which surrounds you and your recent fucked- up behavior!"

Carly spins away from him. Her footfalls echo down the hall. She returns momentarily with a Fendi suitcase—her suitcase—one of a matching set they bought prior to their trip to Barbados.

"Where the hell are you going?" Ryan asks, suddenly chilled.

"To Olivia and Miles'."

Ryan winces upon hearing their names.

"I refuse to stay here one second longer with a lying husband. You want to stand there and lie to my face, fine. You can do it to an empty fucking house!"

She grabs a few things—bras and panties, a suit she tosses haphazardly into the bottom of the case, toiletries. Ryan stares at her dumbfounded, too numb to move. Suddenly, the past few hours are a distant memory.

The next few moments are like a movie shown in slow motion—jerky, erratic, void of sound, images distended. The front door slamming shut brings Ryan back to the here and now.

Reality begins to creep in.

He is standing in the same spot as before; he has yet to move a muscle.

The bedroom is silent.

It is empty.

The house is quiet, too.

Everything that has transpired to harm him returns en masse.

Olivia.

The party.

Miles.

Their joining . . .

Reese.

Sugar walls.

Is it all a dream?

Ryan isn't sure. For a moment, he blinks rapidly, as if that act will somehow show him the truth.

It does not.

No, this is all a dream. He's almost sure.

On the other hand . . .

His torso is still wet.
His wife is gone.
He is alone.
That much Ryan is sure is real.

Chapter 19

The sound of the front door breaks their reverie. Olivia glances up into the warming face of her husband, Miles. Carly follows suit. They had been holding hands as they sat on the couch, an untouched glass of merlot in front of Carly, a near-empty glass for Olivia. But as Miles enters, their hands retreat, like rats scurrying to safety when the lights are turned on.

"Hey, baby. Hello, Carly, what a pleasant surprise," Miles says cheerfully.

Carly tries to smile, but it comes across flat. His wife rises to greet him.

It is 9:00 P.M. The two women have been sitting, conversing for close to three hours. Carly returned to her job after leaving her home, trying without success to plunge headlong into her work—only to leave early, calling Olivia and asking if she'd meet her after work.

Olivia, intense guilt gnawing at her insides the way a vulture picks at carrion, immediately left the office to meet her best friend. They made tea, went for a manicure/pedicure, and then sat on the couch to talk and wait.

Miles is smiling as he puts down his leather bag. He is dressed in dark slacks, bronze, button-down shirt with French cuffs, and a camel hair blazer. His locs are held back by a thick rubber band. Around his neck is a thick dark cord, the end holding a gleaming piece of twisted silver. It meanders through his chest hairs, and Carly, for a moment, marvels for the thousandth time at his generous good looks.

He goes to Carly, who stands and wipes her hands unsurely together before giving him a hug.

"Good to see you, Carly. Better half around?" he asks lightheartedly.

Carly's mood darkens. Her mind races, and Olivia takes over.

"No, baby. Um, Carly's gonna stay with us tonight. Okay?"

Miles shoots her a glance before panning to Carly. "Of course. Everything okay?"

Carly shakes her head. "Not really."

Miles looks at Olivia.

"Um, Ryan and Carly are having some problems, baby." Her eyes are saying, *let it go, Miles.*

"I'm sorry. Anything I can do?" he asks, rubbing her shoulder.

She returns a half smile.

"Yeah, beat some sense into his ass!"

Miles grunts and then heads to the kitchen, leaving the two women alone. They sit while Olivia grabs her wineglass stem to steal a sip. Carly's remains untouched.

Olivia is on pins and needles. Ever since Carly called, she hasn't been able to concentrate on anything else. She knows that she must be there for her best friend—but how? She's partially responsible for this *thing*. Or wholly . . .

Letting Ryan in like that . . .

Allowing it to happen . . .

The only thing that gives her solace—the only thing that provides wiggle room to breathe—is this new thing—Ryan's recent disappearances—and today's outright lie. Carly had immediately asked Olivia to check on the client—this David Ramsey—and what was Olivia supposed to do? She didn't like getting in the middle of her two best friends. On the other hand, if it hadn't been for her in the first place . . .

David Ramsey wasn't even in the goddamn state! It took less than four minutes to confirm that for Carly.

Was Ryan seeing someone?

Doubtful.

Up until this past weekend, Ryan had seemed almost *consumed* with Olivia. Perhaps that wasn't right—but clearly, he had something on his mind, and it had everything to do with her.

That much she knows.

The way he looked at her . . . the way he held her gaze.

The way he made her feel—energized, alive, desirable.

And Olivia had let this thing continue, a snowball rolling down a hill.

Why?

Because it felt good.

We all want to feel desirable. All want to know we still got it going on. Can still hook 'em with just a glance or sensual smile . . .

But after Miles' talk with him, everything changed.

On Monday, he didn't even glance her way.

Stormed out of the office—blowing off the staff meeting. Even Rod, the company president, was surprised at his behavior.

As if he was on a mission . . .

But what?

Or with whom?

Olivia did her best to console Carly, listening to her, nodding her head at the things she said, agreeing with her position. *Yes, girl, men are scum. What can you do? They fuck up constantly, and then expect us to take their sorry asses back. Miles? Yeah, girl, he ain't no better— just hasn't acted up lately . . . but he will . . . they always do.*

Carly takes a sip of merlot.

Puts the wineglass down, then picks it up again.

Thankfully, Olivia muses.

She's going to get Carly to relax.

For the moment, get her to forget her troubles.

And hopefully, keep the truth from spilling out, putting an end to their friendship, marriages, and everything else that is sacred and pure.

Miles undresses upstairs. Slips into a pair of faded button-down Levis, sweatshirt, house slippers. He finds himself wondering about the situation downstairs. He pats his tongue against the roof of his mouth, reaches for his cell, glances at the closed door, and dials.

"Ryan . . . hey, man, it's Miles. Haven't heard from you since Friday. Think we should talk—especially with the recent turn of events. Carly's here. I'm sure you already know that. So holla back, 'cause we need to talk. Figure some stuff out."

He pauses for a moment as he reflects on how to say what's on his mind.

"Listen, man, just want you to know I'm not the bad guy here. I'm your friend. Always have been—always will be. That hasn't changed. So call me, okay?"

Ryan stares at the cell phone screen without answering. He sits in his cage, office dark, save for the halogen lamp on his desk and the laptop screen, which bathes his face in muted light. The cube-space floor below is deserted, vacant. He has been here for hours, attempting, without much success, to work. Rod, spying the light on, ventured up; they chatted for a brief moment about the Malaysia problem, but he left him alone when he could see that Ryan wasn't his normally jovial self.

So, Ryan sorts through e-mails, checks production schedules and line reports, doing it like an automaton, without any real thought behind his actions.

When the call comes in, it makes him jump. He stares at the cell, feeling vomit rise in his throat when he recognizes Miles' number.

That's the *last* person Ryan wants to speak with right now.

After a few minutes of silence, he checks his voice mail. Listens to Miles' voice, his cool words, not a care in the world. Not taunting him, but just saying, sooner or later, Ryan needs to call him . . . talk to him . . . figure this thing out . . . together.

I'm not the bad guy here—I'm your friend.

Ryan deletes the message and snaps his phone shut.

Realizing that no productive work will come this

evening, he shuts down his laptop and extinguishes the lamp.

Ryan contemplates his next move.

Bathed in darkness, it doesn't take him long.

Chapter 20

She is pushed back into the soft velvety folds of the comforter. It is happening all so suddenly, movie on fast-forward, nothing choreographed. But that is what she is loving right now—this primal, instinctual way about him, the way he is presently silent, except for his grunts and erotic groans.

The room is semi-dark—the shades not shutting out all light and commotion from the street below. There are parallel patterns—streaks of light on the ceiling that ebb and flow—traffic racing along, even at this hour—close to 4:00 A.M.

His hands are on her shirt, fondling her beneath the thin, almost translucent fabric. In seconds, it is bunched up her smooth torso, breasts heaving into view. His mouth attacks them first, still clad in the lace bra. He pulls the clasp apart, breaking it with a short grunt, palming both flesh and nipple with large hands, thrusting the meat into his hungry mouth.

She had been twirling a martini shaker in her hand

earlier, this thing she does for patrons—for show—
but this particular time, it came undone, sending
Grey Goose and Puckers showering onto her right
side, soaking the upper half of her tee. She hadn't
had time to change; hadn't had a moment to even
shower since they scrambled into her apartment like
drunken lovers. He sucks at her now, tasting the mixture of dried perspiration and French vodka, gliding
his tongue along the contours of each breast, cir-
cling her now rigid nipples.

This way to him is new—unexpected. He is an animal tonight—no longer in control, no longer re-
fined. Tonight he is a beast, out of control, primal in
his actions, taking her wares, not asking for permis-
sion, no longer wishing to converse.

Her jeans are peeled down, panties discarded like
last week's newspaper. Legs thrust wide, and then,
God help her, it is all happening so damn fast. He is
feasting on her with one bite, swallowing her sex into
his wet, hot mouth.

Reese screams in pleasure. Her hips buck in time
to his licks and his sinful swallows. He is consuming
her now, feeding on her pussy with abandonment,
taking her ring-sliced clit into his mouth, teasing at it
with his teeth, pulling on the jewelry, distending the
flesh . . . one side over to the other . . . fingering her
insides while he works, tasting the juice that begins
to flow like warm nectar. Reese is on fire, grabbing at
his hair, neck, and shoulders, her fingernails digging
into his skin, creating marks, no longer caring, wanting this man to satiate her like no other has.

There are few words between them.

She is screaming, grunting, and crying out. The
room begins to spin; light lines etched into the ceiling becoming infinite figure eight patterns, and Reese

pushes his head away. She knows she will come instantly with a single, feather-like touch. Understands she will gush . . . not wanting to come, not wanting it to end. Indecision, before she pulls him back down, telling him with her actions that it is okay, as if he has a choice, unleashing everything she has to give into his waiting abyss, pounding on his back as her pelvis bucks like a jackhammer . . . ass, limbs, toes, and eyes all twitching in the near darkness. He drinks her in, sucks her down willingly, smacking his lips noisily as her honey bastes his face and chin.

It is a sin the way he devours her.

She is loving life, and he loves her for this momentary digression.

The room slows down, ceases to spin. Reese has a sudden reprieve.

He backs away, fumbles in the near darkness with his belt and pants. She hears him, smells him ready. But she is unprepared when he comes back strong.

Sheathed, raring to go, he enters her fast and furious. Grabbing her ass with both hands, he pummels her sex, using long, thick strokes that send her into outer space. Reese is beyond pleasure. This joining is something she's dreamed of but never achieved—hard to put into words or describe, the feeling simply out of this world—this animalistic, ritual joining.

He is groaning as he pounds her, lips attacking her mouth, teeth mashing against hers as they swallow each other's tongues. He licks at her chin, chews on the stud in her nose, licks delicately at the flesh above her eye before taking it into his mouth and biting down gingerly.

Reese is smoldering. She is beyond fire.

He is a lightning rod.

He is a monsoon.

He is out of control, and she is lava. She is molten and can't stand it, this feeling beyond so fucking good.

"Take me, daddy!" she yells, guttural talk that feeds his fury.

Her eyes lock onto his. Her legs splayed as wide as humanly possible, his thick manhood slamming in and out of her, a well-oiled piston, their rhythm rising to a feverish pitch.

"Fuck me . . . this shit is yours, daddy . . . oh God, this shit is yourrrrrrrrrrrrrrrrrssssssssssssssssssssssss!"

He works harder. No let up, not even for a second.

"Yes, yes, yes, oh fuck, yesssssssssssssssssssssssssssssssssss!" she hisses, like water on a bonfire.

Then he is rising up on his forearms and toes, head jutted back, forehead studded with purplish veins as he comes, crying out, "Oh God!" His eyes squish shut as he orgasms into her, shuddering as the waves overtake him, his body rigid, then soft, yin then yang, melting over her, melting into her, flesh gliding to a stop as he puts his weight onto her. His hands reach gingerly for her breasts, slipping a nipple into his mouth, then kissing her sensually on the neck and cheek, settling his face into the warmth of her nuzzle, stuffing himself deep inside her cavern one last time so that he can wilt. Their heartbeats slowing, becoming one, no longer frenzied, no longer harried, until they both are thinking different thoughts that ebb and flow. Reese finally finds peace, serenity, comfort, and contented sleep in the arms of a new lover.

A single thought is conjured up as he stares at the parallel lines dancing above them, moments before he drifts off and finds nirvana—everything, every single thing that is bad, that has plagued him, is *inconsequential.*

Seemingly, it no longer matters.

Ryan smiles to no one but himself.

These things have no meaning, he muses, when one loses one's self in the decadent flesh of another.

Chapter 21

He watches her march down the steps from her cage, smartly dressed in a plum tweed, four-button suit, looking as fresh as a runway model. He glances away quickly, down to the cell he holds in his palm, staring at it and rubbing the brushed steel with a thumb as he considers his voice mail. He speed-dials, putting the phone to his ear.

"Three saved voice messages."

Today is Wednesday.

Yesterday was Tuesday.

He was absent from work on Tuesday.

Slept in with Reese.

Just didn't have the stamina or the desire to make it in to work after what they had shared.

Folks had been searching for him all day yesterday. He'd finally called Sharon early afternoon, saying he wasn't feeling well and maybe he'd make it in the next day. Hung up before she could question him further.

"Three saved voice messages," his cell reminds him.

Miles—all three.

"First voice mail message—sent yesterday at seven-forty A.M.," the computerized voice says.

"Dude, okay, it's me, Miles. You haven't returned my call. If I were an insecure man, which I am assuredly not, I'd be worried right about now. (Laughs). Seriously, we need to talk. Your wife is still here at the house, so we should talk about that—and more importantly, we need to speak about us—you and me. So call a brother, okay?"

She is meandering through cube-space like a woman on a mission—head up, politician-smile, a purposeful gait to her step. A few employees speak, short back and forth banter. Olivia is polite, but she neither slows down nor changes her expression.

Worry lines spotted from afar.

"Second voice mail message—sent yesterday at six-eighteen P.M."

"Ryan, it's Miles. Please return my call. I need to talk to you; it's important. I've left several messages, and I know you've received them. So please stop ignoring me. You and I need to talk . . . now. Holla back."

She grips the handrail leading to his cage, takes the first step, head held high, her gaze locked in an upward direction.

His direction.

He feels his heart beating faster, blood pressure increasing, the pulse in his neck visibly and audibly up several notches. Thankfully, his cage is empty, save for him. For a moment, she has disappeared from view, but Ryan knows it is only for several agonizing seconds. Soon now, she will be rising into sight, like a submarine emerging into sunlight, breaking through the watery depths to float boat-like along the brilliant surface.

"Third voice mail message—sent today at eight-fourteen A.M. Marked urgent."

"Dude—okay, kid gloves coming off. I'm surprised you have chosen not to return my calls. That's fine, Ry. That's your prerogative. The thing is, dude, I've been fronting for you regarding Carly. You and I both know it. She's been asking a whole lot of questions, and guess what? I was gonna keep up the charade, for everyone's sake, but now, I'm growing tired of your foul-ass mood. So you know what? Fuck it, Holmes. You don't wanna call me back—fine, you're a grown-ass man. Don't call me back. But I hope you're prepared for the consequences once Carly learns the truth. I suggest you get off that high horse and call me back. ASAP, brother . . . before things get ugly."

Olivia rises into view. Ryan snaps the cell shut, exhaling loudly. She doesn't knock, doesn't wait for him to usher her in. She just waltzes in, as if his space is hers.

Perhaps it once was.

Their eyes lock. She closes the door softly behind her. Presses her back against the door as he waits for the tirade to unleash.

Curiously, it doesn't come.

Olivia waits a moment.

The time passes slowly.

They stare each other down, neither willing to give up their position first.

Ryan leans back slightly, palms flat on the smooth surface of his desk as he exhales. Considers better times, not too long ago, when he waited with bated breath for Olivia to invade his space.

"Been a minute," Olivia begins. She still has made no move from the door.

"It has."

"I'd say you're looking well, but that would be a lie. And I don't lie to my best friends."

She pauses, considers the absurdity of her statement before pressing on. "I mean, you're stressed; anyone can see that—with everything that has happened—"

"Please, Olivia, spare me the niceties."

She scrunches up a frown.

"Aren't we in a good mood? Well, at least I know you aren't getting laid, 'cause the bitch sure ain't taking care of you with that foul-ass attitude."

"Fuck you very much, Olivia," he says.

She is ready to fire back a missile, but reconsiders.

"You know what, Ryan? You and I need to talk." She moves to the sofa. "Okay if I sit?"

Ryan gives her a half nod. Says nothing.

"A lot has transpired in a relatively short period of time. I feel as if I'm responsible—feel as if things have gotten away from me . . . it's like . . . like . . . a snowball . . . no, more like a freight train barreling out of control."

Ryan no longer hears her words. He has focused on the imagery of the train's brakes screeching, careening straight ahead, sparks hissing . . . and the ensuing drama behind the icon is haunting.

"Listen, Ryan, things began to spiral out of control after you and Miles talked. Not sure what went down, but that night when you didn't come home, it went from bad to worse—"

"Have you asked Miles what really went down, Olivia?" Ryan asks forcefully, cutting her off as he rises from the desk. "Just curious if you have any idea what's really going on here?"

"No . . . well . . . yeah, of course, I have. But you know Miles. He shares what he wants to share—holds the rest in—been that way as long as I've known him. So it ain't gonna change now."

"Well, not sure what else to say, then."

Olivia stares at him incredulously.

"Please. Ryan, you can start with what *did* happen. Something went down. Let me in."

Ryan is grinning as he shakes his head.

"Olivia, no. You wanna find out what's going on? Wanna know who the true players are in this shit? Talk to your husband, not me!"

Olivia rises, goes to him until a mere twelve inches separate them.

"Bullshit, Ryan. You're my best friend. In the past, there's never been a problem between us. We could always converse about everything under the sun— our relationships, our spouses, our fears. That's why we're best of friends."

"Not this time," Ryan responds.

"What do you mean, 'not this time'?"

Ryan merely shakes his head.

Olivia sucks in a breath and changes tactics.

"Okay—your wife, remember her? Carly hasn't been home in three days. Does that fact bother you in any small way? Just wondering."

"Hey, she walked out on me—not the other way around!"

"Ry, you sound like you're in fucking high school—"

"Hey, you're in my goddamn office, so watch your language!"

Olivia pauses for a split second.

"You got to be kidding me! Carly walked out on your sorry ass and all you can think about is the language I'm using? Nigga, you need Jesus or something strong right now."

She shakes her head in defeat.

"Okay, cowboy, how long is this shit gonna last? How long, Ryan? How long are you going to let your testosterone control you? Hmmm? Think Carly's just gonna sit back and wait patiently for her hubby to come around?"

Ryan is silent, considering her words.

"How long, Ryan? I mean, for God's sake—she's with *child*!"

"Olivia, I did not walk out on her." The words are whispered low.

"No, but you didn't come home, and then you blatantly lied about lunching with a client. Stupid-ass mistake. Real stupid, Ryan. Whatever you're doing, whomever you're doing it *with* . . . and I hope to God that is *not* what is going on here . . . you need to curb your habit and come correct. Now. Before it's too late. I'm telling you this as your friend."

Ryan goes to the wall opposite his desk to glance out the window. Olivia watches him silently. For a moment, neither speaks. Olivia feels a breakthrough coming. So she sits, leaning back into the comfortable folds of the leather couch, using the reprieve to take deep, silent breaths. This shit is killing her— Carly around her constantly not making it any easier. The guilt is like a cancer threatening to slow roast Olivia to death.

Ryan turns and fixes his eyes on her. His forthcoming words are low and steady.

"And, Olivia, let me tell *you* this as your friend— things aren't what they seem. So before you go casting the first stone, make sure your *own* house is in order."

Olivia is taken aback. She is momentarily frozen in place.

"What does that mean?" she spits, volume rising.

"Ask your husband," Ryan responds, before grabbing his suit jacket off the back of his chair and exiting his cage, leaving Olivia to contemplate his barbed words alone.

Chapter 22

The main level of Olivia and Miles' home was filled with about seventy-five people—mostly employees from the firm. Olivia had done this going on four years now, an annual event right after third quarter profits and losses are posted, where she pulls together her salespeople to celebrate their hard work. It had morphed into an annual, all-hands event that everyone looked forward to, a time when folks could hobnob with anyone from Rod, the president of their company, on down to the mailroom clerk, in an atmosphere that commanded mutual respect. Not to mention great food and flowing libations.

Olivia is managing the event like a football coach. All that's missing is her wireless headset. She's issuing orders to her immediate staff for more white wine, bacon-wrapped grilled shrimp, and less spinach quiche; after this song goes off, switch to the hip-hop CD; this smooth jazz that's playing is too much like elevator music right now. Carly walks between rooms assisting, making sure wineglasses are topped off, plates filled, people taken care of. Miles is here, too, making sure he meanders among the crowd, saying his hellos, ensuring folks are comfortable.

Friday night, close to 9 P.M., they've just finished giving out their employee awards, along with the cash prizes that are so coveted. Rod did the honors while employees and spouses looked on in hushed apprehension. Now the music has been cranked up, Miles' specialty, and presently, he's got a reggae dance hall tape in, and folks are loosening up, courtesy of the wine and beer. Some of his co-workers are here, too, folks from his nonprofit, mingling with the techies and marketing folks. Carly is making the rounds, staying busy, but she's been spotted glancing at her watch from time to time. Making excuses when people find out she's Ryan's spouse.

"Oh, my goodness, so good to meet you! Where is he, by the way?" someone asks.

"Haven't seen him this evening." This about twenty minutes later. "Everything alright with him? Noticed he was absent from work one day this week—a first for Ryan, I'll tell you that!"

Even Rod corners her by the stairway, smiling as he takes her by the elbow, whisking her away to a back guest room.

"A moment of your time, if you would?" he asks sheepishly.

Carly nods, knowing this moment would surely come. She had asked Olivia to ensure that Ryan would show. She refused to call him herself. It had been five days, and not a word from her husband.

So two can play this game . . .

But this . . . not showing at his company party, especially since he was one of the senior people, management . . . was suicide. Everyone knew that!

"Good as always to see you, Carly," Rod says, kissing her cheek gingerly.

"You, too, Rod. I was speaking with Lily earlier in the evening." She refers to his wife of 18 years.

"Good. Excellent! Listen, I must cut to the chase, so forgive me. Is everything okay with your husband? He has not been himself lately, and frankly, I'm worried about him." Rod eyes her curiously.

Carly takes a moment to respond. Inhales a breath and lets it out slowly.

"We've had a hard time of late . . . trying to work it out." She wants to say more, but lacks the energy to do so.

"I know," he says, consoling her with his tone and downcast stare. "Lord knows I know. Lily and I have had our share of problems. It's difficult running a company and making time for one's family. Ryan works very hard—sometimes maybe too hard."

Carly is surprised by his candor.

"I just want you to know if there is anything I can do . . ."

"Thank you, Rod."

"Anything. Do not hesitate to get in touch with me. Alright?"

"Yes."

"One question, if I may. Do you expect him to show tonight?" Rod asks, his gaze riveted with hers.

"I did," she responds, checking her watch for the hundredth time this evening, "but now I'm not so sure."

Rod nods.

"I understand. I will leave you, then. Please try to enjoy your evening. Things will work out. I have a good feeling about you two."

Rod takes his leave while Carly remains in the guest bedroom, glancing around at the furniture, the stuffed animals Olivia is fond of collecting, wondering if Rod's words will ring true.

Only time will tell . . .

Miles is sequestered in the corner by the entrance to the gazebo-covered deck. He holds a lime-topped Corona in hand, and is in the midst of an in-depth conversation with a dark-skinned man. They are standing shoulder-width apart; the gentleman holds an oversize wine stem half-filled with Shiraz. They are laughing, Miles' locs bouncing as he nods his head, tips his beer to his lips; the dark-skinned man is clean shaven, bald, a large diamond earring in his right ear. He wears a dark suit, blue silk button-down underneath, no tie, relaxed collar. He is handsome, in a dark, mysterious way.

Carly is watching them from just off the kitchen. She holds her glass of Diet Coke. No more wine now that she's pregnant. She resists the urge to look at her watch. She knows it's after ten. Many of Olivia's folks have left, but the core partygoers are still here, dancing to the reggae vibe, lights turned down low, as libations and conversation continue to flow.

Who is the gentleman talking to Miles, she wonders. He reminds her of a writer or some creative type. Can't put her finger on it, but she'd bet money on it. She has been watching them for the past fifteen minutes. They seem to be absorbed in their conversation, others leaving them alone. Olivia whisks by her, grabbing another bag of ice from the garage—touching Carly's elbow, asking her if she's alright.

Carly nods, says nothing.

Instead, she decides to satiate her curiosity by going over.

"Hey, Miles," she says.

Miles nods. "Hey, Carly." He glances over at the gentleman and says, "Carly, let me introduce you to Aden. Aden, Carly."

He extends his hand, takes hers in his.

"A pleasure," he says, voice two octaves below normal.

Carly smiles. "Likewise." She is glancing between the two men. "Where do you two know each other from?"

"The nonprofit," Miles answers cheerfully. "Aden is a recent addition to our organization as lead psychotherapist."

"Oh? Nice. Where are you coming from?" she asks.

Aden looks at her. "Detroit. I was with the city's youth runaway unit, but after five years, the hours finally got to me. Being on call 24/7 and working emergencies every day just kind of wore me out." Aden has sincere eyes. Carly likes that.

"I can imagine," she says. "Actually, I can't. I tip my hat to folks like you and Miles who are out there on the front line, every day, dealing with the real urban drama—not the stuff you read about in some novel or see on TV."

"Well, thank you," Aden says, flattered.

"Miles, I was wondering if I could steal you away for a moment. Would that be okay, Aden?"

"Of course."

Miles' eyes shine with moisture and Carly accepts the fact that he is a bit wasted. His voice is up a notch in volume, too. He leads Carly out onto the deck where, surprisingly, no one is about. There is a freestanding clay fireplace in the corner, with an oval opening that emits a romantic glow. Carly places her hands in front of the fire and immediately feels warmth.

"God, this is nice," she says.

Miles nods.

"So?" he asks, glancing quickly back at the closed door leading to the house.

"Miles," she begins, without preamble, "this thing between Ryan and me really has me all messed up. I mean, I can't for the life of me figure out what's going on."

"I know. It must be driving you crazy," he responds with reassuring eyes. "I've tried calling him, you know," he adds as an afterthought.

"Yeah, Olivia told me. And that's what I wanted to talk to you about. Well, partly what I wanted to ask you."

Miles is silent.

"I'm at a loss here to explain what is happening. You were one of the last people to talk to him, face-to-face, so perhaps you can shed some light on all of this."

Miles holds his hands wide, grins in the semi-darkness, firelight bathing his face in orange hues.

"Carly, we've been over this before. As I told you, we met for a drink; we were shooting the shit the way we always do, and then we went our separate ways. I assumed he was going home. I know I did."

"Yes, you've explained that before. But what doesn't add up is this: he isn't just shutting me out—he's shutting you out, as well. Correct me if I'm wrong, but I've overheard you tell Olivia that you're getting pissed that he hasn't returned your calls."

"Yeah, well . . . Ryan's going through something. I assume when he's ready to share it with me—"

"Miles," she says, interrupting him, "this is *me* you're talking to. You two are best friends. Up until now, he's told you *everything*. So what changed?"

Miles is silent, considering her words. She is correct, he is angry—actually, beyond angry. The fact that Ryan hasn't responded to his repeated calls has

Miles considering a number of things. He refuses to let this one go . . .

"I can't answer that. Only your husband can."

"Well, is he cheating on me? Is there another woman?" she blurts out, unable to contain her rising frustration, anger, and emotion.

Miles is silent for a moment.

"Naw, Carly, no *woman* I know of." He grins sheepishly, and Carly frowns.

"Okay . . ." Hesitancy. Then, "I mean, did something go down between you two on Friday?" Her eyes are like lasers, boring into his skull.

"Naw . . ." Miles emits a short grunt. Carly looks at him strangely. There is something not quite right here. Can't quite place her finger on the pulse of it . . .

"Miles?"

He snaps his head around, frightening her with the suddenness of his actions.

"I told you, Carly, nothing happened . . . damn!"

Miles steps back, escaping the daunting firelight. Before he descends back down into darkness, Carly spies an evil grin adorning his face.

"What is with *you*?" she whispers. "It's as if you are getting pleasure out of my pain . . ." Her voice diminishes to nothing.

"Perhaps you don't know your husband very well," he says suddenly, loud, face bursting back into orange light. He appears sinister, and Carly feels her heart race.

"Meaning?" she asks cautiously, fingers shaking.

"I don't know . . . nothing . . . Corona talking," he slurs, holding up the now-empty bottle, as if on display. "If it pleases the court, your honor . . ."

He turns away, saunters back into the confines of his home. Carly watches him go. Aden is waiting patiently for him. Their heads tilt toward one another;

Carly witnesses hushed conversations, more laughter, locs bouncing . . . something not quite *right*.

Carly turns back toward the fire, extending her hands toward the red-hot divide.

Not even this orange glow can warm her insides now.

Chapter 23

"Can I have a word with you?"

Olivia's stare burns into her husband's. He glares back, eyes darting between hers and the small group of folks from the nonprofit. They are in the basement family room, sitting on the dark brown sectional, drinks in hand, watching a boxing match on HBO HD.

It's close to midnight.

Olivia is beyond tired.

Beyond irritated at what she's just learned from Carly.

Miles excuses himself, walks with her up the stairs, past the living room where people still congregate. The music permeates the air like a thick fog.

He heads for the deck, but Olivia steers him into the kitchen and out into the garage where it is quiet.

Just the two of them.

After the door closes behind him, she turns and folds her arms over her chest.

"Just what the hell have you been telling Carly?"

"What are you talking about?" His eyes are animated, not able to remain in one place very long.

"Miles—you and Carly had words tonight. You upset her with this bullshit talk about Ryan and her!"

"What the hell did I say?!" he yells, then auto corrects his volume.

"I don't know. That's what I'm trying to find out. But you said something that cut to the bone—'cause she is one upset puppy right now. And I don't need to remind you of just how fragile she is. Do I?"

Miles grins. Takes a step forward. "And I don't need to remind you that we are all here because of you, Olivia." He steps forward again, one hand gesturing with an empty Corona bottle. Volume cut down a notch. "You decided to flirt with my best friend and things got out of hand." One further step until mere inches separate them. "So *you* watch what you say to me about it being my fault. Or should I go tell Carly the truth?"

Olivia is aghast. She opens her mouth to speak, but no words emerge.

"Yes, that's what I thought. Better keep your philandering tendencies to yourself. Don't want your best friend to find out what you are up to."

Olivia gulps.

"Think I'm stupid, Olivia? Think I don't know what happened that night after the party? Shit."

Olivia freezes. Stops breathing. Everything comes to a halt.

Several moments pass as Miles and Olivia stare each other down.

"Watch what you say to me. Hear me?"

Silence.

"I SAID, DO YOU HEAR ME???"

His voice echoes in the tight space.

Miles spins around, twisting on the balls of his loafers. He loses balance; his locs stream out from his head and dance briefly in the air; the beer bottle leaves his fingers. It arcs up ever so briefly before dropping to the concrete ground where it shatters into a dozen fragments.

Olivia's body spasms at the sound, his words, his frenzied misstep, her rapidly deteriorating friendship and marriage. . . .

Hour and a half later.

The party is over.

Everyone's left.

Miles is upstairs asleep.

Olivia and Carly are cleaning up, collecting empty beer bottles, paper plates, 16-ounce plastic cups. They work silently, both tired, both alone with their respective thoughts.

As far as parties go, this one was an unqualified success.

People will be talking about it next week. Great food, good drinking and conversation.

Everyone pleased.

Except for Olivia and Carly.

Each alone in her own world.

Alone . . .

"Olivia," Carly says, breaking the silence. Olivia is in the kitchen, just finished loading up the dishwasher. Carly is blowing out candles, shutting down the stereo, collecting a lone bottle that was missed in the corner of the large room.

"Yes?"

"Can we talk?"

Olivia feels a spike of pain travel down her back.

She stands straighter. Nods once. "Of course. I'm finished here."

Carly heads for the deck. Her hand touches the brass doorknob. "Let's do this outside, okay?"

Carly doesn't wait for an answer from her best friend. Instead, she is through the door before Olivia can consider a response. Olivia turns off the lights to the kitchen and dims the ones in the living room. When she joins Carly on the deck, Carly is sequestered in a chair, pulled up close to the fire. She motions Olivia to sit. Olivia does so, rubbing her palms in front of the growing warmth.

Carly has a handful of branches between her feet. She feeds them into the opening, witnessing the sparks and crackle as the flames come alive.

"Ummm, that's nice," Olivia says, attempting to break the ice.

Carly nods.

"Sorry Ryan didn't show," Olivia says. Pauses a moment before saying, "I'll track him down tomorrow—Rod asked me to—find out what's going on—starting to affect his performance and all."

Carly nods silently, then turns to her best friend. Exhales slowly.

"There's something I need for you to answer, okay? No more bull, no more dancing around the edge, 'cause this is my marriage we're talking about."

"Yeah, of course, Carly, but—"

Carly waves her hand, cutting short any further discussion.

"Here's the thing, Olivia—I know something went down with Ryan. A person doesn't just change overnight, like a switch being flipped. One second on, the next moment off, you know?"

She doesn't wait for a response.

"I think Miles knows something and isn't telling me. I think you do, too. Can't put my finger on it, but I'm willing to bet money . . ."

"Carly, listen—"

Again, Olivia is shut down by a quick raise of Carly's hand before she can begin.

"Olivia," she says softly, eyes locked on hers, "it's late. I'm beyond tired, missing my husband more than you know, not knowing what tomorrow will bring."

Olivia glances down.

"I ask you as my best friend and as a woman—as one who knows me and understands the way I tick better than most—I am asking you now to please tell me the truth . . ."

The tears begin to well. For the moment, they are unnoticeable. But very soon, they will slide down her dark cheeks.

"Tell me what in God's name is going on. Something's happened. Tell me what you know."

The tears have sprouted; they meander down her cheeks slowly. When Olivia glances up and into the face of her best friend, her eyes are wet. Her lips part, then come together.

Carly's face is bathed in firelight. Her features are stone-faced—not a single emotion visible.

Olivia considers her best friend. Sighs heavily, knowing she's about to cross a divide, do something she won't be able to undo. Mind racing . . . like a snowball, a freight train out of control.

Carly takes her best friend's hand in hers. Olivia allows her, numb to all feeling. She sucks in a short breath, frowns for a moment as she wipes away her tears, and begins. . . .

"Remember our party?" she says softly.

Chapter 24

Ryan stares at his illuminated watch for the hundredth time that evening. Reese lays beside him, the covers tousled and pulled back to their knees, hand on her chest, her breath rising and falling in waves. Both are silent, bodies moist, heated after frenzied sex, an afterglow painting them.

It is just past one in the morning.

Ryan feels the buzz that is in his testicles, circulating through his lower extremities like boiling water. Reese feels it, too, her own post-orgasmic tide—the ebb and flow soothing her.

Without opening her eyes or turning to face him, she senses him glancing at his watch again. In the near-darkness, Reese says softly, "Why don't you go?"

A moment passes.

"I don't want to."

"But you should." It is a statement, not a question.

Ryan doesn't respond.

He has been thinking about Carly all night. Knows the party was tonight, knows he needed to show—if not for his company, certainly for his wife. Yet . . . he is here . . . with Reese.

Afterglow of lovemaking . . .

A stronger intoxicant than that of his wife's . . .

Except . . .

He thinks of her.

Carly.

Ryan knows he needs to leave. Go home. Find sleep in his own bed.

Their bed.

He's married.

His wife with child . . .

Jesus!

Reese can sense his discomfort in the way his body tenses. It is slight, almost imperceptible, but she is growing to know him, this man who brings her joy when the sun is down.

So she reaches across to his belly, slides her finger down until she is cupping him, feels him beginning to rise. She then turns toward his form, eyeing Ryan as he lays there, eyes closed and breathing unhurriedly.

Runs her palm against the length of his shaft. Feels him engorge. Moments later, he is rock hard, and she marvels at her power, this ability to make this stranger sprout in her hand. She smiles, feeling herself grow wet again.

"Who are you?"

The question comes from out of nowhere. Ryan has turned to face her, his hand cupped over hers.

"What do you mean?" she asks.

"Simple question. I don't know you. I yearn to know more about the woman with whom I lay."

"Okay." Reese turns onto her back. Her hand remains on him, fingers clasping the shaft as if it were a railing on a darkened stairway.

"I'm just a regular woman. Not much beneath the surface."

"I find that hard to believe."

Reese exhales slowly.

"I was born and raised in a small town in Ohio. Came East to go to school at Hampton—wanted to be closer to our people and get all cerebral—but after two years, I dropped out. Couldn't find my groove, you know? So I hung out in Virginia Beach for a while, bartending at some of the Atlantic Avenue hot spots. That, too, got to be a drag, so I packed up my shit, and me and my hooptie headed here—to D.C. That was two years ago."

"Family?"

"My mom still lives in Ohio. I go back every blue moon or so. Father's been gone forever. One brother. Who the fuck knows what happened to him? Dead? Jail? AIDS? Don't know. Don't really care."

"Wow. I'm sorry."

"Don't be. That's life; shit happens. Everyone I know has a dysfunctional family. So, to me, it's normal."

"Okay." Ryan pauses to consider her words. He runs a finger along the ridge of her navel, enjoying the feel of her soft, black skin. His hand descends, traveling over coarse pubic hair, experiencing her wetness.

"Gonna finish school?" he asks, fingering her flesh.

Reese's eyes are closed. Her tongue emerges from her mouth; it touches her top lip, making it moist before disappearing.

"Perhaps. I've learned that education doesn't make one smarter. And it sure as hell doesn't make one happier. Look at you!"

Ryan plunges inside her using a finger. Reese moans.

"Touché!"

She grins, then cups his balls lightly in her palm as she rocks to his rhythm.

"Can I ask you a question?"

Finger slows. "Shoot."

"What's your fantasy?"

Ryan eyes her.

"Come again?"

"Simple question—what do you yearn for? Everyone has a fantasy or two. What's yours?"

Ryan ponders a bit.

"I guess it's being with a woman who will do whatever I ask of her. Satisfy me in whatever way I choose."

"Hmmm."

"What?"

"You want someone submissive."

"Not submissive."

"Then what?" she asks, squeezing the bulbous head of his cock between her fingers.

"I want a woman to whom I can just say—do this— satisfy me in this way. And she'll do it willingly. No questions asked. You know, sometimes it's not about foreplay, not about loving. It's about satiating one's desires, getting rid of the tension that threatens to bind you up. Sometimes, I just want to cum hard without explaining the details of how and when."

"Understood."

"Do you?" he asks.

"Yes. Most of us cannot ask our partners for what we truly want."

"Why is that?"

"Because we're afraid they'll look at us like we're crazy—that they won't understand our private passions; and that will drive a wedge between us and them. So we keep our fantasies to ourselves."

"True, true."

Reese jerks him measurably; Ryan slowly works her with his fingers. For a moment, they are lost in the actions of each other.

"Tell me your fantasy, Reese," Ryan finally utters.

Her hand settles on his fingers—guiding him over her clit. She traces tiny circles with his hand until he is driving on his own.

"Can you handle the truth?" she asks, closing her hand around him.

"Try me."

"Okay." She is eyeing him, her stare riveted to his. For a moment, they please each other without words—watching the movement of their breathing and their irises that seem to flare in the half-light.

Reese moans lightly.

"That's it," she whispers. "Right there is where it's at . . ."

Ryan's hand covers hers—gripping her fingers, commanding her to squeeze him tighter.

"My fantasy?"

Ryan waits.

She is silent a moment more.

"I want to be violated."

Ryan takes her clit between his fingers and pulls. Reese's breath for a moment is arrested.

"Don't psychoanalyze the whys . . . no questions asked. Just take it, and make it yours."

Ryan checks his watch.

It's late.

He should be going. He should be focusing on mending his marriage.

But this woman won't let go. She is tugging on his cock, and her words filling his other head with decadent thoughts that won't go away.

His fingers descend into the cleft of her plump

ass, fingering her there. Reese's stare is locked with his. She quivers to his touch, holding her breath. She is a river; she is that wet. He fingers her gingerly, and she responds by moving against him, pushing him deeper. It is a new sensation, but one she has yearned for.

Ryan leans in, kissing her hard on the mouth. He devours her tongue. He pinches a nipple, willing her to cry out.

She does.

His finger is gliding in and out of her now, and Reese is relaxing to his touch. She wants more. She wants him inside of her. She moves onto her stomach and spreads her legs wide, raising herself off the mattress. In the half-light she is vulnerable and intensely sexy. Ryan can feel his cock pulsating as she glances back at him with uncontrolled fury. He is rock hard as he mounts her.

Ryan checks his watch again.

Glances down at her loveliness. Oils himself with her juices. And presses himself against her warmth.

Reese reaches behind her and guides him home.

Take me, she demanded of him.

Make it yours . . .

So Ryan does.

Chapter 25

This time, he does not experience the rush of silence that normally envelops him. This time, when he steers into the quiet cul-de-sac, Ryan feels wary and drained, and the shadows that peer back from the redbrick colonial appear sinister.

It took Ryan less than twenty-five minutes to drive home. At Reese's, he showered, to eliminate the fuck-smell that oozed from his pores, and to remove the bite of sleep that tugged at him constantly. *Just a few more minutes,* he tells himself. *Just a few moments before I'm in my own bed, alone.*

He has shut off the recent events of his life. There were so many thoughts and images pawing at his consciousness that he was finding it hard to breathe. So he refused to deal with the totality of it all . . . opting instead for denial; it's a wonderful thing at half-past 3:00 A.M.

For a split second, he finds peace. His mind is on shut-down, the music in his black sapphire 760Li spreading throughout the luxurious interior the way blood spills from a fatal wound. It seeps into his pores that were scrubbed clean less than an hour ago. But not even soap and a fresh loofah can erase what he's done— unfaithful too many times now to rationalize.

Ryan trys not to think about that now.

No.

The music serves as a temporary diversion. It is smooth; it is soft. It is nonjudgmental. It doesn't probe. It doesn't raise an eyebrow. It just *is* . . . along with the quiet ride that somehow disconnects him from the road, as if he's riding above the ground, flying. There is no sound, just a quiet rush in his ears. Is that the music he hears, or does that rush come from deep within his heart, which is trying to speak loudly?

Ryan doesn't know.

He pushes a button; the garage door rises; and the bile that has retreated like a frightened mouse beneath dusty floorboards rises again in his throat, threatening to choke him. The black Ranger Rover is there, slotted in the left space—which means only one thing . . .

Carly is home.

He contemplates withdrawing. But of course, it's too late for that. She knows he's arrived—Ryan's certain of it. He drives forward and parks, killing the engine. Sits for a moment composing himself. Willing his nerves to calm down. The peace and serenity have left him as quickly as they came. Ryan exits the car, closes the door, lowers the garage door, and enters his house.

It is deathly quiet. Too quiet.

Lights off, but with slivers of moonlight squeezing between shutter slats and finding the floor, Ryan can make out their furniture. He removes his jacket, leaves it on the breakfast bar, and heads for the stairs, sucking in a breath. His foot taps the first step when he hears the words: "Don't bother."

Ryan freezes.

Carly is sitting in the oversize, overstuffed love seat that is sandwiched between two walls facing the windows. She is draped in darkness, but as he stares, her features begin to emerge like tree limbs through a blinding fog. Her feet are folded underneath her, and she is wrapped in a Gabi, a soft cotton blanket with colorful embroidered ends from Ethiopia, given to them as a wedding present five years ago.

He removes his foot and turns, going to her quietly.

There are a thousand things sprinting through his mind right now. There is so much to say. It's been a week since they've laid eyes on one another, and yet, he can't speak. He feels an outpouring of emotions. He wants to lean down and kiss her, envelop her with his arms, feel her warmth against a body that has grown cold. He knows what he's done is very, very wrong. On some level, he wants it to all end—for his life to go back to the way it was. Back when it was just the two of them. Before Reese. Before Olivia.

Olivia . . . Jesus.

He's tried not to think about her these past few days. Reese has been instrumental in that regard. When he was lost inside Reese, fucking this woman he barely knows, it was as if Olivia has receded like the tides; she disappeared for that moment, beneath the waves, and he liked that. Not thinking about her all the time. Not feeling consumed by thoughts, feelings of her and what could be.

But now, he stares at his wife. In near-darkness, she presents herself the way she always does: regal, unpretentious, beautiful like some long-ago Egyptian queen, his very own Nefertiti. He observes her features: the sharp nose, the curve to her cheek-bones, thin, sculpted lips, dark eyes that stare at him unblinkingly, smooth, silky, short chestnut hair. She doesn't need studs bisecting her flesh nor flashy tattoos to define her. No. Carly is simply a woman who inspires confidence with a glance . . . a nod . . . a sensual whisper his way.

"Come sit." Her words are clear, carrying across the expanse of living room. There is no trace of scorn in her voice. Ryan takes a seat on the carpet in front of her. She continues. "It's been a week."

"Yes."

"Expected a call from you."

"You walked out on me, not the other way around."

She pauses. "You missed your own company party—not very brilliant, if you ask me."

"Yeah? Well, with everything that's going on, I didn't feel very social."

Carly leans forward. "Okay, Ryan. Tell me about you and Olivia."

The words hit him like a steel door slamming on his teeth. They reverberate in his ears. They sting his cheeks.

"Excuse me?"

"Ryan," she says quietly, "you and Olivia have something between you. Tell me what it is. I've heard it from her. Now, I need to hear it from you."

There it is.

Laid out in front of him.

Nowhere to run. Nowhere to hide.

He notices she is shivering. Body quivering. She works to control her rage. Anyone, including him, can see that.

"I—"

"Please, Ryan," she says, interrupting him, "it's

late. I'm beyond exhaustion, not sleeping, not eating, living with this—not knowing if my husband desires me anymore—"

"Baby, of course—"

"Let me finish."

"K."

"I want honesty right now. I could become a
straight-up ghetto bitch, tearing to shreds everything
you and me built; I could be screaming at you right
now based on what I know, but I'm not. So, please . . .
I'm asking you . . . tell me the *truth*."

Ryan feels like crying. He knows he has hurt her
deeply, understands that his actions are cutting straight
to bone. He reaches for his wife to console her, but
she pulls away.

"Don't. Simply tell me."

"Okay," he says softly. "What do you want to
know?"

Carly sits forward, soft, thin hands on her lap, eyes
burning into his.

"Tell me everything."

It is so easy to lie to the one you love. We tell ourselves we're doing it because we care. Because of the
need to protect them from further harm. We rationalize our actions, convincing ourselves that letting
them know the God's honest truth would only drive
a wedge deeper between us, or worse, place us on a
collision course that could only end in a horrific,
fiery crash without any survivors.

So we lie.

Small ones. Remove the details. Edit out the specifics.

We know, on some level, what we're doing is wrong.
But we're trying to do the right thing. What's best for

them . . . we want the hurt to end. We don't want the
ones we love to suffer any further. So, we spare them.
Or at least that's what we tell ourselves . . .

"It started the night of party," he begins.

Carly sighs.

"No, Ryan, it did *not.*"

He pauses.

"Please don't tell me your defense consists of way
too much food and alcohol. I'm much too smart for
that."

Ryan nods.

"Okay, Carly." He sucks in a breath and exhales
quickly. "I've been attracted to Olivia for some time
now—"

"Do you love her?"

"What?" Ryan's voice croaks. He utters a half-
laugh. Carly's lips are pressed together in a scowl.

"It's a simple question."

"No, Carly. I love you."

She processes his words and nods for him to continue.

"At the party, things got out of hand. I had a lot to
drink. We all did."

"Yes, but I did not forget that I have a husband
and fuck someone else's man."

"Is that what you think went down?"

"Why don't you tell me."

Another sigh.

"As I said, we allowed things to get out of hand.
We"—face toward the ceiling, searching for the
right words—"we . . . I guess *we* acted on our attraction."

"You guess?"

"Alright. We did—we acted."

"So what exactly happened?" she asks.

"Carly, why are you doing this? If you've spoken to

Olivia, then you already know." Sweat is pooling in his armpits, and he prays the beads that have formed on his forehead are not yet meandering down his face. Ryan resists the urge to wipe them away.

"Because I want to hear it from you. So just tell me."

She is remarkably calm. Too much so, Ryan reasons. He knows how he'd react if the tables were turned. He quickly shuts these thoughts down, not wanting to even consider the possibility of Carly with another man.

"It was late. Everyone was asleep. I was thirsty, so I went upstairs to get something to drink. That's when I saw her."

"Olivia was waiting for you."

"No. It was nothing planned. Whether she heard me up or just happened downstairs at the same time, I don't know. But she appeared."

"And?"

Ryan wipes his brow.

"We, uhhh . . ."

"You touched her."

Carly's voice is near a whisper.

"Yes."

"Where?"

"Carly."

"Where, husband?"

Ryan swallows hard.

"Her breasts."

"And?"

He sighs harder.

"Please." His voice is wavering.

"AND?" Louder. "Where else did you touch her?"

"Between her legs."

Soft whisper.

"I didn't catch that," Carly says.

Ryan's hands are fumbling with one another.

"Between her legs."

Carly nods.

"You touched her pussy. Let's call it what it is, Ry. I mean, when you and I are fucking, that's what you call it—right? You've had no problem uttering that word before, so say it now."

"Why are you doing this, Carly?"

Carly laughs. "You're fucking pathetic! I'm not doing anything. You are. So say it, goddamn it!"

"Pussy."

"No. Don't just say, 'Pussy.' I want to hear you say, 'I touched our best friend's pussy.'"

"I touched our best friend's pussy. Happy?"

Long pause. "Ummm-hmmm. What else?"

"That's it."

"Oh?" Carly feigns surprise. "She didn't tug on your dick? You didn't fuck her that night?"

"NO! Did she tell you that?"

"So you didn't fuck her?"

"No, Carly, I did NOT!"

Ryan stands, needing to distance himself from her. He's used to being in control, but things have, in an instant, flipped. He finds himself vulnerable. Weak. It scares him beyond words.

Carly jumps up, the Gabi tossed onto the floor like table scraps fed to a hungry dog. Ryan heads toward the windows, but his wife intersects him, finger in his face, stopping him cold.

"Perhaps not, but you wanted to. You were *so* ready to fuck another man's wife, my best friend . . . hell, *your* best friend, while I lay asleep on the floor below. Right?"

Ryan is silent.

"RIGHT?" Inches separate their faces. Carly does not move, standing her ground. Her hands are back at her sides. "Be a fucking man for once in your life and tell me the truth!"

"Yes," he hisses.

"Alright."

Carly moves to the window, peeking through the slats before turning around. "So, that was it?"

Pause.

"I'm waiting."

"Yes, Carly. That was it."

"Nothing else? No further physical contact of any kind since then?"

Here, Ryan spies the abyss opening up before him. He stands on the edge, glancing downward. He can come clean, right now—tell his wife the truth—cleanse his soul—and God help him, there's a part of him that wishes to do just that. Cleanse himself of this awful secret he clutches close to the vest, this thing that threatens to destroy not only him, but his marriage and friendship, as well.

It would be so easy. *Just tell her,* he muses. *Tell her the truth. Get it over with. The pain will only last a second. Then comes peace.*

"No, Carly . . . nothing else."

Just like that, it's done. And Ryan knows there's no turning back.

Carly considers his words for a moment. She nods silently, returns to her seat, picking up the Gabi, wrapping it back around her shoulders.

"Where have you been tonight?" she asks suddenly.

"Out."

"Obviously. I mean, *where*?"

"Nowhere. Out driving. Clearing my head."

Carly is silent. She is watching him, and he can feel every pore contracting, screaming, it seems, against the lies that conspire against him.

"Driving . . ." she repeats.

"Yes."

"Not *fucking*?" she asks, her head cocked to the side.

"No. Not *fucking*."

"You sure?"

His stare drops, then returns to her a split second later.

"Yes."

"Ummm-hmmm."

Carly suddenly rises and brushes past him towards the stairs. Ryan's eyes grow wide.

"Where are you going?"

She spins on her heels to face him.

"I will not spend one more second in your presence. I'm sickened by what I've learned. Sickened, humiliated, and crushed by your actions." Carly shakes her head petulantly. "I never in a million years thought my own best friend would try to fuck my man. But what's worse is the knowledge that you would let things go that far. You would have fucked her—while her husband and I slept a few feet away. I shudder to think you are capable of *that*. I shudder to think what else you are capable of doing."

"Baby, I am so—"

"Ryan," Carly says, holding up her hand, cutting off any further conversation, "I do not want your apology. I don't want to hear how sorry you are. You can't fathom how much you've hurt me, nor can you begin to make it up to me. So save your words, because they are meaningless to me now."

She proceeds up the stairs, stops, and then retreats back down.

"Do you think you are the only one who feels desire?" Carly eyes him curiously. "Do you honestly think I am incapable of wanting what you want? Please! I'm not dead, you know. I walk down the street and feel what you feel—the same desire you experience to be with another. Yes, Ryan—it happens to *me,* too—it happens to all of us—that feeling—the wondering— what would it be like to lay with that man who just passed me by. The one with the sexy smile and the broad shoulders. I wonder. I fantasize. Just like you do. Do you honestly think I don't?"

Ryan stares at her incredulously.

"Obviously you don't. Your look gives you away! Isn't that typical?" Her foot hits the bottom landing with a thud as she laughs. Ryan instinctively jumps back.

"Men are all the same, thinking they're the only ones who pine away about being with someone else. As if the rest of us are lifeless inside. Well, I'm here to tell you, husband, I'm not dead. I think and feel the same things you do. I have desires just like you. I wonder what it would be like to be with another man. Difference is, I don't act on those feelings."

Ryan gulps.

"If I acted every single time I felt desire in these loins, well then," she says, sauntering up to him until mere inches separate them, "I'd be nothing but a fucking animal, a baboon, a whore . . . nothing more."

With that, she spins on her heels. Carly reaches the landing, pauses, turns to face her husband once again.

"I want you out of this house now. And you are not to return until I sort my feelings out. Whether a week, a month, or more, you—"

"Carly, it's close to 4:00 A.M.!" he pleads.

She ignores him.

"You will not set foot in our house until I say it's okay, or I swear to God . . ."

Ryan's eyes brim with tears. It is he who now quivers.

"Or what?" he whimpers.

Carly advances on him until her spit can be felt on his shivering cheek.

"Or by God, I'll cut this baby from my womb myself."

And with that, she pirouettes, retreating up the stairs until she is gone, out of sight.

PART THREE

Chapter 26

It is relatively easy to find the house on 16th Street, thanks to MapQuest. Parking, however, is another issue. She has to drive around for several minutes due to the lateness of the hour. Finally, about two blocks up and one block over, on a narrow street with thick towering elm trees and dark ivy that covers quaint Tudor homes, she is able to find a vacant space. She glides to a stop, kills the engine, and reaches for her cell.

She glances at the tiny screen—four missed calls, two voice mails. Sighing, she dials her number to retrieve the messages, which are both from Olivia.

"Carly, it's Olivia. I . . . don't even know how to begin—can't find the words to express how deeply sorry I am for hur—"

Carly hits delete.

Second message: "It's me again. I need to say something else. I know I've violated your trust, know I've done something terrible, something you can't possibly forgive me for now, but—"

It is deleted, as well.

She checks herself one final time in the mirror before exiting the vehicle and removing a wheeled travel bag from the trunk. The quiet of the street unnerves her. The block seems sinister from verdant foliage and she is alone—so she moves with a purpose to her step. Finding his house minutes later, she follows the concrete steps to the front door, sucks in a deep breath, and rings the bell.

He is asleep, of course. He hears the bell almost as distant thunder. He's not exactly sure if what he heard is real. But when she rings the bell a second time, and then a third, he is roused from his sleep. He props himself up on one elbow while cocking his head to the side, eyeing the clock on the nightstand to his right . . . 4:48 A.M.

Who on earth could be at his door?

He rises quickly, wraps a bathrobe around his frame, and places his feet in comfortable house slippers before sauntering down the stairs, rubbing at his eyes with the back of his hand. The front door presents itself directly in front of him, a thick aging slab of hardwood with a tiny distorted lens for viewing. He peers through it, frowns, tilts his head as if a different angle will somehow give different results. He takes two steps back, deactivates the alarm, and unlocks the door.

Carly is staring up at Tyler Nichols with puppy dog eyes.

For a moment, neither speaks. He observes the travel bag behind her, and glances up the street before settling his gaze back upon her.

"How'd you find me?" he asks quietly.

"Senior Staff Directory." She displays a weak smile.

Tyler nods, then says, "Need I ask?"

Carly shakes her head. "Please don't. Not now . . ."

He nods again and reaches for her, pulling Carly

into the folds of his bathrobe. They remain like that for a moment, the distant sounds from a passing car the only intrusion.

Tyler releases her an instant later, opens the door wide, and ushers her quietly inside.

Chapter 27

Ryan drains the last of his coffee.

Presently, it's ten minutes to nine. He's been in the office since six. Didn't get any sleep. Grabbed what belongings he could, stuffed them into an overnight bag and left, heading for Reese's, then thought better of it. Needed to clear his head, figure out his next move. His wife had thrown him out of the house. So what was his next play? Go back to Reese? Ryan wasn't sure. Instead, he drove straight to the office, took a shower there, changed, and tried to bury himself in work.

Rodney had called an emergency meeting with all department heads for 9:00 A.M. sharp, having to do with this annoying problem that wouldn't go away. Ryan's domain was manufacturing; the problem was with engineering, or so his people said. The customer in Tokyo was demanding answers as to why their shipment was delayed. Fingers were being pointed in all directions. Ryan thought his people were on top of it last week, but he was in and out of the office, and things had a habit of falling through the cracks when he wasn't around.

The past fifty minutes had been spent around his conference table, head down with his engineers, being brought up to speed, looking at alternatives. Ryan's team seemed convinced the problem was a design flaw and not a manufacturing problem, and this was the part he loathed—going into a department head meeting and pointing fingers at someone else. Therefore, he wanted to make doubly sure his people were correct in their assertion.

Ryan calls the meeting to a close at five minutes to nine. His team gathers their things and leaves. He grabs his jacket and heads downstairs, spying Olivia coming out of her cage. The two do not make eye contact. He is conscious of her movements, and he feels constrained, as if he's moving with an injury.

Rodney is already in his conference room, a large spacious area off of the main space, with floor-to-ceiling glass. He's at the head of an enormous cherrywood table, palms pressed flat, a dull expression on his face. The department heads file in, taking their seats. Olivia is the last to arrive. She takes a chair diagonally across from Ryan, purposely avoiding him as he stares straight ahead.

"Let's get to it," Rodney says. He makes eye contact with each one: Ryan, Olivia, Dennis, from Engineering, Randall, from HR/Legal.

"We've got a problem in Malaysia. Chipset shipments are behind schedule. NTI is complaining big time. At this point, I want to know exactly what the problem is, and what we need to do to correct it ASAP. Ryan?"

Ryan has been listening with his head down so as to not glance at Olivia. Now, he stares at her for a split second before panning to Rod. He opens his mouth to speak.

"As best we can tell, the problem does not lie with manufacturing. The chipsets are failing QC at the tail end. Chinny has gone through the line with a fine-tooth comb, so we're fairly confident."

"But not one hundred percent?" Rod asks.

"Nothing is ever one hundred percent, Rod. It could be with the line, but I doubt it."

Rodney nods, pivots his head to the other side of the table. "Dennis?"

"We see no design problems with the prototype, which incidentally was fabbed to the same specs as this production run. But that doesn't mean the issue doesn't reside in the design. We have seen similar problems on other chipsets, so we can't rule out a design flaw."

"The prototype was manufactured in Malaysia, correct?" Rod asks Ryan.

"No," Ryan answers. "It was fabbed in Taipei. Malaysia had another run when that job came down."

"So it could be the plant, then? Wrong set of instructions programmed or something like that?"

"Again, Rodney, we've gone through the line; it checks out. I suspect we missed something when we went from Proto III to Prod I. A sample from the line has been Fed-Exed to us. We need to put it under the microscope and find the bugs."

"And in the meantime?" Randall asks. "We need to ensure we're not violating any agreement with NTI by delaying shipment." He glances around the table, making eye contact with each department head before settling his gaze upon Rodney. "The size and scope of the contract worries me."

"Which is exactly why we need to do a preemptive

strike. Head off any further issues by addressing NTI directly."

"Little late for that," Olivia says.

Rod snaps his head to her, purses his lips, yet remains silent for a second. Only a second.

"We're about to change that." He doesn't wait for a response before continuing. "I want Olivia and Ryan in Tokyo day after tomorrow. Right now, what we need is damage control with NIT. Olivia, that's your specialty. Ryan, you tag along to appease their technical folks. If need be, you'll re-route to Malaysia on your way home if the line becomes the issue. In the meantime, Dennis, I want all of your available resources looking at the chipsets when they come in. Day and night until we fix this thing. Randall, anything he needs, you give it to him."

"Understood."

"I'm in Geneva day after tomorrow giving a speech to one of the study groups of the ITU. After that, I'll fly on to Tokyo if need be; that is, if you all haven't wrapped things up." He's staring at Olivia and then Ryan.

They both nod.

"I don't need to remind anyone of the potential value of this contract to our company. NTI has shown great faith in us with their initial order. We need to go to general quarters on this one and do whatever it takes to get the problem solved." Rodney stares each department head down in turn.

"Questions?"

There are none.

"Olivia, Ryan, stay. The others, back to work."

When the room has emptied, Rodney clears his throat. "Get the door, would you?" he says to Ryan.

"Ryan, Olivia, I'm just going to say what's on my

mind; not going to make any apologies for my words. So, here it is. I'm not sure what is going on with the two of you, but something's wrong. The dynamics have changed, and that has me worried. Very worried. Normally, you two are like Lucy and Ricky—joined at the hip—hell, each used to finish what the other started. Remember that? But no longer. Like I said, I'm not going to try to second-guess everything that has happened. I know both of you are under tremendous stress; I recognize that. We all do. But I need you to get back to the way things were—where the two of you were *dazzling*. I want to see the fire in your eyes. I need that in Tokyo—need the two of you to appease NTI, make them our brethren again. I'm not telling you how to do your job—because both of you are top-notch, the best this company has. But somewhere along the way, something has changed. Now I need you to put it back the way it was. Kick ass and take names. Okay?"

"Yes, sir," Olivia responds.

Ryan nods.

"Good. Olivia, would you excuse us?"

Olivia rises and leaves without another word. When they are alone, Rodney rises from the table to stretch. He goes to the window, glances out for a moment, hands behind his back before he turns to Ryan.

"Look, Ryan, I'm going to level with you. I'm worried about you. You look like shit and your work is suffering."

Ryan presents a sheepish smile.

"Now I know you and Carly are having problems. I was disappointed not to see you at Olivia's party. Hell, everyone was."

"I know, Rod—"

Rodney waves his hand. "You don't need to explain your whereabouts to me. But I do need you to get back into your zone, because you've left that place and it concerns me greatly when your work begins to suffer."

"I'm sorry, Rodney. Things between Carly and me are just hard right now."

"I know. I know. Marriage is a tough business; you don't have to tell me. But my first priority is to the shareholders of this company. I'm sure you understand that."

"I do."

"Good. So, listen to me—as your friend—whatever you need, you've got it, but get yourself together, please. Get this personal stuff behind you. As your president, I have to insist you turn things around here. There is no choice in this matter. The company cannot tolerate poor performance. I need you back in the zone, Ryan. I need you back up there, and I need you back there yesterday, you follow?"

"Yes."

Rodney moves to Ryan's side, places his palms flat on the table so he can bend down; he is eye-to-eye with Ryan.

"I need to be clear on this, Ryan. So, are we?" Rodney asks.

"Crystal . . ."

"Good, man," Rodney says, placing a hand on his shoulder.

The gesture is meant to console, but all Ryan feels is a deepening chill, spreading slowly throughout his extremities. He doubts even Reese can warm his spirit now.

"Have a minute?"

She glances up from her phone, sees him in her cage—a long time since he's been here—and frowns.

"I'm busy," Olivia responds, then goes back to her messages.

"One minute, Olivia." Ryan shuts the door behind him, but makes no attempt to go farther. "Can we have some privacy?" he asks, referring to the windows. Olivia shakes her head.

"You won't be here that long." She busies herself, not making eye contact with him. Ryan ignores the comment.

"What is going on here?" he asks.

"What are you talking about?"

"You should know, Olivia. My wife throws me out of the house after conversing with you. Jesus, what exactly did you tell her?"

Olivia glares at him while jamming her hand down on the button, forcing the windows to go opaque.

"You have one hell of a nerve coming in here after being AWOL for practically a week. You didn't return my calls, or the calls of my husband. Hell, you didn't call your wife even once while she was staying with us. You disappeared, Ryan . . . God only knows to where; only He knows what you've been up to. So do not chastise me for my behavior."

"I'm not chastising you, Olivia, but my marriage is on the line, and I want to know what transpired between you and my wife!" Ryan works to control his voice.

Olivia simply laughs.

"Guess you should have thought about that before going AWOL! You are quick to point your finger at everyone but yourself. You're the one with the issues, Ryan," she says, rising from her desk, eyes glaring. "You're the one who needs to check himself before checking others."

Now it's Ryan who emits a short grunt.

"You have no fucking idea what is going on here, Olivia . . . none whatsoever. You sit there, secure in your own shit, as if you're sitting safe in a glass house, throwing stones at me. Well, I'm here to tell you, baby, you have no fucking idea what's really going on here . . . none."

Olivia considers his words. She swallows hard and glances away for a moment before leveling her stare at Ryan's.

"Let me clue you in on something, Ry, and I'm only going to say this once—you're on your own. I'm out of this; so is Miles. I fucked up once, but as God is my witness, I will not screw up again. I apologize to you and I apologized to Carly for my part in all of this. But I'm done. So leave me out of it. It's you against your wife. I suggest you handle your business and salvage the best thing that ever happened to you—your marriage. Now leave me *alone*."

Olivia glares at Ryan for a few more seconds before adding, "I may have to work with you, but I don't have to talk to you any longer. Now kindly get the fuck out of my office!"

With that, she punches the button, forcing the windows clear. Head down, Olivia returns to work, and Ryan has no choice but to heed her words and leave the same way he came in.

Miles rubs his cell between thumb and forefinger. It fits nicely in his palm. He glances at his watch, notices he has a few minutes before his next meeting. He decides now is as good a time as any to make the call.

First ring. Second, third, fourth, and then to voice mail. Miles sighs.

"Ryan, it's Miles," he says, a seriousness in his voice. "I need to talk to you immediately. It's kind of an emergency."

Miles holds the phone to his lips for a few seconds more before ending the call. Cradles the phone in his palm as he goes to the window, glancing downward to the courtyard below.

The phone vibrates a minute later.

"Hello?"

"It's Ryan."

"Ryan . . ." A long exhale of breath. "You're a hard one to get a hold of. How are things?" Miles tries to lighten the mood, immensely grateful for the connection to his best friend again.

"You said it's an emergency—is it?"

Miles emits a short chuckle.

"Damn, bro—can two best friends catch up for a minute?"

"I don't have time for this, Miles! Is there an emergency or not?" Ryan spits, voice low, as if he's whispering. But his ferocity can be felt where Miles stands.

"Can you calm down for a second? Ryan, I just want to talk to you. We really need to—"

Miles hears the snap of the cell as Ryan ends the call. He pulls his cell from his ear, stares at it incredulously. Stabs the SEND button to redial.

Call immediately goes to voice mail. He ends the call, then hits SEND again. Curses to the window.

"Fucker!"

Redials twice more before his assistant pops her head in, breaking his concentration. He snaps his head from the window.

"Your eleven-thirty is here," she says before retreating.

"Thanks. Ah, give me a minute," he says distractedly.

Redials. Voice mail picks up again.

Miles sucks in a breath.

"Nigga, I'm so tired of your shit, you know that? So let this be a warning to you. You think you can just move on and not talk to me? Think again. I'm not done with your ass, not by a long shot. Be seeing you, Ryan. Be seeing you real fucking soon! Believe that!"

This time, it is Miles who snaps the phone shut, dropping it on his desktop, clenching his teeth as he wills his heart rate to slow to a dull roar.

Chapter 28

Tokyo City Hall, with a height of 800 feet, is located in Shinjuku-ku, a two-tiered tower design paying homage to Notre Dame in Paris. The second tallest building in Tokyo, only behind Tokyo Tower, an Eiffel Tower replica, and at fifty feet taller than its Parisian counterpart, the world's tallest self-supporting steel structure. This, Olivia muses, would be fascinating to someone who gave a shit right now. Sadly, she is not in that camp. Far from it, in fact.

She and Ryan find themselves on the forty-seventh floor, high above the city, in a lounge area decorated in shades of gray and black. All the furniture is white supple leather over aluminum or steel frame. Candles flicker, providing the only light. Outside, a heavy downpour obliterates the normally unobstructed floor-to-ceiling view. Now, there's only gray—inside and out. The room feels cold and sanitized.

Their host is Tetsuo Kuriowa, the VP and general manager of business development for NTI. He is a thin, wiry man, bespectacled, with an affinity for Rin cigarettes. Over sushi, fresh sashimi, and green tea, he pontificates about the architectural history of Japan, all the while waving his smoke over a shock of blue-black hair. Ryan and Olivia listen intently, sitting opposite each other, their eyes on the rest of the entourage, making minimal eye contact with each other. They barely spoke during the 14 hours in the air. Ryan slept most of the way; Olivia read, worked, and watched several DVDs.

Ryan sighs as he reaches for his third green tea. Anorexic attendants in dull gray uniforms are there to refresh his cup. He produces a weak smile for the one who attends to him and takes a sip while pondering the situation here. The good news is that the NTI folks have been appeased—at least for the short term. Olivia, he has to admit, has done an excellent job of schmoozing with the higher ups. They have been convinced that the problem with the chipsets has been nearly eliminated—a simple bug. Olivia is quick *not* to call it a design defect; defect suggests larger implications. This, she assured the senior staff, was an annoying bug . . . nothing more. The production runs should commence again within a day; NTI should expect their first delivery by courier shortly thereafter.

Ryan's job has been to monitor the situation from his cell phone and Wi-Fi capable iPaq, and report back to NTI's chief technology officer, who will undoubtedly brief the president. Ryan has been on the horn with Dennis every hour on the hour, and checking in with his own staff to get the unbiased, unfiltered reports. The news has been good. True to form, as usual, Olivia is indeed correct. A design bug, something that Dennis' engineers uncovered about ten hours into their examination, and a quick fix, with much help from Ryan's team. Chinny is standing by to receive the mods via FTP, which should take no more than an hour. Afterwards, they will be QCed and then programmed into the line; and the first chips are set to roll off by daybreak, fingers crossed. Ryan says a silent prayer of thanks. Now if only his personal life can be sewn back together as quickly.

Dinner comes to a close about thirty minutes later. The elevator ride to the lobby is swift. Most of Kuriowa's entourage follows them down, so there is zero opportunity for discussion in the cramped steel quarters. A car service is waiting outside to take them back to the Dai-ichi Hotel Tokyo, located next to the renowned Ginza district and walking distance from the Imperial Palace. The ride should take no more than twenty minutes; instead, it takes close to fifty due to maddening traffic and the inclement weather. Olivia and Ryan make small biz talk, and a quick debrief with Rod on speakerphone as the rain pummels the streets and their vehicle. Ryan's head lays gently on the leather headrest, his eyes attempting to focus on vibrant neon that whizzes by. Soon, he is seeing without really seeing, his mind projecting images onto his retinas as the drumming of the rain soothes him. He is thinking of the three women in his life: his wife, Carly; his lover, Reese; and his best friend, Olivia, who sits silently beside him checking voice mail messages.

When they first boarded the plane, he was still waiting for an opportunity to talk to Olivia—to really talk, get back to the way things were, if that was indeed possible. There was a sense of hope that lofted him as the Boeing 777 lifted off from Dulles; this romanticized view that all would be forgiven—that somewhere over the Pacific, Olivia would gaze longingly at him the way she did six months ago—back when she thought of him as beautiful.

Indeed, Olivia had called him beautiful once. Ryan smiles now at the remembrance.

But all of that evaporated the moment Olivia settled into her business class seat, retrieving her laptop and legal pad, her body language making it perfectly clear that she had no interest in conversing with him on anything other than work.

Now, 48 hours later, Ryan's view of Olivia has changed. She no longer commands the same level of respect. Less than an hour ago, as he watched her grasping a piece of sashimi gingerly between chopsticks, he realized that her manicured fingers were no longer enticing. Her head was tilted back as she laughed at a joke Tetsuo Kuriowa made about the hip-hop mogul, P. Diddy, breasts heaving, spreading the buttons of her crisp white cotton blouse as she cackled. Ryan observed all of this silently, watching her disinterestedly. Once, not long ago, he would have been captivated by that laugh and the ropy muscles at the base of her neck that undulated like a serpent; but not now. He glances over at her for a second. She eyes him for a moment before turning her attention back to her fucking cell phone. They are sitting 24 inches away, but it might as well be 24 *thousand*. He feels nothing. Nothing but growing contempt.

Shift to Carly.

For several seconds, her image is there—right behind his forehead, like a nagging headache—his wife sitting alone in the dark a few nights ago, regal nose, high-yellow cheekbones, thin, sensuous lips. Cut to a quick memory of the way they used to make love, as husband and wife: Ryan on top, Carly's tight, lithe body wriggling underneath him, marveling at the way his length would disappear inside her, only to reappear moments later; Carly's eyes closed to mere slits, mouth half open, hardly a sound emerging; but he could sense desire in her eyes.

Stop it.

Shift to Reese.

He has to.

The pain is right there beneath his forehead—a throbbing, mind-numbing migraine. Threatening, like a stroke, to strike him down where he lays his head.

Their last night together, Reese and Ryan—the same night Carly threw him out of his own house. He nuzzled behind her, entombing himself deep inside her, connected in a way that stirs him even now.

"What?"

Ryan turns toward the sound. Olivia is facing him now. "Excuse me?" he says.

"Can I ask you something?"

"Oh, now you wanna talk?" he retorts.

Olivia ignores him.

"Just what exactly did Miles say to you that night when the two of you were alone?"

Ryan lifts his head and abruptly turns to face her. "What?"

"I want to know exactly what Miles said. Something went down between the two of you . . . something concerning you and me, but I suspect it's more than that. He's being evasive, I know that. I just don't know what exactly was said."

Ryan responds with a snort-laugh.

Olivia glares. "Just what is your problem?"

Ryan leans in. "I'll tell you just what my problem is! You sit there with your 'everything's alright in my world' attitude, staring down your nose at me like I'm some pauper in stinking rags, and you have no clue how fucked up your own house has become!"

"And what is that supposed to mean?"

"It means, honey, your shit is fucked up."

Ryan puts his finger in her face. "And you need to check yourself and your man before you tell me about getting my own marriage in order."

"Okay, Ryan, you know what?" Olivia leans into him so to not be heard by the driver. "Why don't you cease speaking in tongues and just tell me what is really going on?"

Ryan shakes his head.

"You deserted me," she says. "You turned your back on your best friend. You left me to rot out in the open all by myself. You have some fucking nerve not speaking to me, leaving it all up to Miles to sort out."

Ryan laughs out loud. "Miles! He's the most comical out of all of us. You and Carly are so fucking concerned about my comings and goings. Well, let me tell you, honey, it's your husband you need to be concerned with. Not me!"

Their car pulls to a stop under the huge awning of the Dai-ichi Hotel. As the driver steps out to open Olivia's door, her face turns up in a snarl.

"Fuck you, Ryan!" she roars as one mule hits the wet pavement.

Ryan grabs her arm before she can duck out.

"No longer interested, Olivia. But why don't you ask your husband instead? That is, if he can remember which team he's batting for."

Next morning, Ryan sits alone after finishing breakfast. He scans the headlines disinterestedly before brushing the paper away. Pulls his cell out and places a call to Olivia.

No answer.

When he goes to a house phone and asks to be connected to her room, Ryan finds she's already checked out.

"When?" he asks.

"Last night," the desk clerk informs him with perfect English diction. "Had us book the first flight out to the States."

Ryan thanks her.

Hangs up.

Checks his watch. Four plus hours until his flight to Malaysia.

Plenty of time to take a stroll in the brilliant sunshine.

Chapter 29

Olivia steers around the corner, the dazzling sunshine temporarily blinding her. For the first time in close to sixteen hours, her heart rate slows. She can feel the light at the end of the tunnel; a hot shower, some rum vanilla herbal tea, and a long nap will revitalize her spirits. It's good she is home early; good she's arriving in the middle of the day when Miles is not around. It was smart to leave Tokyo when she did—in the midst of that madness with Ryan—because her whole demeanor was becoming polluted. The office doesn't expect her in until tomorrow. Perfect. She desperately needs to decompress. To clear her mind of those thoughts that have swilled around like scum against a city pier.

When she pulls onto her street, Olivia breathes easier. Seeing her home always does that. The grass is immaculately cut; the hedges trimmed with the skill of a barber. Parked beside her mailbox—the shiny one with the brass numbers embedded in black metal—is a silver Audi coupe. Temp tags. Olivia stares at it as she presses the garage door opener. She wonders why the sports car is parked right there—next to *their* mail-box. Residents usually park their cars in their garages or in driveways; the street is hardly ever clogged with cars. In fact, someone a few years ago raised this very issue at their homeowners' association meeting—the fact that they've all spent this money on garages and gleaming asphalt driveways. So, the message was clear— use them, and don't park on the street. And most comply.

This thought is fleeting, however. The last thing on her mind right now is why this Audi is parked in front of their mailbox. Instead, a steaming hot shower is calling her name, along with a mug of rum vanilla herbal tea. Perhaps watch television—catch *Oprah* later on this afternoon. When was the last time she got to do that? she muses.

Olivia glides into the kitchen, dropping her purse onto the countertop. She wheels her carry-on to the base of the stairs, contemplates dragging it upstairs to their bedroom before nixing that idea. Flinging off her mules, she climbs the steps slowly, suddenly aware of something.

A noise . . . a sound . . . something not quite right.

She reaches the top landing and pauses, cocking her head to the right towards their bedroom. The entrance is less than thirty feet away, past the guest bedroom and full bath. There are definitely sounds emerging from their bedroom—muted voices.

TV?

Clock radio?

Olivia wrinkles up her nose, suddenly aware of a scent she can't quite place. She grips the handrail before pushing off, toes curling into the carpet.

When she comes to the door, she pauses for a half beat before entering, glancing left to their large bed.

The covers are rumpled and unmade. She takes in the clothes on the chaise lounge, before settling her eyes on Miles, who lies beneath the white sheet. His mouth is open, lips forming a silent "O." The scene is surreal—like from a foreign film.

Before she can question her husband, before he has an opportunity to respond to the inquiry that has been birthed on her own lips, the bathroom door opens with a flourish, and someone walks into view. The person is male, bald-headed, and nude, just out of the shower, Olivia can tell, because water droplets cascade down his taut chocolate body. Olivia's eyes connect with his—Aden's—Miles' co-worker, before panning left to her husband. The scene has shifted from surreal to unbelievable.

In the blink of an eye, Olivia's world has shattered. Her heart rate spikes and threatens. Now it's no longer about soothing hot showers, sipping herbal tea on the back deck, or long uninterrupted naps—not anymore. Now it's about her new life that has suddenly become a car wreck.

Olivia takes in Aden, who has retreated to the bathroom, wrapping an oversize fluffy towel—her fucking towel, she notices with disdain—around his athletic frame. Suddenly she finds herself sick, and pivots on the balls of her feet, running from the room and into the hallway, past the guest bedroom, past the bathroom, down the stairs as the muffled voice of Miles calls out her name, stinging her ears. She hits the bottom landing, almost twisting her ankle in the process, practically losing her balance as she skids on a mule; running into the hallway and ripping open a door, descending onto one knee then another, hugging the toilet as she vomits, heaving uncontrollably as her eyes water and burn.

Miles is at her back, his touch on her shoulder, feather-like, but it is vile and almost foreign, so she shakes him away.

"Baby, it's not what you think—"

"GET THE FUCK AWAY FROM ME!" Olivia screams.

She heaves, vomits some more. After flushing, she shoves Miles with a force that amazes even him. Rinses out her mouth, spits into the basin, wipes her eyes with the back of her hand, and recoils from the stench of her own throw-up.

Out the door, on auto-pilot now.

Into the hallway.

Back into the living room.

Breezing past Miles, who's slid on his pants, his chest and feet still bare.

To the kitchen, yanking open the refrigerator, grabbing the first thing she sees—a liter of Coke— twisting off the top and guzzling the liquid down as if her insides are on fire and this is her only fire hose.

"Take it easy, baby . . . use a glass."

Olivia stares at him in disbelief.

She flings the open bottle at him; it spins on its vertical axis as it leaves her grip, Coke spilling forth in an ever-expanding arc. Miles ducks, the bottle and its contents coming to rest on the carpeted floor twenty feet away.

"HAVE YOU LOST YOUR FUCKING MIND!?" Olivia yells. "I catch my husband in bed with another man, and all you're concerned about is me drinking from the bottle?"

Miles creeps closer. "Olivia, listen. It's not . . . baby. We just stopped by for lunch . . . and Aden took a quick shower . . ."

His palms are up, like some deity.

"Do I look like I was born yesterday, mother-

fucker? Or should I say, fatherfucker? I can't believe
this shit." Olivia turns her back on him, rummages
through the open fridge, grabbing at deli meats and
cheeses. She rips open plastic wrappers, stuffing the
food into her mouth as if she is crazed and ravenous.
Bits of cheese fall from her mouth onto the tile. She
ignores this while Miles comes up behind her, hand
again on her shoulder. Olivia recoils like a disturbed
cobra.

"DON'T TOUCH ME, YOU FUCKER!"

"You need to calm down," Miles responds.

Behind them, Aden has appeared. He's fully dressed
in a navy sports coat, tan pleated slacks, and camel-
color lace-ups. A large diamond is sparkling from his
right ear. Miles turns, glances at him for a moment
before returning his stare to his wife.

"I think it's best that I leave," Aden says softly.

"You think?" Olivia snickers.

Aden disappears down the hallway. Olivia hears
the front door open and close. She stares her husband down.

"Olivia, listen—"

"No, fucker, you listen," Olivia says, getting in his
face. "I want your cock-loving ass out of my house.
NOW! I got nothing else to say."

"Ain't gonna happen."

"Excuse me?"

"You heard me!" Miles exclaims. "Last time I
checked, I pay half the bills up in here. My name's
on the deed, too."

"You think I give a fuck about whose name is on
the deed? I just caught you in bed with another man.
Miles, you are fucking disgusting—"

SLAP.

When the intense dizziness subsides, Olivia finds
herself facing away from him. Her cheek stings. Rais-

ing a hand to her face, she can feel the rising welt. She glances backwards.

"You hit me." The words emerge as a mere whisper.

"I'm not leaving," is Miles' response.

Olivia stares at her husband as if she's seeing him for the first time. The weight of what has just transpired crashes down upon her. She has no idea who this man is standing before her. Surely he is not the man she married.

Her husband was kind. He was gentle. On so many levels, he was amazing.

But all of that was past tense.

Now, it's all been erased . . .

Olivia stares at Miles in disbelief, taking in his features that once upon a time made her happy and content.

She grabs her purse and retreats to the living room, slipping on her mules, reaching for the handle to her carry-on, and pulling it behind her. Entering the hallway, Olivia passes her reflection in the mirror as she heads for the door. She steals a glance, spying one half of a reddened face that makes her wince.

Olivia leaves the house without glancing back.

At the end of the street, Olivia has no choice but to pull over. She's crying uncontrollably. There are so many thoughts slamming into her skull that she swears her brain will burst.

She puts her car in park and reaches for her cell phone while trying to control her shaking limbs. She stares at it for a moment in her lap, the thing swimming in and out of focus as tears meander down her chin. Should she call?

Yes.

She has no choice.

Carly answers on the third ring.

It takes Olivia ten seconds to spit the words out.

"I . . . I just caught Miles in bed . . . with a man . . . he slapped me . . . not sure what to do . . ."

Olivia's former best friend listens for a moment.

"Another picture-perfect marriage down the drain," Carly responds finally, without a trace of compassion. "Welcome to my world."

Then the line goes dead.

Chapter 30

Miles sits behind an oak desk, fingers steepled beneath his chin. Across from him in one of two chairs is Aden. Both men are quiet, staring off into space, alone with their thoughts. Five days have passed since this thing transpired between Aden, Miles, and Olivia.

"I feel bad," Aden says, breaking the silence.

Miles glances over at him.

"Don't. What's done is done. Besides, it was bound to happen sooner or later."

He stares out the window; his office is on the second floor of a U-shaped building overlooking a courtyard. A throng of adolescent boys play basketball while a half dozen onlookers cheer them on. Aden stares at Miles, urging him to continue.

"I mean, I love my wife, don't get me wrong. But this is something that needs to be done."

"What is?"

"This feeling I have inside me. The way I am."

Aden smiles.

"You mean, the way you like guys?"

Miles shoots him a look.

"You know it goes deeper than that."

"I know. I was just trying to bring some levity to the situation."

"Seriously, I can't help who I am . . . or what I've become. I'm still struggling with all of this, trying to sort everything out—and I genuinely hope Olivia can get past this."

"You know I'm here for you, Miles."

"Yes, I know that. Thank you."

"Have you spoken to her?"

"Nope. Olivia won't take my calls. I figure it's best that I stay away—give her time to cool off."

"I've been thinking . . . about your situation. I think you should consider staying with me."

Miles stares at him sharply.

"Are you out of your mind? You and I work together. I'm the director here. Hell, I hired you. How's that gonna look? Aden, please!"

"I don't mean permanently. But I hate the thought of you being miserable at night, all by yourself."

"Aden, it's not going to happen. Besides, I think I have my living situation all worked out."

"You do?"

"Yeah. I have an old hang-out buddy who used to play for the Redskins. Retired now—knee injury. He's got a couple of properties around town that he keeps for out-of-town guests or when he's in the mood to throw a party. Anyway, I called him; he owes me a favor . . ."

"I'm not gonna ask," Aden replies.

"Then don't."

"May I ask where this place is?"

"It's right off of Connecticut Avenue, by the National Zoo. A quiet street of row houses."

"Great!"

"I'm moving in there tonight after work. He told me I can have it for a few months, until my situation is straightened out. Best thing is that it's already furnished, so I don't need to bring anything but my clothes."

"Damn, you work fast."

"That's why I'm the boss," Miles says, winking at Aden, "and on top. Don't forget it, my man."

"How could I?" Aden says wryly.

"Ohmigod, this is soooooooooooooooo nice!"

Ryan grins while swatting Reese's ass.

They are at the Buckingham on West 57th Street, around the corner from Central Park. Reese is on the oversize bed, hugging the fluffy pillows. Ryan is at the window, staring into the faltering twilight.

"Can we order room service?" she asks excitedly.

"You're like a little kid. Whatever you want, Reecy, but I thought we'd take a stroll and get something to eat while we're out."

It is Monday night. Ryan's been back close to a week now, and staying with Reese. She doesn't seem to mind—not at all. The Rhyme, where she works, is closed Mondays and Tuesdays, so they decided to get away. Ryan needs some serious R&R, and Reese isn't about to complain about an all-expenses-paid getaway.

An hour later, they find themselves in the Theater District, walking down Seventh Avenue towards Times Square. Ryan's dressed casually in jeans and a light sweater; Reese wears her favorite low-rider jeans (the ones Ryan loves because he can see her ass tattoo without having her bend over), and a bright red tee shirt that accentuates her (as if they need accentuating) D-cup breasts; afro puffs traded for thick zigzagging cornrows. They duck into a huge Asian eatery where they order spring rolls, stir-fried pork with orange and sesame, and Szechuan shrimp. Ryan sips on a Tsingtao beer; Reese, a Long Island Iced Tea.

"Nice to have somebody serve me for a change!" Reese exclaims.

"I hear that."

The food arrives quickly. They dine while the conversation around them buzzes loudly.

"It's nice to see you other than late at night after the bar closes," Ryan says.

Reese laughs.

"Welcome to my world. Relationships—hell, everything is tough when you work tending bar."

"Why?"

"Because our life is inverted from everybody else's. When you're awake, we're asleep, and vice versa. We live the lives of vampires. Even going to the bank is tough. You gotta make it there before closing time, and that's a hell of a thang when you sleep in until four!"

"I don't hear you talk much about your friends," Ryan says.

"Most of my friends work with me or down the street from me. Lacy is my gurl. She's the other bartender at Rhyme, and Boo-Boo, the bouncer at Felix, is my drinking buddy."

Ryan nods as he reaches for another helping of stir-fried pork.

"Boyfriend work at The Rhyme, too?"

"Excuse me?"

"Just asking."

"About my boyfriend?" Reese's nose ring sparkles in the dim restaurant. "I don't have one. Unless you qualify." She eyes him curiously. "Why?"

"Just asking." Ryan grins. "You haven't mentioned

your past relationships, or any relationships for that matter."

"Well, you never inquired," Reese quips. A spring roll crunches under the weight of her teeth. "We spend a lot of time discussing your world."

"Okay . . ."

"Don't get defensive, I'm just saying . . ." She pats his hand.

"Anyway, tell me about your last boyfriend," Ryan ventures. Reese stares at him for a while before nodding her head.

"Not much to tell. I was dating this guy named Cory for a while. He worked at The Rhyme for a minute as a bar back, but got fired for being late."

"How long did the two of you date?"

"A few months."

"What was he like?"

Reese purses her lips and emits a short grunt.

"I don't know. Just a guy. Kind of quiet, except when he got around his friends. Then, of course, he thought he was the shit!"

"And you broke up because?"

"Um, there wasn't one particular thing, to tell you the truth. He and I were just on different wave-lengths, you know?"

Ryan is silent, watching her. The stud bisecting her right eyebrow captures his attention. He thinks about how he likes to put the metal in his mouth while making love.

"What?" Reese is asking, finding herself suddenly self-conscious.

"Nothing. Just trying to imagine this Cory brutha—wondering what he looks like, the way he dresses, that's all. Contemplating what your type is."

Ryan's cell phone vibrates. He glances down, checks it, and frowns.

Carly.

Calling from her cell phone.

Ryan checks the time.

Ten-eighteen P.M.

He silences it and returns his stare to Reese.

"As you were saying," Ryan says.

"Actually, you were saying . . ."

Ryan's mind is abruptly two hundred miles away . . . with his wife, whom he has not spoken to since being kicked out. He should take the call, he muses. But not here with Reese in his face.

Should he excuse himself? Head to the restroom where he can talk in private?

No.

Why should he jump just because Carly decides to reverse her silence?

He stares at Reese, smiles weakly as he asks if she is going to finish the Szechuan shrimp. She shakes her head. So he scrapes what remains onto his plate and attacks it with his chopsticks. Reese finishes her drink, then excuses herself to grab a smoke. Ryan is grateful for a moment alone.

Time he needs to think.

What if there's something wrong with the baby?

What if she wants to take him back?

Doubtful.

He grabs another bite of the shrimp, washing it down with a fresh Tsingtao.

But what if . . .

Ryan checks the phone for a voice mail.

There isn't one.

Stop it, he commands himself. *You're on a much needed vacation.* His logic tells him he's here because of Carly . . . because she kicked him out.

Not true exactly, but his faulty logic doesn't auto-correct.

His cell vibrates again.

Carly.

This time, he answers it.

Listens intently, his brow furrowing, tension drawing itself around his features like a noose.

Moments later, Reese returns.

She can spot his distress from across the room.

"What's wrong?" she asks immediately.

Ryan is signaling for the bill. He stands, pulling money from his wallet and throwing it haphazardly on the table.

"It's Miles," he answers, eyes cutting swiftly from left to right.

Reese shrugs. "And?"

"He's in the hospital. Someone fucked him up real bad."

Reese exhales a breath as she stares straight ahead.

"He's on life support," Ryan utters. "I've gotta go."

Chapter 31

"I don't fucking believe this! You're actually leaving!"

Ryan ignores her. He never unpacked, other than his toiletry kit, which he now grabs from the bathroom and tosses into his bag.

Zips up as he turns to face Reese.

"And I don't believe you're actually tripping off this shit. I've got to go, Reese. This is an emergency!"

"Exactly whose emergency is it? I thought you were done with Miles. Wasn't he the one who sucked your dick?"

Ryan glares at her.

"You can be so fucking ghetto sometimes. He's my friend—"

"*Was* your friend—"

"He's on life support, for Christ's sake."

"Oh, so now you care about what happens to the nigga? Two days ago, you were buggin' about how he wouldn't leave you alone! Wasn't Miles the one leaving you those harassing messages? Now suddenly you've changed your tune."

Ryan stares at her—standing there, hand on hip,

her nipples poking through the red tee, a hint of dark round stomach flesh between the bottom of her shirt and the rise of denim. For a second, he ponders throwing Reese to the bed, stripping her jeans down to bare knees, and taking her from behind. The thought, however, is fleeting. Carly is in the forefront of his mind—her words twenty minutes ago cutting him to the bone.

"And what about our vacation, Ryan? Goddamn it, we just got here."

"Look, I don't have time to get into this, okay? I'm needed back home."

Silence.

"Oh, so that's it." The smirk on Reese's lips is unmistakable. "*She* calls, and you immediately run back home."

Ryan shakes his head.

"You know what? Enjoy yourself, Reese. The room is already paid for." He pulls out his billfold, peels off four fifties, and tosses them onto the bed. "This should cover your incidentals." Reese makes no move to pick them up.

"What I want is for you to stay . . . here with me . . . and not run back to your *wife* just because she calls."

"This isn't about her," Ryan retorts, grabbing his carry-on from the bed.

"Really? Seems like it is."

"Well, it isn't." He heads for the door.

"I don't want your money!"

Ryan stops.

Turns.

Puts down his bag.

Silently walks back to the bed, scooping up the bills he'd deposited there.

"Suit yourself."

Then he's out the door.

* * *

It is after one in the morning and Ryan stares at Carly. They stand by her SUV in the shadow of the hospital complex, a light breeze blowing Carly's hair around. It is moments like this when he feels an overwhelming love for his wife. Seeing her now—arms folded across her chest as she leans against her Range Rover, a thinner more angular face, presumably from not eating, soft light eyes and creamy butterscotch skin— makes Ryan want to scoop her up in his arms and hold her tight.

He arrived by train hours ago. Spent time with Miles, even though he was so heavily sedated that he didn't wake up, and with Carly and Olivia.

To say Miles looked horrible was an understatement.

He lay there, eyes swollen shut, concussion, jaw dislocated, two broken ribs, a punctured lung, on a ventilator . . . it was too much to take in. Ryan almost cried when he spied his friend.

Details sparse—Miles had left work around five and was headed for his car when he was viciously attacked. They'd found the top half of a splintered baseball bat by his rear fender, dipped in Miles' blood.

The police interviewed Olivia, spoke to Carly, and had a short chat with Ryan once he arrived. Looking for leads. Persons of interest. Those who might wish Miles harm.

Aden had shown up . . . briefly . . . not staying for more than two minutes in the room conferring quietly with the nurse. Olivia watched him with hawk eyes, but kept her composure.

And her silence.

Aden spent some time huddled in the hallway with the police officers as they took a statement and asked pointed questions about his relationship with the victim.

The doctor is cautiously optimistic. Miles has serious injuries. They are watching the swelling in the brain and the lung puncture, in particular. He'll make it—eventually he'll be fine—but it will be a week, at the very least, before he is released, and much longer before Miles can consider himself back to normal.

Ryan sighs, then moves into Carly's space and rubs her shoulders with his palms. She does not stop him. His hands descend, massaging her forearms and elbows.

"I'm sorry."

Carly is unsure whether he refers to their situation or Miles'. So, she just nods.

She had filled him in on Miles and Olivia's "break-up" while he was on the train. Ryan was in shock. The reality of everything coming to a head was sobering indeed. He had hugged Olivia when he first arrived. During their brief contact, he felt nothing. Her eyes said it all—whatever had transpired between them—whatever had gone down between them once upon a time—dead and gone.

She briefly smiled, thanked him for coming, but that was it.

The wind picks up, chilling them both.

"So," he says, attempting a half smile, "what do you make of this?"

"Of what?"

"All of this?" he responds.

Carly ponders his question before responding.

"It's surreal. Like a soap opera. It would be somewhat comical if it weren't happening to *me* . . . to us . . ."

Ryan nods.

"Lately, I've been thinking about Barbados. About

how the four of us were inseparable back then. About the incredible time we shared. I remember while on vacation watching those around us and seeing the look of pure jealousy on their faces, as if they could never fathom having this kind of closeness with another couple. Perhaps I was just naïve to think our closeness, that wonderful bond of friendship, could truly exist . . . let alone last."

"No, Carly, don't think that."

"No?" Carly glances up into Ryan's eyes. "Look what you and Olivia both did to your spouses, and to each other. And now look what has come back to haunt her. We'll never be what we once were."

"Don't say that!"

"Ryan, I, more than anyone here, would give anything to go back to the way things were. But look around you! Miles is in the hospital. His wife left him because she caught him in bed with another man! You cheated on me with our best friend. You've been secretly running around here and there, most recently in New York City, probably with your new woman."

"Carly, hold on."

She turns, unlocks her door with her remote.

"Where's your car, Ryan?" she asks.

"Across the way."

"It's late. I'll drive you there." As an afterthought, she adds, "Don't need two attacks in one day."

The interior warms quickly.

Carly turns to face her husband.

"Can I ask you something? Did you know about Miles?"

Ryan is silent.

"I don't get it; I really don't. How does something like that happen? I mean, they were married for God's sake . . . five years, just like us. And all of us were best friends. So how does that shit go down right under our noses?"

"I don't have the answers, Carly. I truly don't."

"Did he come on to you?"

The question catches him off guard. Ryan gulps.

"Oh, my God . . . when?"

"Carly, please let's not do this."

"Are you kidding? Ryan, I'm so fucking numb right now I can't feel anything, you hear me? If there's any chance of us starting over, I need to know. Everything . . . and I need to know now. No more games. No more trying to protect me. That time is gone. Ryan, look at me." She takes his hand in hers. "If you love me—if you want to stay married to me—if you want for me to have this baby, to have a family—if you desire for us to move on and start over, then you need to tell me . . . everything . . . now."

Ryan is staring at his wife's hand curled around his. He raises his stare, vision blurred by the beginning of silent tears.

Head down, he ponders her words.

Everything—every single thing that has transpired over the past few weeks visits him now.

Ryan shudders.

The snowball, which has been rolling down a hill, has become an avalanche. . . .

Crushing everything in its wake . . .

Leaving nothing . . . not a single thing but stark silence . . .

Why am I doing this? Ryan muses.

Why have I allowed this to spiral out of control?

Is this what you want?

Your wife, whom you love, estranged from you?

Is this what the future holds?

Living alone—with a stranger you barely know?

At that moment, Reese seems a million miles away.

What they have between them is nothing—nothing but an affair of the flesh.

A good *fuck*.

She for him.

He for her.

Nothing more.

Ryan sucks in a breath and lets the pain wrack him, shaking his shoulders as the tears fall.

An avalanche.

Out of control.

Crushing everything in its wake . . .

Leaving nothing . . . not a single thing but stark silence . . .

Ryan raises his gaze to stare at his wife. She is silent, watching him. He wipes his eyes and cheeks, then exhales slowly and purposely before telling Carly everything . . .

Everything she wants to know.

Chapter 32

She cries out.

Over and over again.

The pain is overwhelming. Like a knot, it constricts, tightens, threatening to suffocate. Nothing, not a single thing, relieves.

She knows now.

Now, she knows it all.

This thing that started off between Ryan and Olivia became something involving him and Miles.

Two men.

A blow job.

Oh, my God!

As if to add insult to injury, enter a twenty-something bartender who nursed her husband's wounds.

Licked them is more like it.

Some bitch named Reese.

And he said it was just physical. Sexual.

Sexual . . .

She almost laughs out loud.

She knows it's never just sexual . . . at least not for the woman.

She cries out again.

And again.

He hears her.

Hears her screams.

Cannot take it one second longer.

So, he goes to her shrouded in darkness. Kneels by the bed, stroking her forehead and cheek. Joins her on top of the covers that are dappled with sweat. Form supine, he holds her, whispering how everything will turn out all right.

It's like a bad dream. Sometimes life is like that. But she's a trooper; she is strong; and she will pull through. One day, she'll look back and realize she's made it.

She allows him to grip her tight as the ripples attack her. Face in her hair, he spoons her close while reassuring her.

She'll be okay . . . in time.

In time, everything will be all right.

She turns to face him. "I'm cold."

So, he submerges them beneath the covers. Holds her there, bodies rocking gently against her cries that slowly grow quiet.

Her face pressed against his, tears on his cheek as their limbs intertwine.

"I'm sorry," he says. "So sorry."

Lips brush against hers lightly. The feeling is fleeting, but comforting.

She does it again. Drawing strength, like sustenance. And again.

Mouths open, exploring with their tongues.

Exhaling of breaths as tears dry on their cheeks.

"So sorry this is happening."

He moves down her torso, taking in the rise to her pert breasts, the smooth hollow to her navel. Downwards farther, his nose presses against the fabric of her cotton panties, a trail of kisses in his wake.

Hands on his face, then his ears, moving upwards to his shortly cropped head, pushing down, exerting light pressure, not wanting to force, but needing this release so damn bad she can taste it, like salt on her tongue.

He removes her panties, sliding them down her thighs. She opens her legs willingly and intakes a sharp breath when he touches her *there*. Light tongue flicking against flesh that is already moist. She closes her eyes, tilts her head back, arches her back off the bed and the sweaty sheets, gives in to this feeling that's like a drug—one that will take her pain away. Spreads her legs wider as he licks at her glistening folds, the way a child does an ice cream cone. Slow, deliberate licks . . . top to bottom, bottom to top . . . tasting the nectar that flows freely from her opening.

She can't stop it. Not this feeling that is like a freight train barreling through a sleeping town.

When he sucks on her clit, she cries out.

But this time, the pain has diminished; it has gone. Increasing his pace, he gives her what she desires as she stares wide-eyed at the ceiling. Her back and ass are off the mattress, legs shuddering as her breathing increases. Nothing else matters, except for the passion that explodes inside with the frenzy of a train wreck, causing her to cry out and scream, grabbing his head as she shudders and shakes. He sucks her juices, drinking them down, taking all of the pain away, one silky ounce at a time.

In the morning, Carly awakens, her eyes fluttering for a brief moment before focusing on the sleeping form beside her.

She feels no remorse.

No pain.

Only a good kind of dull ache she hopes will linger between her legs for a long time.

Carly turns on her back, away from the immobile form of Tyler Nichols, and asks God for thirty more minutes of uninterrupted sleep.

Chapter 33

Reese doesn't hold her surprise when she enters her building a little after 8:30 in the evening, almost running smack into Ryan who's heading out. He has a leather garment bag slung low across his hip; in each hand he grasps a dozen items on hangers. His eyes show his astonishment as their bodies brush against one another.

"Reese."

"Ryan."

"Didn't expect you home . . ." he says, then adds, "this early."

"I see that. Caught an earlier train. Manhattan's just not that fun by oneself."

Ryan nods.

"Let me get these to the car. Be right back."

Five minutes later, he reenters her apartment, shutting the door quietly behind him. She is waiting for him by the window, hand on the rattan chair, cigarette dangling from her lips, tendrils of smoke wafting upwards lazily. She takes a long drag, inhaling into her lungs as her breasts seem to expand. Then slowly, she exhales through her nostrils, eyeing him without speaking. She nods once unhurriedly.

"I see you're leaving."

Not a question, but a statement.

"Yes."

Ryan stands there, making no attempt to move into the room or get close to her. Reese purses her lips.

"So it's like that? Just up and leave without even a proper good-bye?"

"Not sure I know what you mean, Reese."

"Oh, please! You had every intention of sneaking out of here without so much as a note saying shit. What were you going to do? Send me a text message? IM me?"

A quick drag on her cigarette breaks the uneasy silence.

"You're pathetic, you know that?" she adds with a sneer.

"Look, I was going to tell you; of course I wasn't just going to roll out."

"Really?" she asks, her voice dripping sarcasm.

"Yeah, Reese, really." Deep breath. Steps forward into the room. "It's time for me to move on—for *us* to move on. This thing we had was what I needed at the time. But—"

Reese is rolling her eyes.

"As I was saying, I need to get back to what's most important to me."

"And that is?" she asks.

"My wife . . . my family."

"Oh, now you have a family?"

"Yeah, matter of fact, I do. My wife's expecting. *We're* expecting . . ."

Reese takes a moment to take that in.

"When were you gonna tell me?" she whispers.

"Just did."

Teeth sucking.

"So, basically, what you're saying is you don't need me anymore."

"Reese, it's not like that." He goes to her, strokes her shoulder. She peers over at him quietly. "You knew what my situation was before we got together."

"Nigga, please! You had absolutely no problem eating my pussy the very first night, and no conscience when it came to me sucking on your dick!"

"Look, I appreciate everything you've done for me. We had fun, but it's over now. I can't keep doing this. I need to get my life back in order. I'm sorry, Reese, but I belong *there*, not here."

Reese laughs.

"You bruthas are all the same. You run away from your drama-infested existence when the shit gets too thick. You find a strong black woman to nurse you back to health. Then, once you're feeling fit, it's back to the damn drama that sent you running in the first place.

"When you came to me, you were lost—like a snot-nosed kid—you had nowhere to go—had no idea what you were going to do next. Hell, you were being harassed by your own best friend—a brutha who was gunning for you in the worst way—wanted to suck that big black dick of yours so fucking bad he could taste it! You had no clue. You came sprinting to me— and who was it who took you in? Who listened to you cry? Who was it that dried your tears, told you it was okay, got you back on your feet again, showed you love? Me, Ryan. Me, myself, and I. Not that redbone wife of yours with the straight hair and proper English diction. Not your faggot-ass friend. Not his conniving-ass wife. None of the above. It was only me."

Ryan sucks in a breath.

"Reese, you're angry. But where did you think this was going? Did you think I was planning on leaving my wife? Did I ever utter those words to you? Did I ever say this was anything other than temporary?"

She laughs again.

"See, this is what cracks me up. When Miles was harassing you, leaving all those messages on your cell phone three or four times a day, who did you turn to? Who was the one who protected you from him?"

"What are you talking about?" Ryan asks, creeping closer.

"Miles—your so-called friend. Remember the things he said? Remember what he said he'd do if you didn't go to him?"

"So what! I never asked for protection. What are you saying?"

Reese chuckles, puts out her cigarette, blowing smoke diagonally from her mouth.

"Okay, play dumb. It's cool with me."

"Just what are you implying, Reese? Don't fuck with me. What are you saying concerning Miles?"

Reese steps in his face, glancing upwards into his eyes.

"You weren't man enough to handle your business. So, someone else did . . ."

"WHAT?"

Reese saunters back, laughing.

"Go on, boy. Go back to your pretty little wife and your pathetic life. Reese is gonna be okay. I'ma do my thing. Now give me my key and get the fuck out!"

Ryan has turned red in the face, but maintains his composure while fishing the key from his pocket. He places it in her outstretched palm and turns to leave. Suddenly, he pivots around to face her.

"If I find out you had something to do with Miles' injury . . ."

"What? You gonna fuck me up? Please! You know how I like it—brutal and hard. So bring the pipe and lay it on me! 'Cause that's *all* you're good for."

"Fuck you, Reese!"

"Well, okay, baby. One last time for old times' sake," she snickers.

Ryan shakes his head morosely as the door slams behind him.

Chapter 34

"May I speak to Luther?"

"Speaking."

"Luther, my man, what's up? It's Ryan."

"Hey, Ryan, long time no see. How ya livin'?" Luther asks excitedly.

"I've been good. You?" Ryan steers across the Southeast/Southwest Freeway.

"Ah, I'm great. The man keeps me running, but I can't complain. How's that hottie wife of yours?"

"Carly? Um, she's good." As an afterthought, he adds, "We're expecting."

"Man, that's great. Congrats. Give Carly a hug for me! So what's up?"

"It's kind of a delicate situation. I kind of need some info—you know, the 411 on somebody, and I thought, who better than my ole frat brother, Luther?"

"Ah, sookie sookie now. Who is it? Girlfriend you've been screwing or about to screw? Just playing, man!"

Ryan gulps a breath.

"Actually, it's a friend of mine—an acquaintance

more like it. I've been wondering about her. Name's Reese. She tends bar in Adams Morgan. I'm curious about her background, if she's ever been in trouble with the law, that kind of thing."

"Hmmm. I can do that."

"Yeah, recently I've been wondering whether she has a violent past."

"Alrighty then! Give me her info. United States Secret Service has its benefits, you know?"

"That's why I called you, bro."

He waits until he can't wait any longer. Then he picks up the phone and dials her number.

She answers on the fifth ring.

"Ryan."

"Yes." A pause as he composes his thoughts. A moment ago, he knew exactly what to say. Now, those thoughts have evaporated into the ether.

"What? It's late."

Ryan checks his watch for the hundredth time. Close to midnight. She's right—it is late.

"Just wondering when you're coming home."

This time, Carly takes a moment to compose her words.

"I'm not coming home, Ryan," she responds in a soft, consoling voice.

"What?"

"I'm not coming home." Firmer this time. "At least not tonight," she adds.

"Okay . . ."

Ryan takes a moment to process these words. He hears noise in the background—her background, as if someone else is there. His wife is not alone. That much he is certain.

"Um, Carly, I was hoping we could talk, you know? I figured since so much was said last night—"

"Listen, Ryan, now's not the time to get into this, okay?"

Pause.

"Okay," he responds.

A moment later, he asks, "Are you working late?"

"No, I'm not."

Pause.

"Then where are you, Carly?"

Sharp exhale.

"I'm staying with a friend, okay?"

"Which friend, Carly?"

"Ryan, let's not do this. It's late; I'm not alone; and we're about to eat."

He utters a short laugh.

"Damn, you and your friend sure eat late!"

"Yeah, well, what can I say? Suddenly it appears I've found my appetite."

Ryan's mind races, the possibilities that her statement conjures forces his head to throb.

"Come home, Carly. You're my wife. I want to work this out." The words are uttered soft, almost to a whisper.

"It's too late for that, Ryan. Surely you know that."

"Why?" he retorts quickly. "I don't understand. I thought you said last night there was an opportunity for us to start over. You said you wanted things back the way they were. Didn't you say that?"

More background noise.

A rustling sound.

Ryan's heart is beating loudly in his chest.

"It's simple. You cheated. You had sexual relations with not one, but three different people—two of whom I thought were our best friends. That's something one does not recover from. Damn it, Ryan! Anyone looking at your actions from the outside would swear they've witnessed a whore at work. A man whore . . ."

"Carly, I'm truly sorry for what I've done. I apologized last night and I want to begin again—"

"And what? You think apologizing another hundred times is going to change my mind? No, Ryan. It will not. You've gone too far. First, with Olivia. Then, with Miles. And now, with some hoochie bartender whose name escapes me. No, husband, you're mistaken if you think things can be the same again."

Long intake of breath followed by a rushed exhale.

"Carly. Please—"

"Ryan, I want you and your stuff out of our house by the weekend. Is that clear?"

Pause.

"Where are you staying?"

"Where I lay my head is no longer a concern of yours. I'm giving you your single life back, Ryan. Consider yourself a free agent. Go do what you want to do. 'Cause I sure intend to do just that."

More background noise followed by a hearty laugh.

Male voice.

This time, Ryan is one hundred percent sure of what he heard.

He shudders.

"Baby, you don't mean that," he utters, her words resonating sharply in his ears.

"Oh yes, I do. In fact, I've begun *already*."

The snowball, which has been rolling down a hill, has become an avalanche. . . .

Crushing everything in its wake . . .

Leaving nothing . . . not a single thing but stark silence . . .

Ryan's heart goes dead.

Just like the phone he holds.

Flatlining in the palm of his quivering hand . . .

Chapter 35

The dark-skinned, gaunt security guard has his navy pants with the solid black line down the edge laying low on his hip bones. He pulls them to navel height while eyeing Reese curiously. Glancing quickly over to the flowers she holds in her hand, he pans his gaze across her chest. He smiles, displaying a platinum grill.

"Delivery for Carly Juliet."

"Sign here," the guard says. "What's your name?"

She returns a frown.

"Delivery woman," Reese replies.

"Let me call up," he says, all smiles.

"You do that." She moves away from the desk and toward a low leather couch. Two sets of double doors surround the front desk. The security guard's stare is burning a hole into her chest, but she transfers the flowers to her lap, hiding his target from view.

She holds a small vase filled with mini carnations, orange gerbera daisies, orange spray roses, and yellow poms. Nice arrangement. Safeway bought. She can hear the security guard on the phone with Carly or someone from her office. He enunciates the word "flowers," then says, "I don't know . . . doesn't say." He hangs up a second later.

"Miss Delivery Woman, Mrs. Juliet is on her way down."

Reese moves the flowers out of her face and mouths, "Thank you."

He glances to the left and right before uttering, "You should lace me with your digits. Brutha would love to call you sometime." A flash of platinum teeth.

Her mood sours.

"My man would not be amused," she retorts.

Security guard doesn't miss a beat.

"I won't tell if you don't."

Reese sighs audibly.

A moment later, Carly sweeps through the double doors. Reese sizes her up: butterscotch skin, short, flat-ironed hair, thin waist, smallish breasts. The attire surprises her. Jeans, off-white wool sweater, tan boots. She expected an Ann Taylor fitted suit. Guess folks behind the camera can wear whatever they want.

Carly's gaze settles on her and the flowers in her lap; she frowns.

"I'm Carly Juliet. These are from?"

She stands, thrusts the vase into Carly's hands, and reaches into the back pocket of her jeans, extracting an envelope.

"Your husband, Ryan."

"Figures," Carly hisses. She turns with flowers in hand, dismissing this delivery woman without a second thought, when she is halted by a hand to her elbow.

"You need to hear this. Your husband wanted me to make sure you got this."

"Got what?" Carly asks.

She pulls the card out of the envelope, flips it open, and holds it at eye level for her to read. Carly's eyes grow wide.

"This: Your husband doesn't want you anymore. Know why? Because he's got a new, sexy young thing. That's right—I'm your man's woman now. And he don't need a my-shit-don't-stink, I-can't-satisfy-my-man prissy bitch like you. Ryan's traded you in for a newer model!"

Carly steps back, taking a defensive posture.

"Who do you think you are, showing up at my job, bitch?"

"I'm Ryan's new squeeze who's claiming what's rightfully mine. So cease these games you be playing; he don't want you. He don't want to be married to your ass no more. That's why he's fucking me now."

Carly is staring at Reese as if she's just spotted a six-inch long centipede.

"Did you know he fucked me in the ass? Oh yeah—Ryan loves him some Reese-ass!"

Carly rears back and flings the flower vase at Reese. It smacks her in the chest before careening to the floor. The carpet breaks its fall; the glass, thankfully, doesn't shatter. Still, water splashes at Reese's feet as carnations, orange gerbera daisies, and roses scatter around her.

"BITCH, no you didn't!" Reese screams.

Several things happen simultaneously.

The security guard jumps into action, bolting around the shining desk.

Carly moves backwards, ID card swiped as the double doors fling open.

She is through them in an instant.

As they close behind her, she turns and smirks at Reese who stands there, mouth agape, a mess of flow-

ers and an empty vase gathered at her drenched an-
kles as Carly mouths two words, FUCK YOU.

Then she is gone, making Reese look like the fool
she is.

Olivia answers on the second ring.

"It's Carly."

Short pause.

"Hey, girl." Relief mixed with trepidation.

"How's Miles?"

"He had an uneventful night, so that's a good
thing. Right now, we're taking things day by day."

"I understand. Tell him I was asking about him."

"I will."

Longer silence.

"You have lunch plans? There's something I need
to share with you."

Olivia mulls over her request.

"I do, but I'll cancel them."

"I'll meet you in an hour—usual spot."

Olivia hangs up and breathes a sigh not filled with
relief.

Ninety minutes later, Olivia and Carly sit facing
each other over a small table in the back of a Chi-
nese restaurant. A pot of green tea is positioned between them. Small ceramic mugs steam in front of
them. They order perfunctorily, then wait for the waitress to leave, giving them privacy.

Carly begins without preamble.

"There's something you need to know," she says.

"Okay." Olivia places her palms flat on the table-
top, as if bracing for bad news.

"I had a conversation with Ryan the other night—after we visited Miles in the hospital."

"Okay."

"That was the first time we've had a chance to really talk, and I found out some things that concern you. I think you should know, since they involve you and your marriage."

Olivia gulps. Gone is the outward confidence. All that's left is a scared little girl. She nods for Carly to continue.

"The night of the party, you and Ryan had intimate contact."

Olivia's lips are mashed together. She signals her agreement by nodding silently.

"What you don't know is that Ryan came back upstairs after Miles interrupted the two of you. He waited for things to quiet down, then crept back to the first floor, expecting you to do the same."

Olivia's eyebrow arches.

"Someone did meet Ryan on the first floor. It was dark, very late—the rest of us seemingly fast asleep. I know I was passed out. Perfect conditions to consummate your relationship."

Olivia's brow furrows.

"But we *didn't* consummate anything. I've already told you that."

"Yes, but Ryan did. He had oral sex. He let someone go down on him." Carly pauses to let the weight of her words sink in. "It was dark. Ryan thought it was your mouth on him . . . but it wasn't."

Olivia's mouth is agape.

"It was Miles. Your husband."

"Ohmigod," her words whispered.

Carly watches Olivia's face shudder. She can see that the news goes deep, hitting hard. She did not know. This much Carly is certain.

"This explains . . ."

"What?" Carly asks.

Olivia glances away, then back at Carly.

"Ryan kept talking about what happened after the party. This is what he was referring to. Jesus!"

"Yup. Fucked up, don't you think?"

Olivia slurps at her tea. Gestures to the waitress. She appears, and Olivia orders something stronger.

Far stronger.

She's shaking her head peevishly.

"One more thing . . . Ryan and I are through. He told me about his new muse, a twenty-something ghetto bitch who had the nerve to show up at my job this morning."

"Ohmigod, are you serious?"

"As a heart attack. The bitch can have him 'cause I don't want him. As I told him last night, he's a free agent. I'm granting him his single status. So there you have it."

Carly raises her mug to her lips and finishes her tea. She plants it on the table, rises, and places a twenty down.

"I've lost my appetite, Olivia, but this should cover it."

Her used-to-be best friend glances up, tears watering her eyes.

"Carly, I'm so sorry . . ."

"Yeah. Don't I know it?"

Chapter 36

Tyler opens his front door and grins.

"Was wondering when I'd see you again."

"Is this a bad time?" she asks.

"'Course not. I'm always delighted to see you." Tyler gestures for Carly to enter. She remains there, holding onto the handle of her travel bag.

"Tyler, I hate to barge in on you like this, especially at this late hour, but something's come up."

"Carly, get your ass in here! It's late and it's cold outside."

She walks inside as Tyler closes the door behind her. Warm air assaults her.

"You're right. Damn, it is cold out there!"

"So, what's up?" he asks, giving her a quick peck on the cheek. Carly reaches for him and hugs him tight for a moment, enjoying the way his body feels against hers.

"Shit's all messed up," she says, pulling back. Tyler takes her hand and leads her into the living room. They sit on the couch overlooking the dark fireplace. "After everything that's happened with me and my husband, the bitch he's been sleeping with had the nerve to show up at the job today."

"What the fuck? Carly, I'm so sorry." He takes her hand in his.

"I know. It's so damn ghetto; I'm still having trouble believing it myself. She had the nerve to taunt me in the lobby of BET! Can you believe that? Anybody who exhibits that kind of behavior is definitely out to lunch. Bottom line is this—I don't trust the bitch as far as I can throw her. If she has balls enough to come to my job, then she might try to mess with me at home. I'm not taking any chances."

"You're doing the absolute right thing. I told you before, you're welcome here for as long as you want or need a place to stay."

"I appreciate it, Tyler. I'd just feel better staying somewhere other than my house for a couple of evenings. Let things calm down, you know? Plus, I want Ryan to get his shit out by the weekend, and I don't want to hear him whining."

"Carly, it's better that you don't go home. You have no idea how crazy this woman is. Have you contacted the police?"

"No, not yet. I don't have any info on her. I was planning on calling Ryan and telling him to keep his bitch on a leash. Wanted to settle in here first, though."

"Whatever you need . . . I got you, Carly!"

"Tyler, you're wonderful." She grins. "Listen, about the other night . . ."

Tyler cocks his head to the side, giving her his full attention.

"You were wonderful, Tyler, just what the doctor ordered."

"Okay . . ."

"But right now, I don't need or want the complication of a relationship—not when my life is literally a freaking mess—a nightmare, more like it. I really dig your company, and you've been an angel to me during my time of need. But sex is going to complicate things and I can't deal with further complications right now."

"Understood."

"Do you? I'd rather not stay here if this is going to be . . . difficult. I mean, I was a full participant the other night, and the things you did to me felt so damn good, but I don't want you thinking it's going to happen again."

"Carly, what you need is a friend right now . . . a shoulder to cry on. I'm that person you can count on. I'm that friend. So don't worry a second longer. I hear you, and I promise I won't do anything to complicate your life further."

"Thank you, Tyler. You truly are the best!"

She hugs him close for a moment before patting his cheeks playfully.

"I know. Don't forget it!"

Tyler stands and gestures upstairs.

"Your bedroom is as you left it. If you need anything, and I mean anything, don't hesitate to let me know." He walks to the staircase, settling his hand on the banister. "And if you do change your mind—you know, if you happen to have a late-night change of heart—I believe you know where to find me."

Tyler winks at Carly.

"Consider me a friend," he adds, before ascending the staircase, out of view.

"Yeah," Carly says under her breath, "that's what I'm afraid of."

He descends the stairs to The Rhyme, adjusting his eyes to the indigo light that seems to seep from behind the bar. He spots Reese immediately—how can he not? She's wearing the pink Von-Dutch baseball tee—the same one she was wearing the first night he stumbled in here—except tonight, she's donned a baseball cap that looks sexy as hell. Her oversize breasts give the impression that they are reaching out for him, calling his name—and for a split second, he feels the pulse in his pants race, feels the tightening of his manhood against denim fabric. He considers fucking her just for old times' sake, but then regroups, reconsiders this course of action.

He's not here for that.

Up to the bar, a scowl on his face.

She wears the same.

"Well, well . . . look what the cat dragged in," she says, taunting him.

"Reese."

"What can I get for you, Ryan? You here because you missed me?" Reese laughs at her own words.

He begins, skipping pleasantries.

"I want you to leave Carly alone. Going to her job wasn't cool, and it won't be tolerated. So here's a warning to you—quit that shit now before things heat up."

"Or what, Ryan? What are you or Mrs. Juliet gonna do? Kick my ass? Report me to the authorities? Do I look like I give a fuck?"

"Look, Reese," Ryan leans in, "this has nothing to do with her, so leave her out of it. Okay?"

"Please! It has everything to do with her," she hisses, head down low so the other bar patrons don't hear. "I need for her to know who she's dealing with. And you, too, I guess, 'cause it appears your memory ain't all that swift."

"I'm not interested in hashing this out with you, Reese. I'm asking you nicely—but I'm only gonna ask you once—leave Carly alone before things escalate to the next level. And I don't think you want to go there. Leave it alone, Reese. Leave my wife alone before a side of me you've never seen before emerges."

"I just love it when you're all hot and bothered." Reese is mere inches from his face now. "Makes my love box all wet."

"You're a freak, you know that?" he retorts, pushing back from the bar.

"You have no idea."

Ryan is halfway to the stairs when she yells, "Damn shame about your friend, Miles."

He pauses in mid-step, turning to face her, his face reddening.

"He really should have been watching his back. You and that pretty little wife of yours need to do the same."

"Excuse me?"

Ryan takes a step towards her.

"It's a crazy world out there, Ryan, all I'm saying." Their eyes meet, stares lock.

Neither one blinks.

"Not safe at all. You'd be wise to remember that," she says, before whirling around to tend to other patrons.

Three days later, the phone rings once . . . twice . . . three times. On the fourth ring, the answering machine picks up.

"Hey, Ryan, it's Luther. I misplaced your cell number, so I'm leaving you a message at home.

"I've got the 411 you requested last week. Give me a call back when you get a chance and I'll share the particulars. Some interesting stuff, to say the least, so holla! Kisses to the lovely missus. Peace out."

That evening, Carly listens to the message.

Hits rewind.
Plays it again.
And without remorse, hits delete.
Poof.
Message erased.
Just like that.

PART FOUR

Chapter 37

Seven months later . . .

He stands at the crowded bar, yelling his order, a black and tan, to be heard over the din of patrons. He's at Blue Fin on Broadway and 47th Street, surrounded by an attractive after-work, pre-curtain crowd that's snug in the all-glass corner bar with its view of Times Square. The music is trip–hip hop and loud. He's alone, dressed smartly in a dark gray, four-button suit with an open-collared blue shirt. His shoes are polished and his cuff links shine in the twilight. He nods to the bartender, an anorexic Asian woman with jet black hair that descends straight to her ass like one of those Caribbean waterfalls. He takes a sip and moves off to find a place to sit.

Ryan is both tired and invigorated.

Tired because of an all-day meeting across town he's just returned from. Invigorated because he's finally done, it's Friday; and he decided on the spur of the moment to extend his time here in New York—at least for another night. He has nothing to go home to, so why not?

He'd pulled off his tie, ran some water over his face, and came here. The night is young, and New York City always makes him tingle with that special something—as if all the energy from outside the pane is being infused into his veins this very instant.

Seven months.

God, how time has flown.

As Ryan scans the crowd, meeting the eyes of several attractive women, he takes a moment to recount what's transpired.

Things with Carly have gone nowhere.

She stuck to her guns and made him leave their home. He found a one bedroom in Northeast that's Metro-accessible and close to a bunch of eateries and nightlife. Not that he's taken advantage of the nightlife, but it's nice to know those things are close by.

They speak very infrequently—he and his wife. At first, he was calling her nonstop, but after several weeks of her not returning his calls, Ryan gave up.

Her pregnancy is going as expected.

Reese—he hasn't seen or talked to her since that night he confronted her at The Rhyme. Moving on . . . both of them . . .

The job is going well. He's managed to pour his energy back into work, much to the delight of the president and his staff. He and Olivia are cordial in front of the worker bees, but gone are the days when they were close buddies.

Miles?

Ryan hasn't seen him in months. He knows he's basically healed, but the two of them just don't speak anymore.

Nothing to talk about, as far as Ryan is concerned.

So, here he is . . . Friday night, Manhattan, a delightful night full of possibilities laid out in front of him, if he would even consider them.

Ryan is thankful for the time alone. Time to get on with his life . . . time to think about Ryan and his own needs. His future. His happiness.

Towards the rear of the bar, a group of happy hour–goers stand to pay their bill and leave. As the bodies shift, Ryan spies a woman sitting where the bar curves ninety degrees. She is cocoa-colored, with dark hair that is pulled back with a single hair tie. Her top is tight-fitting and low-cut, parading lovely breasts for all to see. Their eyes meet and she displays a dazzling smile. Ryan is momentarily taken aback; is she smiling at him? She seems to nod imperceptibly to him, and Ryan finds himself making his way over to where she sits.

"Is this seat taken?" he asks.

"It is now," she replies coolly, as her eyes give him the quick once-over.

Ryan sits. "Thank you."

"No, thank you. The pleasure is all mine." She smiles again.

Ryan sips his black and tan before setting his glass down and turning to face her.

"You are lovely. Can I tell you that?"

"You can tell me anything you want."

"Alrighty then!" Ryan laughs, holding out his hand. "Ryan. And you are?"

"Jennifer. A pleasure to meet you."

"I think you said that already."

"See," she says, lightly touching his shoulder, "you've got me repeating myself!"

"Damn, I'm good," Ryan retorts.

"That remains to be seen," Jennifer says with an eyebrow arched.

"Feisty with attitude to boot—I dig that. So, what do you do, Ms. Jennifer?"

"Me? I'm in consumer marketing."

Ryan nods.

"Work in Manhattan?" he asks.

"Oh no, I'm an out-of-towner. Just here with my girl for the long weekend."

"Oh, so where's your girl?" Ryan glances around the packed bar.

"She's around somewhere—enjoying herself. Probably talking to some man."

"I see. And do you have big plans for the weekend while you're here in the Big Apple?"

Jennifer eyes Ryan before answering.

"You really wanna know?"

"I asked the question, didn't I?" he says.

"Now who's being feisty?"

"Touché. Go on—yeah, I really wanna know."

Jennifer nods a few times before locking her stare with Ryan's.

"I'm here to fulfill a fantasy." Her eyes don't blink.

Ryan nods once, takes a sip of his drink. "Care to elaborate?"

"Sure." Jennifer places her cosmopolitan to her lips before responding. "I hope you don't think badly of me . . . but, I've always been intrigued by the idea of a threesome. It's something I've thought a lot about. Recently, I got out of a three-year relationship."

"I'm sorry—"

"Don't be. Shit happens. Anyway, now I'm free to explore my desires unencumbered, so to speak—no one holding me back. And my girl is like, let's do a weekend getaway to NYC . . . you know, what happens in Manhattan stays in Manhattan . . . so here I am!"

"Damn. Who's the lucky bastard?"

"I don't know. Haven't met him yet."

"Excuse me? I'm not following."

"I haven't met him yet. I'm hoping—*we're* hoping—to get things popping tonight or tomorrow night."

Ryan stares at her for a moment.

"You're serious?"

"I am."

"Wow," he says. "I mean, look at you—you're fine, dressed to the nines, and—"

"What? A good-looking sistah can't get her groove on?"

"Naw, I didn't say that."

She laughs.

"Look, I've labored over lost love for months. I'm so tired of that shit—of moping around at home, not going out, not meeting anyone. It's my time, Ryan. I need this, you know?"

"Yeah, I do." Ryan shakes his head.

"What?"

"Nothing—it's just that I know exactly how you feel. I've recently gotten out of a relationship myself."

"Awww, you're just saying that to get in a girl's pants!" Jennifer slaps him on the shoulder. Ryan grins.

"Not me!" Hands in the air.

"Oh, so you're gay or something?" she asks mischievously.

Ryan pauses for a moment. His smile, for an instant, is erased. But then, it's back, just like that.

"Not hardly."

Jennifer leans in, one hand on his lap as she gets closer to his ear. "Can I tell you something?"

Ryan turns to her, but says nothing.

"My girlfriend and I have been here since yesterday afternoon. We partied until four o'clock this morning. Had a ball, met a ton of guys—but none who've passed the bar if I was administering the test. I'm not looking for a long-term relationship, Ryan. Not looking for companionship. I'm here because of a need—a desire. I want to feel like a woman should. I want to feel heightened sexuality. I want to feel alive again."

Ryan is silent.

Hand goes to him. He is warm in her grasp.

"I'm turned on by you, Ryan. You've got the looks and this 'command' to you."

"I'm turned on by you, too."

"Then we should do this—you, me, and my girl. You'd like her."

Jennifer rises, putting a hand on his shoulder. She leans in, the scent to her perfume intoxicating, the pull to her breasts hypnotic.

"Running to the ladies' room, but do me a favor— don't go anywhere, okay?"

"Not going anywhere, Jennifer."

"And give consideration to what I just said. We could make beautiful music together, the three of us . . . I can tell."

Jennifer leans in and Ryan assumes she's going for a cheek peck, but he is surprised when he feels her lips on his. The kiss is soft, unassuming, and wonderful. Then she opens her mouth and Ryan enters, feeling the longing well inside him like a groundswell. He is focused on her feel—the softness of her breasts that press against his chest, the wetness to her mouth. He conjures up images of the two of them entangled with this faceless, nameless friend, and the thought dazzles him to the core. Desperately, he wants to lose himself in this stranger, this woman he does not know, but Jennifer pulls away.

He watches her go, marveling at her bouncing hips and succulent ass beneath her close-fitting skirt. Her spike-heel boots make him gasp.

Ryan gulps air before reaching for the black and tan.

Finishes it in several gulps, then signals for another.

Jesus.

What he'd give to lose himself in the flesh of total strangers tonight.

Chapter 38

She picks up on the third ring.

"Hey, it's me."

With the noise level in Blue Fin being what it is, Ryan had no choice but to find quieter pastures in order to make his call. He left a bar napkin over his fresh black and tan and headed upstairs to the lobby of the W Hotel where he found a quiet alcove.

"Hi." A lukewarm response. He feels this snowball that has become an avalanche, deep in his gut. It is an all-too-familiar feeling, one he'll never get used to.

Ryan sighs heavily. "It's been a while. Just wanted to check on you. How are you feeling?"

"Okay," Carly says. "I'm ready for this baby to come. I'm tired and irritable all the time, not to mention the fact that I hate being overweight."

"You're not overweight; you're pregnant," Ryan says.

"Whatever, same difference."

A moment of awkward silence.

"How are you doing?" she asks.

"I'm surviving. Not much more than that."

Another moment of awkward silence.

"Listen, Carly, I know we haven't spoken in a while, but I'd like to see you. This not knowing where we stand is driving me crazy."

He pauses, hoping she'll say something.

She does not.

"I miss you, baby," he continues. "And it's killing me that you're not involving me in your pregnancy . . . *our* pregnancy."

Slow exhale of her breath.

"Ryan, what do you want me to say? You cheated on me. You expect me to just forgive and forget? Well, I can't do that."

"Carly, I want us to be a family again. I want to come home. Do you understand that?"

Carly is crying now—softly, but Ryan can hear it distinctly through the phone.

"Baby, please don't cry. I didn't mean to make you cry."

"Guess you should have thought about that before you fucked our best friend and that whore."

The words are like barbs; they cut deep. They are wounding, drawing blood. The avalanche has morphed into an out-of-control freight train, brakes screeching as sparks from its wheels fly. Ryan winces hard.

"Carly . . . baby . . . I can't keep doing this, living in no-man's land, not knowing if we are getting back together or what. I want to come home. I want for us to be a couple again. Please . . ." Ryan hangs his head low, his words barely above a whisper.

"Ryan," Carly says, her voice strong and clear, "there is no *us*. You broke *us*. You killed *us*. Do yourself a favor and stop living in the past and move on. Move on, for God's sake, Ryan . . . move on."

With that, Carly ends the call, and Ryan knows with sudden finality that his future is sealed.

He closes his cell, and heads to what awaits him downstairs in the curve of a bar.

"Hey, sexy, I'm back! Let me introduce you to my girl."

Ryan is back on his stool, head hung low when he hears the sound, feeling a hand on his left shoulder. For the past four minutes, he's thought of nothing but this last conversation. Ryan knows he and Carly are finally through. He's tired of chasing after something that isn't coming around. He's tired of apologizing, tired of trying to explain the pain that still roosts inside him, just tired of all the bullshit.

When he hears Jennifer's voice, it's like smooth jazz on a romantic, candle-lit night. He fills his lungs as he raises his stare, pivoting on his stool to face the lovely Jennifer . . .

And comes face-to-face with a bartender named Reese instead.

How long they traded back and forth stares, he cannot say. It was one of those moments where the air seemed to be sucked out of the room, and all motion came grinding to a halt. He knows that conversation around him continues unabated, and yet it feels as if all eyes are on him.

Ryan tries to pry his stare away, but he cannot.

Reese is having similar trouble.

Jennifer's eyes dart from Reese to Ryan and back to her friend again, trying to comprehend the situation. She shakes her head petulantly.

"Am I missing something?" she asks hesitantly. "Do you two know each other?"

Ryan is silent.

Reese disengages her gape with Ryan and turns to her friend.

"This is Ryan."

"Yeah," Jennifer responds, "I know who this is," she says a bit irritated.

"No, girl," Reese continues, "this is *the Ryan*—from back home." She stares at her friend for a moment before comprehension registers on Jennifer's face.

"Oh, my God! Ryan?"

"That's my name."

Ryan's smile breaks the ice. Reese follows suit. For a moment, no one speaks. They stare each other down, except this time, there are smiles all around. Reese speaks first.

"It's good to see you, Ryan. You are looking well."

"You, too, Reese."

And it's true. She does look good. Damn good.

Ryan hates to admit it, but there's something different about her. Standing before him is a kinder, gentler Reese; her expression is softer. Perhaps it is her attire. Reese is clad, like her friend, in knee-high boots and a tight skirt that hugs her curves like a glove. Her blouse is all-revealing, and Ryan can't help but steal a glance at those ripened melons that he used to adore. The ensemble oozes sexuality, and Ryan can't help but find himself turned on.

"Wow," Jennifer says, cutting through the morass of memories, "this is *too* deep!" Her expression sours as if she's just connected the dots, realizing that tonight's plans are unraveling before her eyes. She sighs heavily. "And to think we were so close."

Ryan laughs. It's all he can do. Standing before

him is the woman whom he cheated with months ago and her gorgeous, in-search-of-a-fantasy friend. Moments ago, he sat contentedly, wondering how this fortune passed to him. But as quickly as it arrived, it retreats, like a summer thunderstorm. All he can do is laugh out loud.

"What?" Reese asks.

"You . . . your friend . . . and me. The likelihood of us running into one another in a city of eight million people—the absurdity of it all."

"What can I say?"

"I saw him first!" Jennifer cries, coiling her arm around Ryan's neck. Reese takes a seat to the left of him, eyeing him and then her friend.

"Technically, that's incorrect."

Jennifer thinks for a moment, then exclaims, "Shoot! But he's so damn fine." Her words fade to a whisper.

"True, true."

Ryan locks stares with Reese. He is thinking of his conversation with his wife minutes ago. To his right, Jennifer snakes a hand down his inner thigh. The sensation causes his suit pants to draw tight.

"I think I need a drink," Reese says.

Ryan signals for the bartender. "We all do." He smiles sheepishly. Jennifer is on his right, fingers stroking his lap, digits that creep ever so close to the expanding outline of his awakening dick. Reese is to his left, shoulders rubbing him seductively as she settles on her stool. Her breasts are like beacons, shining brightly, lighting the way.

Ryan shakes his head while contemplating his next move.

Only in New York City . . .

* * *

Hours pass.

He didn't plan for that to happen.

But it did.

Exit strategy unraveling before his eyes.

He had planned on having one drink before taking off.

This was one group activity he had no intention of pursuing.

But something about Reese kept him planted on his stool.

There was none of the controlling, in-your-face person he had come to know all too well. Now she was laid-back, relaxed, laughing and chatting along with the two of them. They talked about *everything* . . . politics, films, traffic, New Orleans, the islands, Africa, reparations . . . everything but *them*. Reese dissecting the Asian bartender's every move, reviewing her drinks as if she were Siskel and Ebert. It was quite refreshing, and Jennifer's company was delightful indeed.

One more drink, Ryan promised himself. What could it hurt?

By eleven-thirty, Blue Fin hadn't thinned an inch. They ordered food and ate at the bar: fresh tilapia stuffed with lump crabmeat for Ryan; Caesar salad topped with grilled salmon for Reese; and crab cakes for Jennifer.

Another round of drinks after the plates were cleared, and then coffee.

Ryan rises unsteadily, checking his watch—midnight—knowing it is now or never. Leave now, or stay the night with the two of them.

He pays the tab and kisses Reese on her cheek. Turning, he takes Jennifer's palm in his.

"It's been a pleasure. I wish we could have met under different circumstances." Jennifer nods silently. "I'll walk you to the door," she says.

Ryan meanders around tables, Jennifer tagging behind him. The night air assaults them when they get outside, but it feels good. Ryan glances up and down the street, trying not to appear like a wide-eyed tourist. Jennifer settles close to him, her breast on his arm as she nuzzles against him.

"You should stay."

"Not a good idea."

Jennifer moves closer still. Ryan wraps an arm around her waist, grateful for the warmth.

"You should come back to our room with us."

"Definitely not a good idea."

"It's okay with her, you know."

Ryan gazes into Jennifer's eyes before allowing his stare to descend to her nipples, which have hardened in the nighttime air. Her hand is above his belt, hanging loosely, but now it drops until she finds what she's looking for; she cups his manhood firmly, feeling him through the suit fabric of his pants.

"Room 813, W Hotel. Please, baby."

Ryan's eyes are closed. He holds onto this stranger he barely knows; they rock together to a silent beat. He faces her, pulling her into him as they rock, her hand between his legs, stroking him to razor–like sharpness.

The snowball that became an avalanche. The freight train that screamed out of control.

He knows he is lost without Carly.

Yet he can't do a damn thing to win her back.

That much is clear.

His relationship with the woman back inside is dysfunctional, to say the least.

Reese is, without a doubt, poison.

Yet, he stands here in the deepening cold, contemplating ravaging her and this beautifully intoxicating stranger, sweaty bodies intertwined in some frenzied out-of-control dance that stirs his loins.

But that would only complicate matters.

Only drive the wedge deeper, spreading the chasm wider still—a trench that cannot be filled.

Ryan removes Jennifer's hand and raises it to his lips, kissing it gingerly. Turning up his collar and sighing heavily, Ryan heads north on Broadway.

Silently, Jennifer watches him go.

Chapter 39

Glancing down at his watch to note the time, 1:17 A.M., he feels rather than sees the door in front of him open. Raising his head, he comes face-to-face with Reese, who is clad in a thick terrycloth robe that drapes all the way to the floor. She greets him silently, moving out of the way so he may enter.

He does so slowly, aware of the dozen or so candles that decorate the room. It looks more like a mini-apartment—soothing earth tones, warm fabrics, large, comfortable-looking bed; modern artwork, vertically thin windows overlooking Broadway, a glass coffee table with an assortment of books, a fresh white orchid in the corner.

He stops in the center of the room as Jennifer enters from the bathroom. Her dark hair hangs free and is wet, fresh from a hot shower. She, too, wears a hotel robe, its ends hanging free, breasts hinting invitingly. She smiles when she sees him, gliding to the edge of the bed. She kisses him once on the mouth before lowering herself to the mattress and pulling him towards her. Silently, she unbuckles his belt as Reese's robe drops to the floor, revealing her dark nakedness. Quickly, he is in Jennifer's mouth— no fanfare, no foreplay—and Ryan groans while groping Jennifer's pert breasts.

He is dizzy as the world spins on its axis.

Ryan has been here exactly fifteen seconds and is now being fellated by this stranger. Reese comes up behind him, wrapping her hands around his waist, closing the gap until she is pressing her breasts seductively against his back. Jennifer's head bobs rhythmically, taking him deep into her mouth with a longing hunger that surprises him. Her fist grips him decisively, oiling him up and down as she slurps him deep into her throat. She stares up at him as Ryan is mesmerized by her actions.

He can barely stand.

The feeling is indescribable.

He has reached behind to palm Reese's ass. Ryan kneads the flesh, and she responds by grinding against him, spreading her thighs so Ryan can find her sweet spot. He sticks two fingers inside; Reese gasps as Jennifer continues to suck on him, his mind reeling from the exhilaration.

Ninety seconds.

The pressure within his loins is maddening. He is making love to Jennifer's lovely mouth, her jiggling breasts heaving as Reese uses her tongue to bathe him from behind. His mind is shattering into a million pieces. He is going insane; he can feel it as the seconds mount. The room continues to spin, candle-light appearing like a kaleidoscope as he is bent forward by a strong hand. Ryan snakes his hand downward until he finds Jennifer's sex, wet to his touch.

One hundred and ten seconds.

He must taste her. So he does.

On the bed, legs splayed wide, he lowers his face

Devon Scott

to her knees and kisses her there, working upwards to the space where her thighs meet. He touches her pubic hair with his mouth, letting his tongue run in lazy circles, first concentrating on her clit, and then moving downwards to her opening. She is moaning now, grabbing his head gingerly as she begs him not to stop. And he doesn't. Increasing his feeding as he reaches for Reese, following the rise of her flesh as he pinches a nipple between his fingers.

Reese moans while parting her legs.

Ryan finds her opening, slipping a finger effortlessly inside. The two women lay side-by-side, legs spread as Ryan pleasures them both. He kisses Jennifer's sweet spot, then moves over to do the same to Reese's. Jennifer watches in earnest as his fingers find her core, as he licks at Reese's folds in the way she used to worship.

Hard and raring to go, Ryan enters Jennifer first. He feels her shudder beneath him as Reese kisses Jennifer's breasts. They are like this for a while, rocking together on the bed, Ryan enjoying the sensual tempo from this stranger.

After a time he moves to Reese. He fills her in one fluid motion, watching her mouth open in a silent scream of pleasure.

His eyes are closed and his head is thrust back as he pummels her without mercy, gripping her as he gives her what she desperately needs, taking what he desperately desires.

Then it's back to Jennifer, on all fours as her head rests in Reese's lap.

Fucking her with abandonment, Ryan a missile, a piston thrusting in and out with lightning-fast fury, oblivious to the erotic moans and screams around him.

Fuck Carly, his mind shrieks in silence as he pounds Reese from behind.

Fuck her, Ryan muses again as he releases into the quivering folds of a stranger named Jennifer.

They kiss quietly—Ryan, Reese, and Jennifer—before lying down exhausted and spent.

Ryan fails to notice the blinking red light behind the white orchid in the corner, capturing their escapade on mini-DV.

Chapter 40

Three weeks later . . .

Carly's hand rests on her swollen belly. She's dressed in a pair of men's sweatpants, size extra large, and a maternity top. Her breasts are engorged. Her back and nipples ache. The tea that sits in front of her tastes bitter. So, too, does the pistachio ice cream embedded with the chocolate chunks. She pushes them aside and struggles to stand, taking in her surroundings. She is in the living room on the first floor, a room she's come to loathe, like the rest of this house— every square inch of space reminding her of the life she and Ryan used to share.

Carly is exhausted. She's always exhausted now. Yet, restful sleep eludes her. So, she grabs her Black-Berry off the coffee table and thumbs the control wheel, erasing e-mails as the TV drones on.

It is 11:47 P.M.

At this hour, the room is the color of indigo.
Olivia is on her back, nude, arms stretched over-

head, her palms pressing into the cool cherrywood headboard of their bed. Her legs are spread wide, ass off the damp mattress, eyes scrunched shut, as if afraid of what they might see should they suddenly open. The three-hundred-thread count sheet does little to stifle the heat radiating from within.

There are no sounds up here on the second floor, back of the house facing the tall woods. For a moment, she concentrates on the silence, willing herself to hear something—anything. When she does not, she rises, kicking the covers from her clammy form, and goes to the window, thrusting it wide open.

The coolness of night assaults her. So does the sound of nocturnal creatures.

Her nipples harden instantly from the cold, and for a moment, this is all Olivia can grasp and hold onto: the yin and yang of hot and cold, and the similarity of these sexual/asexual desires rooted inside her. The cold air attacking her skin and boiling loins feels good . . . but only for a few seconds.

Glancing back at the empty bed, Olivia tries not to wonder where her husband lays tonight.

Or worse.

With whom . . .

While holding her cell to an ear, she fills her lungs with a deep drag before exhaling through her nostrils.

She's standing in the alley, not because she can't smoke inside, but because the others are so damn nosy.

"Naw, girl, I'm not good. You know that nigga hasn't called? Yeah, can you believe it? You'd think after that pussyfest, he'd change his tune. But that's okay— 'cause I got something for his ass."

She switches ears, takes another drag before toss-ing the butt away. She watches the orange sparks col-lide with cobblestone.

"Oh yeah, girl—he's got a surprise coming! Just you watch. The nigga's gonna be sorry he forgot about me! Anyhoo, gotta get back to the grind—later!"

Reese snaps her cell shut and reaches for the back door to The Rhyme.

She's wearing a smile—the first one in about three weeks. . . .

Three-forty A.M.

Darkness is a drug.

It envelops, soothes, and consoles all it touches.

Finally, after hours of fretful tossing, Carly has grown still.

Only to wake to a sound.

It is indistinct, but she perks up immediately, as if she hasn't been sleeping at all.

Pulse in her neck sprinting, covers clutched close to her breast, head cocked to the side, trying to pin-point the sound.

There. Again. Softer, but distinct this time.

Definitely something . . .

She rises quickly, throwing off the comforter and gliding effortlessly on the balls of her feet to the win-dow—pushing the wooden slats slowly aside.

Nothing. The deck and back woods are dead quiet.

To the front of the house now. Slowly, purposefully. Into one of the guest bedrooms. To the window—again, edging wooden slats aside.

A lone, late model vehicle, its running lights on, is pulling away from the curb. D.C. tags, but the num-bers are illegible from here. Flash of brake lights be-fore the car hangs a quick left and vanishes.

Taking the steps carefully, Carly surveys the living room and kitchen areas before moving to the front door, face pressed against the wood, taking a quick peek out through beveled glass.

Nothing.

The street is, like the backyard, deathly quiet.

To the alarm in the hallway; all indicator lights a steady green.

Disarming it, she returns to the front door, takes a sharp intake of breath before opening it.

There—down by the corner of the braided welcome mat—a thick package, hastily wrapped in brown grocery bag paper, its ends covered with masking tape.

Addressed to her.

Carly glances quickly up and down the street as the wind stirs, causing her teeth to chatter.

She hesitates before picking up the package. In this post 9-11 era, it could be a bomb. But her curiosity gets the best of her. So, she reaches for it, and returns to the comfort and safety of her home. Locks the door, resetting the alarm quickly.

Doesn't breathe until she's ripped the package open.

A videotape.

No label.

Carly doesn't cry until she's viewed its contents. . . .

Chapter 41

"Hello, fucker!"

Ryan is disoriented by the lateness of the hour, but not so much so that he fails to recognize the voice.

"Reese. Do you know what time—"

"Yeah, I know exactly what time it is. Long time no hear, nigga! Three weeks and two days to be exact."

"First off, I'm not your nigga. Second, I've been busy, and it's really late. What do you want?"

Reese draws in a breath, exhales before speaking.

"Oh, so it's like that? Nigga gets a shot of some double chocolate pussy and then it's lights out— radio silence. Okay, cool. A sistah was just ringing you up to say hello and shit. See how the wife is doing."

Ryan sighs.

"My wife is fine, Reese."

"Is she? I don't think so."

Ryan jolts up in his bed. The apartment where he is staying is cramped, the one bedroom hardly capable of fitting in all of his stuff. Most of his life is stacked neatly in boxes in the living room; the rest is in storage.

"Excuse me?" he says, reaching for the lamp on the nightstand.

"You deaf? I said, I don't think so. At least not after seeing your ass in action."

"Just what the fuck are you talking about? I told you to stay away from my wife!"

"Your acting debut. The video, nigga." A short laugh.

"What video?" Ryan asks, rising from the bed.

"Oh, you know—me, you, Jennifer, New York City. Gotta tell you, you sure were working it that night. You might be an asshole, but you sure can lay the pipe!"

The cell has dropped from his palm, but Reese doesn't know it yet. It lies on the top folds of his blanket while he races to the kitchen. Snatching up the phone, he dials his home number—well, her home number now since it no longer belongs to him—and waits an excruciatingly long time while the phone rings and rings and rings.

Shit.

Meanwhile, Reese has figured out Ryan's gone. She unleashed a few "fuck yous" before hanging up.

Back in the bedroom, Ryan grabs his cell and snaps it shut. It rings an instant later.

"If you're fucking with me, Reese—"

"Oh, we're way past that, lover. See, I figure the only thing a nigga like you responds to is *violence*."

With the phone to his ear, Ryan pulls on a pair of jeans.

"WHAT?"

Reese is calm—almost too calm.

"Violence. It got your attention before; it's gonna get your attention again."

"What the fuck are you talking about?"

"Miles. And now I'm gonna fuck up everyone you

hold dear—gonna fuck them up real bad until you have no one left. Yup, violence is the only answer 'cause you don't wanna act right!"

"YOU LISTEN TO ME, you cunt, touch my wife and I'll fuck—"

The avalanche is careening out of control, swallowing everything in its wake—leaving nothing but death.

The line goes dead.

Ryan stares in disbelief at his phone.

Hits speed dial for Carly's number.

Nothing.

Hits redial.

"Come ON!" he yells to the empty room.

Nothing.

Shit.

Eyes the time . . . 3:57 A.M.

Where the fuck can she be?

Pulls on a sweater and boots. Reaches for his wallet.

Thumbs 911 as he sprints out the door.

"Nine-one-one emergency. Please hold . . ."

"You've got to be kidding me!"

Ryan is in the parking lot, racing for his car. He's got the engine cranked and heat running before the call goes through.

"I need the police sent to my house—this is an emergency—my wife may be in danger! Hurry!"

Ryan gives the 911 operator the information:

Crazed lover—ex-lover.

Pregnant wife, not picking up the phone.

He's at least twenty-five minutes out.

No way can he reach her in time.

The operator asks a few questions before dispatching the police.

"A patrol car is on the way, sir."

Ryan ends the call.

Hits speed dial again.

"Carly, pick up, PICK UP!"

Nothing.

A freight train out of control.

Fuck!

Redial. Again. And again. And again.

Nothing.

Fuck. Fuck!! FUCK!!!

He races the car out of the complex, almost side-swiping a bunch of parked cars in the process.

"Calm down, calm down; don't kill yourself. Get there in one piece," Ryan recites to himself.

Glances down at his cell. Where could she be? An immediate pain shoots through his abdomen as he considers the fact that she could be with Tyler Nichols again.

Put it out of your mind!

He contemplates calling Olivia and Miles. Carly could be there, although doubtful.

Takes a few seconds to decide.

Speed dials their number.

After four rings, he hits END and then redials.

Down 16th Street, which is desolate this time of night, thank God, he races through several red lights, knowing he'll surely be caught on camera at one of these intersections.

Fuck it.

No answer from Olivia and Miles.

No answer from Carly.

WHAT THE FUCK?

Ryan steers onto the Southeast/Southwest Expressway. A few cars share the road with him. Ryan floors the accelerator as he considers his options.

Glances down at his cell while gritting his teeth. Then makes the call.

"Hello?" The voice is groggy, almost weary.

"Hey, Luther," Ryan says apologetically, "sorry to wake you."

Taking 295 south, he steers his vehicle towards Maryland and the home he used to share with his wife.

The speedometer reads 79 mph.

"Ryan? What time is it?"

"Yeah, it's me—and it's late. It's an emergency, or I wouldn't . . . wouldn't have bothered you."

"What's the matter?" Luther is wide awake now, voice matter-of-fact and clear.

"That chick I asked you to check out—she's stalking my wife . . . threatened her. And this time, I think Carly's truly in danger!"

"Slow down. How come you never called me back? I left several messages at your home regarding her. Dude, she's definitely a nut job!"

"WHAT?" Ryan almost screams into the phone. He presses down on the accelerator hard; the car lurches in the cold, dark air.

"I checked her out, just like you asked. Misplaced your cell number, so I left a number of messages at home. That was, like, six, seven months ago, right?"

"Sorry, man, things have been really fucked up— never got them."

"Okay. Give me the thirty-second version. All of it." Ryan does.

"Jesus. Okay, you need to know this: your girl was

jailed for assault—twice—and get this—the people she assaulted were dudes!"

"Fuck, I gotta go. Got to reach Carly."

"Ryan—hang on—let me call this in."

Luther drops his cell and reaches for his other phone. Punches in a number, and Ryan can hear bits of the conversation.

"Give me your address at home," Luther commands.

Ryan does.

"Okay. I'm back. I've got a partner who lives out that way. He's off-duty but on his way. He'll check it out and make sure your wife is safe."

"Thank you. Jesus—assault? Jail—when was this?" Ryan asks.

"Shit, I don't remember the details, but I believe it was several years ago down in Virginia Beach. She did thirty days the first stint; second time, fucked up this guy she was seeing real bad. Put his ass in the hospital. She did six months in lock up for the crime. Crazy bitch!"

"Luther, I've got to get home. I've got to reach Carly."

"Understand, bro. Just don't do anything stupid. Let law enforcement do their job."

"Way too late for that," he whispers before ending the call.

Chapter 42

He arrives at the home he used to share with his wife, back when life was simple and honest—no deceit, no lies. The reddish brick colonial stands majestic in the nighttime air, the cul-de-sac quiet and dark, save for the flashing blue and red lights from the cruiser sitting in the driveway.

Ryan pulls up alongside and cuts the engine before jumping out. A cop's flashlight is in his face almost immediately.

"I'm the one who phoned this in. I'm the husband."

"Let me see some identification," the cop responds.

"Is she safe? Is my wife okay?"

"Sir, identification please." The cop's tone is firm.

Ryan pulls his wallet out and proffers his license. The cop shines his light on it for a moment, then back up at Ryan's face. Satisfied, he returns the license to Ryan.

"No one's home—or so it seems. The place is locked up tight. Can you let us in?"

Ryan shrugs. "I don't have the key . . ." and as an afterthought he adds, "anymore." Then says, "Let me see if the garage code's changed."

He scrambles up the drive to the garage door, flips up the plastic sleeve hiding the keypad, and punches in four numbers.

Nothing.

Shit.

Ryan turns to the cop and shrugs sheepishly.

"Let's see if she still keeps a key out back."

He jogs around the house, passing azaleas, the odor of fresh mulch hanging in the air. Onto the deck and over to one of a half dozen potted plants. Lifts one up.

Nothing.

Another, then another—Ryan checks them all.

No spare key.

"Nothing more we can do here," the partner says. "Place appears secure; no signs of a break in."

"But where is she?!" Ryan exclaims.

"We have no idea. Here's my card. You can call me day or night should you require further assistance." The cop heads down the deck stairs. Ryan follows.

"But what about this woman? She's crazy."

"Your wife?" the first cop asks.

Ryan glares at him.

"No, the one stalking her—and me!"

"Sir, I'd suggest you file a restraining order against this person if you think you or your wife's safety is in danger. The county courthouse opens at eight-thirty, and you can get an emergency order the same day."

Ryan stands in the driveway, watching them go.

A moment later, another car pulls up, an unmarked sedan with its lights flashing.

A beefy black guy emerges, Glock slung on his hip.

"You Ryan?"

"Yeah. Luther sent you?"

"Yup. Name's Chris. What's the deal?"

Ryan briefs him. Chris takes it all in, nodding as Ryan provides the details.

"Where do you think your wife is now?"

"Haven't a clue." Ryan doesn't mention the thought that has been nagging him for close to forty minutes now—that she's with Tyler. "I called our . . . um, best friends. They don't answer either. She could have gone over there."

"Where do they live?"

"Not too far from here—about twenty minutes at this time of morning."

Chris pulls out his cell phone.

"You want me to go check them out?"

Ryan shakes his head.

"Naw, I'm sure they're fine . . ."

"You sure?" His stare bores into Ryan. "If you're worried, then it's better to err on the side of caution. Won't be no trouble for me to swing by."

"It's cool. I appreciate it, though."

Chris nods.

"K. Give me your cell number."

Ryan does. Chris dials and Ryan's phone rings.

"Now you have my digits. Holler if you need me."

"Will do. Thanks again."

Chris returns to his vehicle, kills the flashing lights, and backs away. Ryan is left standing in the driveway, alone.

He knows he should go to Miles and Olivia's, but will feel foolish if Carly's not there. He whips out his cell again and speed dials his wife's number.

Nothing.

Tries Miles and Olivia again.

Nothing.

A freight train out of control.

Dials Reese.

His call goes immediately to voice mail.

Jumping into his car, Ryan knows what his next move will be.

Chapter 43

The drive takes under fifteen minutes. The sky is already beginning to lighten, black indigo giving way to a deep ocean blue. Soon now, heaven will show itself in all of its glory. Ryan hopes by then he won't be too late.

No one is answering their phones.

Not Carly, not Olivia and Miles, not even Reese.

He's given up, taking the shiny metal thing that fits into the palm of his hand and dropping it on the seat beside him.

He turns the radio on, but the music at this time of morning merely aggravates. So, he drives in silence instead.

Turning onto their street, Ryan steers his vehicle to a stop in the driveway.

Olivia and Miles' home.

The lights are off. The street is dead silent. Only tree limbs move to the wind's dance, a low howling that seems to whistle as it attacks branches and leaves.

Ryan cuts the engine, gets out. Goes to the front door, and without fanfare, rings the bell.

Then again.

And again.

Nothing.

Peering though the window doesn't buy him a thing.

He rings them up via his cell again.

Nothing.

He goes around back, onto the deck. Out here, the wind is more pronounced. Out here, it screams, throwing up haunting shadows that dance on the weathered wood. Ryan goes to the bay window and door. Instantly, his heart rate spikes.

Right side, six inches up from the door handle, a pane is missing.

Ryan jumps back, his boots crunching on shattered glass.

He checks the handle and it gives.

Heart rate spikes again.

Should he call the police? Luther?

No time.

Ryan sucks in a breath and enters.

It is as he remembers.

Suddenly, it is all coming back to him.

Try as he might to thrust these thoughts out of his mind, and instead concentrate on the task at hand, something inside him won't let him.

The images come back like a rushing stream; they invade his psyche all at once.

The party . . . *He was in fact just standing there, head pounding from a night of crabs, Coronas, apple martinis, and cigar smoking. Just the last two were more than enough to make his head spin.*

One-thirty in the morning, standing in the kitchen of his best friends' home, Olivia and Miles asleep upstairs, Carly crashed on the futon in the level below—and Ryan, his cotton-mouth and tongue begging for moisture as he rummaged through the fridge searching for something to drink. He found a liter of Sprite and, not having the strength to search for a cup, tipped the bottle to his lips and hungrily drank.

As he dropped it into the refrigerator slot, he stepped back to close the door.

That's when he saw her.

Olivia.

What he saw took his breath away.

Ryan moves forward slowly from the kitchen. Dancing shadows from outside paint disturbing images onto the carpet and floor. Ryan stays close to the walls, knees bent, gripping the black handle of a long carving knife he found in the sink, its gleaming blade pointing in front of him, the only usable weapon he could find. He steps down into the living room, considers calling out the names of the home's occupants, but thinks better of it.

Olivia was clad in a button-down shirt—little else. The shirt hung open. He could see the dark patch of pubic hair that spread over her mound—and a large purplish nipple peeked out from the side of the shirt. Her hair hung free, locs surrounding her beautiful darkened face. Between her lips hung a burnt-out cigar. She moved forward on her toes, like a dancer; she seemed to glide toward him effortlessly. He glanced quickly toward the closed doorway that led to the basement stairs. Behind her, the back of the family room couch was sprinkled in shadows; the rest of the room was indigo.

Like it is now. Dappled in shadows. The effect is eerie. He feels terror crawling up his limbs. Not only from the present, but also from the past . . .

Ryan wrestles to admonish these thoughts that roost in his brain, threatening to incapacitate him.

He needs to stay sharp.

He desperately needs to focus.

Ryan couldn't wrestle his gaze from her body, which seemed to writhe as she moved near—the illusion of a serpent—and the fullness of her spoke to him. Not like Carly, certainly not overweight. Just curvy hips, meat on the bones like his mama. Legs and thighs that spoke of substance and full breasts that hung invitingly. When she was within touching distance, her eyes never leaving his, the cigar now inches from his face, his cock swelling in his boxers with the certainty of a raging flood, he reached for her. Her legs parted, her eyes unblinking. His fingers traced a line down the cotton fabric of the man's shirt, past buttons, parting the halves, and resting a hand lightly on her breast. Gently, he circled the hard nipple before dipping down farther past her navel, which—

A sound. Distinctive. Coming from upstairs.

This, he is certain.

Ryan moves cat-like to the other side of the room. The pulse at his temple is pounding now. His heart is in overdrive, adrenaline being pumped to every corner of his extremities. He should call for help.

Backup is what he needs.

She reached out and expertly slipped her hand inside his shorts. His cock came alive as she palmed the bulbous head, stroking the shaft, raking her fingers lightly over his balls. He reached out, finding her opening effortlessly, slipping a finger inside. His thumb found her clit and began a rhythmic massage. Her legs parted farther. He pulled out abruptly and brought a glazed finger to his mouth. Tasting her, sucking in her juice, eyes never leaving hers.

Up the stairs now, staying close to the edge, wanting to take them two at a time, but knowing this would give his position away.

He knows not what awaits him at the top of the stairs. It could be anything . . . or anyone. But Ryan knows all of this—everything that has transpired—every single thing that is about to happen—is his doing.

It is his fault.

A snowball rolling down a hill . . .

Becoming an avalanche . . .

A freight train out of control . . .

Her hands spread lengthwise along the edge of the furniture, her back bending forward and down, lifting up the shirt in the process—Miles' shirt. She spread her legs wide, exhibiting in all of its splendor her heart-shaped, chocolate-colored ass.

At the top of the stairs he pauses, hearing it again.

A sound.

Distinctive. Rustling-like.

Inching closer to their bedroom, a bedroom that Miles and Olivia shared during happier times, times when they all were part of a family.

Ryan and Carly.

Miles and Olivia.

He gripped himself decisively, readying to impale his hardness into the wetness of her sweet cavern.

His ear goes quietly to the door, gripping the knife with purpose.

God, protect me from what's on the other side of this door.

His other hand reaches for the doorknob, inhaling a breath and exhaling silently, preparing himself for his destiny.

Suddenly unable to contain his hunger, he lunged forward with a purpose that surprised even him.

Ryan thrusts the door open.

Spies Olivia alone on the bed.

It is her eyes that find him first. He will never forget that look. For as long as he lives, Ryan will never be able to shake that image from his brain.

Olivia's wrists are bound behind her, mouth

gagged with a dirty white sock, and her legs held open by a broomstick that is bound to each ankle with electrical cord. He has to blink to be sure, but this is no dream—a beer bottle is inserted deep inside her, almost to the hilt.

It is the gaping look from her that Ryan will never forget.

The heartrending stare that speaks volumes.

You did this to me, it says.

An avalanche . . .

A freight train careering out of control . . .

Ryan groans audibly, dropping the knife while reaching hastily for his cell.

Chapter 44

It's been a long time since he's laid eyes on Miles.

He seems to have aged. Worry lines traverse his face.

Olivia, too.

They sit together, estranged husband and wife, huddled on the couch while being interviewed by two police officers. Olivia's stare is vacant, lips mashed together while her husband does most of the talking. They make little eye contact—Olivia and Ryan. She has made it clear he is no longer welcomed here.

Can you blame her?

A pair of patrolmen have Ryan sequestered in the hallway, going over his story.

Olivia has provided a description to the police. It's Reese, no question.

"So let me get this straight," a tall, well-conditioned cop the color of butterscotch asks, while his partner, a shorter but equally fit white patrol officer, eyes Ryan with outward disdain. "This woman, Reese, she's your girlfriend?"

"No. We used to—" Ryan searches for the right word.

"Date?"

Ryan doesn't answer.

"Friends with benefits?" This coming from the white partner. Then adds, "And just so I'm clear," he consults the pad in his hand, "you're married, right?"

Ryan gulps. "Right."

"So you think she's in danger—your wife?"

"Yes, that's what I've been trying to tell you. Have you put out an APB or something on Reese? She's crazy! She's responsible for this and for Miles' injuries, too. She all but confessed to that crime. And don't forget the fact that she's done time . . . for damn assault!"

The black cop eyes Ryan, but says nothing. He walks away for a moment, going into the living room. Ryan can see all of them from where he stands. Miles is consulting with the three officers; Olivia's stare remains vacant, poking through his flesh as if he's a ghost.

The black cop returns.

"We're putting out an APB on Reese. She's considered armed and dangerous. We won't take any chances with this one."

Ryan nods.

"What about my wife?"

"Can't do much until she's located," the white cop replies, flipping closed his notepad, signaling the interview is over.

"I'll go back to our . . . um, her house, to see if she shows."

"No, go home. I'm sure she's among friends and is fine," says the black cop. "Olivia's given us the name of your wife's friend—a Tyler Nichols—we'll check him out now, see if she's with him. If not, we play the waiting game . . . until she turns up." His hands spread wide as if in offering; his eyes have softened a bit.

The white cop, on the other hand, is feeling no such compassion.

"Hopefully Tyler's not a friend with benefits," he says with a smirk. "Know what I mean, partner?" Stare locked onto Ryan.

No longer wanted, no longer needed, he announces his departure.

No one sees him to the front door.

He's shut the car door and turned the ignition when Miles raps on the driver's side window.

It startles Ryan. He fumbles for the switch, lowers the window.

"How long have you known?" Miles says.

"Known what?"

"That Reese was responsible for my assault." His face is level with Ryan's, eyes unblinking.

Ryan hesitates, ponders the question.

"Not going to kick your ass or anything, Ryan. Just trying to understand how it came to this—you not having my back. I know things are fucked up between us—all of us—but there was a time when we were friends, when I'd have done anything for you . . ."

"Yeah . . ."

"Was it two days, two weeks, two months? How long have you known?"

"Look, Miles, I never knew for sure until tonight . . . an hour ago . . ."

Miles pulls a loc from his eyes.

"Regardless of what went down between us that night after the party, I'd never in a million years do anything to hurt you or your wife. And I'd never put you or Carly in harm's way. Know that. I may be many things, Ryan, but I'm not *that*. . . ."

Ryan can't look him in the eyes. So, he pans his stare away.

"Miles, I don't know what to say other than I'm sorry—"

But he's already walked away.

Chapter 45

Dawn had already erupted by the time Ryan steered his car home.

Home.

No longer a home. Now, merely a one bedroom in a Northeast apartment building that's recently been refurbished. The rent is close to what he's paying for the mortgage on the house. Pays extra for underground parking. Ryan pulls into the nondescript concrete space that is relatively quiet given the time. Just past 6:00 A.M. and on a weekend. He kills the engine and sweeps his gaze around, feeling a sudden burst of insecurity surge through him.

She could be here.

Reese.

Waiting among the shadows.

He reaches down for the leather slapper he keeps under his seat, and grips it decisively in his hand as he exits his vehicle.

Checks both ways and behind him—nothing—before heading for the elevators.

One comes two minutes later.

Ryan lives on the ninth floor.

He decides to make a pit stop to grab his mail since he didn't do it last night. The elevator door opens on the lobby level; Ryan cuts right toward the mailboxes, enters the mailroom quickly, and walks swiftly over to the wall of mailboxes. He finds 908 and inserts his key as his peripheral vision picks up a movement from the left. At the same moment, the hair on the back of his neck rises. He senses some-one behind him. Ryan spins around, the slapper arc-ing upward, poised and ready to strike.

In that instant, Ryan comes face-to-face with Carly.

"What are you doing here? I've been looking everywhere for you!"

There are dark circles under her eyes, but other-wise, it is the same Carly—beautiful, regal. She clutches a brown and white purse in one hand. Her other draws circles around her engorged belly.

"The police showed up at Tyler's."

Ryan glances past her quickly before returning his gaze to her.

"Are you okay? Do you have any idea what has been happening? God—I've been scared shitless worrying about you. Olivia was attacked earlier this evening. And I think she's coming after you." Ryan drops his stare for a split second before meeting Carly's gaze. "It's Reese. She's out of her fucking mind!"

"I know."

"What? You *know*?"

"Yes. She paid me a visit—gave me this." Carly reaches into her purse and extracts the videotape.

"Jesus. Carly—I'm so sorry you got dragged—"

"Can I use your restroom? And I need to sit back down," she says.

"Of course, of course. Come." Ryan leads her out of the mailroom and to the bank of elevators. He punches the up button. The elevator door opens promptly.

They ride in silence, Ryan thumbing the videotape, feeling humiliated—for all of what has transpired. Carly is quiet, holding her stomach. Ryan watches her in the shiny reflection of elevator door metal. She could be furious; she could be an inferno. But, as usual, she is none of these things. She carries her head high, and Ryan experiences a blast of shame.

"I'm a week late, you know?" Carly says softly.

"Pardon me?"

"My baby—she's a week late. If she's not here by Tuesday, they're inducing labor."

Ryan ponders her words.

My baby.

"Oh." Suddenly feeling sheepish for not even knowing their baby's due date, he quickly adds, "She?"

Carly turns to Ryan and smiles.

"I know it's a girl. I mean, I don't *know* know, but mothers know these things. It's a girl alright—can feel her kicking right now."

Ryan's eyes brim with tears. He thinks of all the things they could be doing in preparation for this baby: decorating the nursery, baby-proofing the house, lying in bed together, he rubbing her shoulders, spooning each other while they watch late night movies and talk about their child's future.

And so on and so on . . .

Instead, this avalanche . . . this freight train out of control.

"May I?" he asks.

Carly nods, taking his hand and placing it gently on her abdomen. Ryan cocks his head to the side, feeling. His eyes suddenly go wide.

"Oh, my God! I feel it."

"Her. A feisty thing. She's coming out kicking and screaming. You watch."

The door glides open. Ryan checks both directions before helping Carly out of the elevator. They take slow, steady steps. Ryan takes his time, thankful for the reprieve with Carly.

They reach his apartment . . . 908.

Ryan checks the handle. Door locked.

He inserts his key, tells Carly to hang back for a second as he opens the door, taking a step forward and flipping on the light. He grips the slapper as he moves further into the hallway. His place is quiet. Nothing seemingly out of place.

Back out into the hallway to escort Carly inside.

She takes in the small living space: a low futon, faux leather recliner, wood coffee table, and halogen lamp—all could have been bought at Ikea or Target. A hallway leads to a bath and the bedroom at the far end.

"Nice place," she says.

"No, it's not," Ryan retorts. "Bathroom's on the left. Do you need help?" Ryan tries to smile, to ease the angst he feels. Carly just stares at him.

"I think I can manage."

Carly turns to head for the bathroom. Ryan drops the videotape on the futon, prepares to sit down. They both hear the distinctive sound at the exact same time.

Coming from the bedroom at the far end of the hall.

Carly freezes.

So does Ryan.

The bedroom door opens slowly.

Out steps Reese.

"Isn't this comfy?"

Reese is clad in a pair of tight black jeans, a brown tee shirt, and matching Timbs. Her top is two sizes too small. Her breasts strain sensuously against the fabric. In her hand, she holds an aluminum baseball bat. The bat hangs low, its head to the ground.

There's no mistaking her intentions.

"What the fuck are you doing here?" Ryan exclaims.

He's jumped in front of Carly, who makes a hasty retreat to the window.

Her eyes are laser points boring into Reese.

"What do you think? I've come to collect my man—and to tie up loose ends."

"I'm not your man, you crazy bitch!"

"Oh really? What do you think, Carly? Didn't it look like he's my man on that videotape?"

Carly is silent. Her breathing is deep, even; her hand clutches the two-tone purse tightly. She steps forward.

"Not speaking? That's cool," Reese says, moving leisurely into the room. The bat drags along the hardwood, making a scraping sound. "As long as y'all both know who's with who."

Ryan slides backwards until he is several feet from Carly.

"How'd you get in here?"

Reese grins.

"Shit, the security in this place is second-rate, yo! All I had to do is sashay up to the front desk—and you know this dimwit Indian guy is behind the desk, reading a freaking comic book. I flash my sexy smile, squeeze the girls together—like this"—Reese rings her shoulders in, mashing her breasts together—"and Saheed is hooked. Fed him a line about being your best friend from outta town here to surprise you. Told him I'd suck his dick if he let me in without anyone knowing."

Reese grins, all proud of herself.

"Bullshit!"

"Yeah? Well, here I am, Einstein. Do the math."

"The police are looking for you. They know all about you—your assaults in Virginia Beach, what you did to Miles and now Olivia—"

"Hold up." Carly speaks for the first time. Reese glances over at her peculiarly. "That was you?" she asks, hand raised, finger pointed accusingly at Reese.

"Yeah, bitch, all my handiwork." She hoists the bat to waist-level. "Now shut the fuck up before someone's baby gets hurt!"

Carly takes another step forward.

"I don't think so."

Arc of movement, almost a blur from her right side.

Purse drops. A key ring, lipstick, makeup bag, and a half-eaten roll of Mentos spill to the floor in rapid-fire succession. Before Reese or Ryan can react, Carly is holding a gleaming revolver between her palms.

"Oh, hell no!" Reese yells, flinging the bat in Carly's direction.

Ryan's eyes are the size of silver dollars.

He screams.

"NO!!"

The gun discharges.

Lightning flash as a deafening roar tears through the room.

Reese's eyes grow wide as the slug tears into her breastbone.

She pirouettes on her heels, like a dancer, before slamming into the wall face-first, dropping to the cold floor with a sickening thud.

Hard.

Ryan vomits.

Instinctively, he leaps backwards, nearly tripping over the supine form of his wife.

Carly lays motionless on the hardwood floor, one leg folded underneath her, arm cocked at a grotesque angle, a slow yet steady ooze seeping from a gruesome head wound.

The revolver still in the grip of her right hand, its barrel smoking.

"NO!!!" Ryan screams again.

Vision blurs; walls, floor, window, furniture—all become a kaleidoscope of out-of-focus patterns.

Then everything goes black.

Epilogue

It is a picture-perfect day. Temperatures in the low seventies, a light breeze blowing gently. He drives up to the house, marveling at the sheer beauty of this home as he does each time he arrives—a two-story yellow Victorian with a wraparound porch. The verdant grass is cut low to the ground and is luxurious, and it never ceases to amaze him how he conjures up images of little children rolling and laughing among the shiny blades of Kentucky fescue. He longs to be one of them.

He turns into the driveway, slows to a stop, and honks his horn once.

Immediately, the front door opens and a young black girl, no older than three, barrels out.

"Daddy, Daddy, Dad-deeeeeeeeeeeeeeeeeeeeeeeeee-eeeee!" she squeals with delight.

No doubt she is her father's daughter—same complexion, same brown eyes, exact same way of arching her eyebrows and displaying a frown when considering a question or anything posed to her. Her hair is worn in two thick plaits that bounce down her back. Jeans, a light top, and sneakers, which pulse red light when hitting the ground, are her attire.

Ryan exits his vehicle and squats down, allowing her to run into him with all of her energy.

"HEY, baby!" Teeny hands scramble for his neck, clutching him as if petrified of letting go.

"Daddy, Daddy, Mommy said not to tell you, but I'm gonna anyway!"

She's wearing a bright red Dora backpack, which she refuses to hand over.

Ryan buckles her into the car seat, kissing her on her forehead.

"What is it, Alexandria? What did Mommy say not to tell me?"

He's moved around to the driver's side and takes a single glance back at the front door to the Victorian while revving the engine. He turns in his seat to face his excited daughter.

Alex puts her finger to her lips, blows hard.

"No telling!" she says.

"I promise."

"Pinky swear?" she asks.

Ryan laughs. "Pinky swear."

Satisfied, Alexandria continues. "Mommy said I'm going to get a little brother for Christmas! Daddy— Santa's going to bring me a brother!"

Ryan's face has gone white. It's as if the air has been sucked out of the vehicle. He remains perfectly still, mind on auto-pilot, not hearing his daughter's additional words. A spike has just entered his cortex, severing the senses. "Daddy, is the day after tomorrow Christmas?"

Silence.

"DADDY?"

"No, baby," he whispers, "Christmas is a long way off."

"No telling, Daddy . . . pinky swear!"

"Okay, okay."

All color has drained from his face, yet his daughter doesn't notice. She's too busy rummaging through her Dora backpack. Ryan puts the car in reverse, easing his foot on the gas.

Off to his right, the front door opens and Carly runs out, hands waving in the air.

Ryan lurches to a stop.

"Oh, thank God," she stammers, out of breath, face looking as fresh as a Dove commercial. "Thought you had left already. You'd have one helluva weekend without this!" she says, displaying Alex's blanky. Alex turns her head, spies the blanket, and emits an ear-splitting screech.

"OHHHHHHHHHHHHHHHHHHHH, Mommy said a bad word!" she exclaims while snatching the blanket through an open window.

"You're welcome, sweetheart," Carly says sarcastically.

Alex immediately calms down.

Ryan takes a moment to stare at his ex-wife. She looks so happy, so content. You can see it in her eyes, in the relaxed lines to her sculpted nose, and her beautifully sensual mouth. Ryan opens his to speak—congratulations are in order. But then he shuts this thought down, snaps his mouth shut, remembering his pinky swear. Besides, what exactly is there to say?

For close to two years now, Ryan's fought hard to wrestle these thoughts from his mind—thoughts that would make any man go insane:

If only he had been faithful . . .

If only he had turned away . . .

It is the sight of her that triggers his fixation and obsession, so he sighs.

This . . . all of this . . . could have been *his*.

Carly has been, for the past few moments of ensuing awkward silence, watching Ryan. She cocks her head to the side, as though wanting to ask if everything is okay. But she smiles instead, knowing the answer to her own silly question.

Back on the porch, Carly is joined by Tyler Nichols.

He reaches for her.

Arm in arm, they watch Ryan and Alexandra go.

Enjoy the following excerpt from
OBSESSED

In stores May 2009!

Chapter 1

"I call shotgun!" Zack squeals.

"Boy if you don't get in your car seat," Kennedy exclaims.

They stand outside of their stone, three-level, one-garage townhouse located on Taylor Street in North-east D.C. The street they live on is tree-lined and quiet. A community made up of mostly middle-to upper-middle class whites and African-Americans, a few immigrants from Pakistan or Afghanistan who keep to themselves. Crime is minimal, due to an aggressive neighborhood watch program and surveillance cameras installed in the driveways of several homes.

All of the rowhouses, as they're called in the District, are stone, some the color of dark mud, others the reddish-brown hue of autumn or the dull gray of slate. All are well kept, with small yet manicured bushes and shrubs. Michael and Kennedy bought this home shortly after they were married six years ago. They were looking for something they could stretch out in and raise a family. The location is decent, as far as the city goes, quiet, Metro-accessible, and a short drive from

the private school that Zack attends and the association where Kennedy works as a lawyer downtown.
Michael, who is also an attorney, but works instead
for a government agency, can make the short drive
downtown as well or take Metro.

Their luggage—Michael's garment bag, Kennedy's
two suitcases, and Zack's gym bag and backpack are
sequestered in the back of Michael's Range Rover.
Kennedy's BMW is tucked in the garage. Michael jumps
in the front seat and starts the engine as Kennedy
supervises Zack buckling in. Once everyone is set,
they take off.

The drive to Jeremy's takes about ten minutes, his
home north of Children's Hospital and Catholic Uni-
versity. Michael double parks on the narrow street, as
Kennedy gets Zack to the sidewalk. He quickly hugs
her and races up the stoop to the second floor, ringing the bell as his father gets out, leaving the engine
running.

"Hey, can I get a hug or something?" he yells to his
son.

"Oh, yeah. Sure, Dad." Zack races back down, backpack bobbing against his thin shoulders. Arms reach
up around his father's neck and hug him. "Buy me
something in New York, PLEASE?"

"Is that all I'm good for? Lord!" Michael grins.

Jeremy yanks open the door and the two high-five
each other before racing inside. Jeremy's mom, Lori,
comes outside, a good-looking thirtysomething woman
of color, dressed comfortably in sweats and running
shoes. She waves at Michael as Kennedy climbs the
steps. They meet halfway.

"Hey, girl," Kennedy says, embracing Lori. "Thank
you so much for taking Zack this weekend."

"You know it's not a problem," Lori says. "We're
going to have a great time. I'm taking the boys to the

movies tonight, and we've got plenty of things to keep them occupied all weekend."

"That's great. Zack's been talking about this sleep-over all week."

"Jeremy too. You guys have fun. Don't worry about a thing—I've got your number if we need to reach you," Lori says before dropping her voice down a notch. "Wish I was going away with my husband. You need to have enough fun for both of us, you hear me?" She winks at Kennedy. Kennedy grins back.

The ride to Union Station takes less than fifteen minutes. Michael parks on the upper level and together they lug their bags into the Amtrak station. They have a 3 P.M. reservation on the Acela Express and a half hour to spare before the train departs. Check in is a breeze. In this day and age of self-service technology, they retrieve their boarding passes from an automated kiosk and grab a caramel frappuccino and a Danish from the Starbucks across from the waiting area. They take adjoining seats close to their gate and collectively breath a sigh of relief.

"The vacation begins," Kennedy says, placing a hand on Michael's lap and leaning in until their foreheads touch.

"Love you, baby," Michael responds, taking her head in his hand as he kisses her lips gingerly. Kennedy, for a moment, loses herself in the closeness of her husband, loving the feeling as she always does of her tongue on his. She opens her mouth wider, inviting him in, then pulls back, suddenly aware of her surroundings.

"Love you more," Kennedy remarks back, in breathless anticipation of things to come.

Chapter 2

Their train rushes along, past buildings, warehouses, and backyards. Trees fly by as Michael glances out the window. Kennedy sits across from him, Amtrak-issued blue blanket draped over her lap, no one beside either of them. The ride is comforting—the train rocking slightly back and forth and it hurls north toward Wilmington, Philly, Newark, and their destination, New York City.

The car is not at all crowded. Michael thought every seat would've been taken, seeing how today is Friday afternoon. But the traveling gods are watching over them. Kennedy sits with her legs crossed, foot tapping to a beat only she can hear on her iPod. In her hand is her trusted BlackBerry Pearl, which she is never far from. Head down, her fingers peck incessantly over the tiny keyboard—type, pause, type, repeat.

Michael has brought several magazines to read. They lay untouched on the seat beside him. The motion of the train is therapeutic, making him groggy. He's got the rest of the trip and the weekend to flip

through the pages, so he lays his head back on the
cushion and closes his eyes. He drifts off only to be
awakened by a vibration on his hip from his cell
phone. Opening his eyes, he observes the expanse of
water as the train passes over a low bridge. The effect
is that they are gliding over the water, traveling via
hovercraft or low-flying helicopter. Michael reaches
for his own BlackBerry as he stares at the scene before him for a moment more. It is peaceful and
serene.

Back to the vibrating BlackBerry.

He owns a silver Curve.

His wife, a black Pearl.

Michael checks the oversized screen. An IM message. He open it and has to smile. It's from a woman.

The woman sitting across from him.

HEY HANDSOME

He glances up. Kennedy's head is down, but she
raises it momentarily. Their eyes meet; she smiles, seductively, then lowers her head, fingers never leaving
the keyboard. He responds.

HEY MS. SEXY THANG. WHAT'S ON UR
MIND?

This time Kennedy doesn't look up. She's busy re-
plying, foot continuing to tap as her iPod whirls
away.

YOU

Michael makes eye contact with Kennedy. He
raises his eyebrow as if to say, "Yeah? Go on . . ."

Head drops back down and she types and sends.

THINKING ABOUT U MAKING LOVE TO ME

Michael grins. His fingers go to the keys, composing a response.

REALLY? DO TELL

When Kennedy is concentrating on something she inadvertently taps her tongue against her teeth. Michael observes her doing this now, and he finds it incredibly sexy.

IM WET

Michael looks up into the eyes of his wife. She's staring at him, eyes unblinking, her smile driving him wild. Michael cocks his head to the side and opens his mouth to speak.

"Right now?" he asks, his voice low.

Kennedy slowly removes the ear buds and shuts off the iPod. She leans forward.

"Find out."

Michael leans back and sighs. "Damn," he whispers. He fingers the Curve, typing a response.

UR MAKING ME HARD

Their stares lock once again.

Kennedy uncrosses her legs and stands, moving Michael's pile of magazines in order to sit beside him. She re-drapes the blanket over both of them. She nuzzles close to him, her hand slowly gliding up his thigh. Her head is facing him and the window, lips dangerously close to his ear.

She whispers: "Will you fuck me later?"

Michael's breathing spikes. His eyes scan over the

other passengers, but they are lost in their own reverie.

"Yes, baby."

Her hand creeps upward, dropping to his inner thigh. Fingers splayed, feeling the rise as he hardens.

"And eat me?" The words are puffs of air against his ear.

"You know I will. Love tasting you . . ."

Her fingers are on him, finding the outline of his manhood and massaging it. She squeezes his dick, feeling it grow between her fingers. Michael licks his lips and leans back further as Kennedy unzips his jeans. She catches his stare and smiles—that seductive smile that drives him insane.

Michael unbuttons his jeans. A moment later Kennedy's hand is massaging his cock through his boxer-briefs. He's fully hard now, and Kennedy clutches him in her hand, the fabric and her fingers constraining him. She slips her fingers beneath the boxer-briefs, and is rewarded with the fullness of him. Fully engorged. Her fingers wrap around his girth and squeeze as she nibbles on his neck. Her lips graze his earlobe, tugging on it playfully.

"I love that you're so big . . ."

Michael turns his head to her.

"You make it that way, Ken."

Kennedy begins a slow stroke, taking her time, but maintaining pressure as she jerks him.

"I want you in me."

"Does Amtrak have the equivalent of a mile-high club?" Michael asks, playfully.

"I wish."

Kennedy glances around at the other passengers. There is no one occupying the seats directly across the aisle from them. She glances back at her husband momentarily before lowering her head, pushing the blanket down in the process. Michael's eyes grow wide. Her mouth consumes him in an instant. Kennedy takes him deep and fast into her throat. Several up and down strokes of his hard dick in her hot mouth, her hand providing the friction, before she sits up, covering him up quickly.

Michael is speechless.

Kennedy kisses him on the mouth passionately while giving his cock a final tug. Then she places it back inside the confines of his underwear. The entire deed lasted less than five seconds, but it was exquisite in its approach and execution.

"Always wanted to do that," she says with a gleam and a longing in her eyes.

Chapter 3

The bellman finishes depositing Michael and Kennedy's bags in their hotel room and gives them a quick tour. King-size bed, room done up in shades of purple and red, eclectic photographs on the wall, an oversized chaise longue made of comfortable upholstery. In the bathroom, an enclosed glass shower stall for two and a separate Jacuzzi spa that's big enough for the both of them. Michael palms the bellman a ten-spot and closes the door. Kennedy rushes him and wraps her arms around his neck, pulling him close and offering up her tongue, which he readily takes.

"I LOVE it!"

"Me too," Michael responds.

"This view . . ." she says, going to the window. They are on the fifty-first floor facing west. The Hudson River shimmers in the distance. It is dusk, and lights in the neighboring skyscrapers are beginning to blink on. They stand at the window for a moment, admiring the picturesque view as Michael stands behind his wife holding her waist. They remain that way for a moment before Kennedy turns to Michael and says with a grin, "I'm starving."

They find a restaurant walking distance from their hotel in the Theater District, an Italian spot with plenty of atmosphere that serves generous portions, family style. Their entrees: veal parmigiana and clams in red linguine sauce. They share a very good bottle of Pinot Grigio between them while waiting for the food.

Michael, much to Kennedy's contentment, sits not across, but beside her in a cozy booth. While sipping their Pinot, Kennedy and Michael recount the ups and down of their week. Their rule—they are only allowed to spend about an hour bitching about their respective jobs. The rest of the time is to be spent on positive rhetoric. Not that either of them focuses on the negative. Their jobs are fulfilling, and for the most part they have bosses who are supportive and coworkers who are pleasant to be around. They chat about Zack, his school and friends, their family, and each other.

Once the veal and clams arrive, Michael has Kennedy laughing about one of his friends/coworkers. Marc is a senior attorney at Michael's agency—he's white and a few years shy of retirement. The Sean Connery lookalike is comical—he's constantly hitting on the young interns and associates. He likes them young—fresh out of college—anyone older than twenty-two or twenty-three won't do.

"The guy is slick," Michael exclaims, while forking a sliver of veal into Kennedy's mouth. "He knows the boundaries with respect to his job. So, as to not seem like he's harassing these women, he attempts to hire them as his personal dog walkers for his two German shepherds."

"I don't like him," Kennedy says.

"I know you don't," Michael replies, laughing. "But you have to give him credit—he is relentless—and it seems like every other week he's getting one of the nubile young things over to his Georgetown condo under the guise of getting to know his dogs."

"Nubile young things? Michael, if I didn't know any better I would think you actually admire him," Kennedy says.

"Ken, I admire his perseverance. The guy doesn't give up, even though he's not getting any!"

Kennedy's turn.

She has a coworker, a paralegal named Jacqueline. Jackie, as she's called, is dating this uptight dentist named Freddy. Michael remembers meeting them at an office function earlier this year. The dentist said all of two words the entire evening.

"Jackie went down South with him for his homecoming last weekend," Kennedy explains. "While there she happened to ckeck his phone and saw all of these text messages from other women."

"She just happened to check his phone?" Michael asked.

"I didn't get into all that."

"Okay . . ."

"Anyway, she finds these messages and they were definitely inappropriate for him to be having with anyone who was not his girlfriend."

"Like?"

"Like, 'I made it safely, baby' and 'missing you and what you did to me last week.' "

"Ouch." Michael takes a sip of the Pinot and forks some of Kennedy's clams into his mouth.

"So, get this. Freddy is sleeping when she's doing all this. She goes into the hallway and calls these women on his phone. Two answer. She asks who the fuck these bitches are, and what relationship they are to Freddy."

"Oh boy. Shit hits the fan," Michael says.

"Sure does. One woman tells her out right, 'I was dating him, but he tried to fuck me without a condom and I wasn't having that!' "

"You're kidding? He should know better," Michael exclaims.

"I know. The other woman says that she is Freddy's cousin."

"What? Just how gullible is your friend?"

Kennedy laughs. "Jackie confronts Freddy—she wakes his black ass up, and guess what he says?"

"I can't even imagine how the good dentist handles this one."

"He says, 'I can't believe you went through my phone without asking!' " Kennedy laughs some more as she pauses to enjoy her food. She has a touch of red sauce on her bottom lip, so Michael takes his napkin and dabs at the spot.

"Typical male response," Michael says, "Deflect the conversation away from the real issue."

"Exactly. What's truly sad is that she started to doubt herself."

"Hold up. I'm sure she pressed him about what the women had said regarding not using a condom? I mean, how can he *not* address that?" Michael asks.

"Well, Freddy managed to do exactly that. He refused to speak to her, and the next day he went to a football game without her."

"She's an idiot," Michael exclaims. "Freddy treats her like shit because he can. Because she lets him."

"True. The whole thing sickened me to hear. It made me realize how lucky I am to have what we have." Kennedy leans in and kisses Michael on the cheek. "I'm blessed to have you in my life, Michael," she says.

Michael glances her way and smiles.

"Does this mean I'm getting some tonight?"

Kennedy groans while rolling her eyes.

"You could fuck up a wet dream, you know that?"

After coffee, no dessert, they walk back to the hotel, hand in hand. When they are inside their room, Michael throws off his running shoes and opens the drapes wide so that the splendor of Manhattan invades their window. He climbs onto the bed as Kennedy begins to undress.

"I guess we should start getting ready," Kennedy says.

"Good idea. Ladies first."

Kennedy retreats to the bathroom and closes the door. Michael reaches for his BlackBerry Curve and checks e-mails and voice mails. Afterwards he presses a few keys, enabling the Chaperone feature on his phone to locate his son.

A few moments later an address displays on the screen.

District of Columbia address.

Jeremy's house.

Technology is a godsend.

He wonders what Zack is doing right now. Undoubtedly huddled in front of Jeremy's Xbox 360 playing *Test Drive Unlimited*, *Top Spin 2*, *Amped 3*, or *Call of Duty 2* (his favorite).

Michael lays his head back and naps.

Kennedy makes a grand entrance close to an hour later. What Michael sees takes his breath away.

"My goodness . . ."

She stands before him, her hourglass-shaped body

clad in a form-fitting little black minidress that stops
at the top of her thighs. Plunging V neckline that is
open right above her navel. Less than half of each
breast is confined by fabric; the rest of her smooth,
lovely flesh is on display. Black shiny, needle-heeled
boots end slightly above her knees. Her hair is flat-
ironed straight down her back, shiny and flawless. The
only jewelry—a pair of diamond-drop earrings in
fourteen-karat white gold—and makeup that looks
professionally applied. Michael is speechless. He goes
to her, slowly, marveling at her as if she's an appari-
tion, reaching out to touch her, inhaling a scent of
heavenly perfume.

An hour ago his wife was standing before him. Now
this creature has emerged, something else. Something
brand new to consider. A vixen. A siren. A dream.

Michael is inches from her face. His heart is pounding, and he is growing hard. He focuses in on the
raisin and champagne-blended eye shadow. The red
Bordeaux lipgloss. He resists the urge to lick her lips
and taste her. Consume her right here and now. He
is that hungry.

"Who are you?" he asks, dubiously, in breathless
anticipation.

And she responds: "My name is Celestial, and I'm
your deepest, darkest fantasy come true."

GREAT BOOKS,
GREAT SAVINGS!

When You Visit Our Website:
www.kensingtonbooks.com
You Can Save Money Off The Retail Price
Of Any Book You Purchase!

- All Your Favorite Kensington Authors
- New Releases & Timeless Classics
- Overnight Shipping Available
- eBooks Available For Many Titles
- All Major Credit Cards Accepted

Visit Us Today To Start Saving!
www.kensingtonbooks.com

All Orders Are Subject To Availability.
Shipping and Handling Charges Apply.
Offers and Prices Subject To Change Without Notice.

Look For These Other
Dafina Novels

If I Could
0-7582-0131-1

by Donna Hill
$6.99US/**$9.99**CAN

Thunderland
0-7582-0247-4

by Brandon Massey
$6.99US/**$9.99**CAN

June In Winter
0-7582-0375-6

by Pat Phillips
$6.99US/**$9.99**CAN

Yo Yo Love
0-7582-0239-3

by Daaimah S. Poole
$6.99US/**$9.99**CAN

When Twilight Comes
0-7582-0033-1

by Gwynne Forster
$6.99US/**$9.99**CAN

It's A Thin Line
0-7582-0354-3

by Kimberla Lawson Roby
$6.99US/**$9.99**CAN

Perfect Timing
0-7582-0029-3

by Brenda Jackson
$6.99US/**$9.99**CAN

Never Again Once More
0-7582-0021-8

by Mary B. Morrison
$6.99US/**$8.99**CAN

Available Wherever Books Are Sold!

Check out our website at www.kensingtonbooks.com.